Finnegan sat across from her. "All right, Aurora," he said. "You wanted to negotiate, so negotiate. What made you decide you need my help after all?"

She sat up straighter, considering her words. "You know the situation in Alyssinia, I assume?"

"I heard you burned a village to the ground."

"I heard I burned several villages to the ground. You should not believe all you hear."

"Not all that you hear, no. But there's a grain of truth in there somewhere. There almost always is. And I've seen what you can do."

"You've yet to see me burn down a village."

"But I've seen your magic before," he said. "I believe you're powerful enough for the rumors to be true."

"Alyssinia is in trouble," she said. "There are soldiers all over the kingdom, tearing towns apart. Homes are burning, there are riots in the capital. The king has been burning villages, just so that he can blame the destruction on me."

"And you intend to stop him?"

"I do."

"And you think I'm going to help?"

She leaned forward. "I know you want me on your side," she said. "I know there's something you need from me. You knew about my magic before I did; you came to Alyssinia because of it. You need me. So why don't you tell me what *you* want?"

KINGDOM
OF
ASHES

RHIANNON THOMAS

An Imprint of HarperCollinsPublishers

HarperTeen is an imprint of HarperCollins Publishers.

Kingdom of Ashes
Copyright © 2016 by Rhiannon Thomas

Library of Congress Control Number: 2015947486
ISBN 978-0-06-230357-8

Typography by Torborg Davern
16 17 18 19 20 PC/LSCH 10 9 8 7 6 5 4 3 2 1

First paperback edition, 2017

For Alex, BFF and writing partner in crime

ONE

WANTED: ALIVE, FOR TREASON AND CRIMES AGAINST THE *realm*.

For a thousand gold coins, even Aurora could believe that the smiling girl in the picture was a murderer.

Aurora tore down the poster and crumpled it into a ball. She had been on the run for a week now, but she had not run far enough. Even this small jumble of houses by the forest edge knew to expect her.

She had been so naïve, to think she could do this. Dirt itched under her fingernails. Her hair had matted around her shoulders, and blood had congealed around the blisters on her feet.

She did not know where to go. She did not know how to build shelters or catch food. She didn't even know how people outside the capital spoke, so she stood out wherever she went. And now the kingdom was covered with wanted posters, promising riches to whoever might capture her. The king's guards could not be far behind.

But Aurora had to go into the village. She had never felt so hungry before. She had never had to hope that she would come across a forest stream, or figure out whether a berry was edible, or spend her day worrying about whether she would eat. She had never once considered where her food came from or doubted that it would appear, had left so much uneaten to be tossed away. . . . She needed more food, or she wouldn't make it much farther, and the king's guards would catch her either way.

Besides, who would think she was the princess, if they looked at her now?

The village was quiet in the early dawn. A few people walked along the street, but they were mostly half-asleep, or so absorbed in their errands that they barely glanced at Aurora as they passed.

Aurora could smell baking bread. She followed it to a shop with a sign above the door showing a single ear of wheat. Aurora closed her eyes and breathed in, savoring even the *smell* of food. Her stomach ached in response.

She looked around. No guards or soldiers in sight. She would have to take the risk.

A little bell rang as she opened the door. A middle-aged woman worked behind the counter, arranging steaming hot loaves onto trays. "Welcome, welcome," she said, without looking up. "Pardon our appearance, it's been one of those mornings. What can I get you?"

"Uh . . ." Aurora stepped closer. The woman glanced at her, and then paused, a bun held inches above the tray.

Aurora tensed. She glanced at the door, ready to run.

"My goodness, girl," the woman said. "You look a fright. What *have* you been up to?'

"Oh," Aurora said. "I've been traveling." She struggled not to cringe at the words, the way she spoke so *crisply*, in her old-fashioned accent.

The woman tutted. "So many traveling these days. Not enough food, is there, not enough work, so everyone thinks they have to move. It's not safe for young things like you to be out there. Not safe at all."

Aurora stepped closer. The fresh bread smelled too delicious to resist. "I wanted to buy some bread."

"Oh yes, yes, of course. I would give you some for free for your troubles, honest I would, but things are tight for us here, too. I really can't spare it."

"That's all right," Aurora said. "Thank you. I have money." She reached into her satchel and pulled out the purse that Finnegan had given her. The woman's eyes widened as the coins clinked together. Aurora made sure to tilt it toward herself as she opened it, concealing the flash of silver and gold. She picked out a few copper coins and pulled the drawstring closed.

The woman recommended the local specialty, so Aurora ordered two loaves. "If you want somewhere to stay," the woman added, as she placed the loaves in a paper bag, "you should try the Red Lion down the street. Good people there. Discreet, you know."

Aurora tightened her grip on the bag. "I have nothing to hide," she said. "But thank you for the advice."

The bell rang again. A younger girl ran in, her braid bouncing behind her. "Mum!" she said. "Mum! There are soldiers here."

Soldiers. Aurora turned so quickly that her hip slammed against the counter. Had the guards been following her? Or had someone spotted her in the five minutes she had been here?

The woman glanced at Aurora. "How do you know, Suzie? What did you see?"

"They're coming out of the forest. I was delivering the bread to Mistress Jones, like you told me to, and the soldiers marched into the street and started ordering everyone out of their houses."

The baker paused for a moment. "That's no reason to stop your deliveries, is it, Suzie? People'll need their bread, whatever happens. Quick, take the next lot to the Masons. Don't worry about the soldiers."

"But—"

"Do it!"

The girl gaped at her mother. She shot Aurora a curious look, and then nodded.

"All right," she said. "I'm going. I just thought you'd want to know." With another glance at Aurora, she sped back out of the door.

"Thank you for the bread," Aurora said, trying to keep her voice from shaking. "I'll look at the inn, like you said."

"Nonsense, child." The baker strode around the counter. "Better get you away quickly, hadn't we, if they're looking for you."

"Looking for me?" Aurora tried to frown, pushing her panic away. That was the right look, wasn't it, for innocent confusion? But the baker would have none of it. She grabbed Aurora's wrist and pushed her toward the door behind the counter.

"At least go out of the back door, then. No point in dealing with soldiers if you don't have to, if you ask me. It's a quieter street back there, and not too far from the edge of the village."

She ushered Aurora into a cramped storeroom, with sacks of flour resting against one wall and a huge counter covered in trays of rising dough against the other. The low ceiling was held up by two beams, and the baker swerved around them as she headed for the back door. "This way, this way," the baker said. "No point in hiding you, they'll only look, and then how will you get away? This door here now."

Someone knocked on the back door. "Open up!" a man shouted. "King's orders. We need to inspect the property."

The baker jerked back, her hand tightening on Aurora's wrist. She turned toward the shop front again, but the bell above the front door rang. Two soldiers marched into the bakery. They stopped when they saw Aurora, eyes widening. They might have known she was in this area, but they had not known she was in here. She should have hidden as soon as she heard they were looking for her.

The soldiers pulled out their swords, one shouting to the others outside. Aurora wrenched her wrist free of the baker and ran for the back door. A soldier kicked it open, and three men advanced into the storeroom, swords raised. Aurora scrambled back. She grabbed the dagger in her bag.

She had been foolish to think entering a shop would be safe. Now they would catch her, they would drag her back to the capital, back to King John's booming laugh and his stony eyes and his threat of the pyre.

The nearest soldier grabbed for her arm. She dodged, panic and defiance swelling inside her, and fire shot across the storeroom floor. The soldier's cloak caught, and he tore it away, yelling. The burlap bags burned too, and the wooden pillars in the center of the room. The baker screamed, and Aurora jumped around her, around the shouting soldiers, running for the door.

Her whole body seemed to blaze. She dodged, and she ran, out of the storeroom and onto the street.

More soldiers hurried toward the commotion at the

bakery. Aurora spun on the spot. There had to be somewhere she could run.

"Stop!" one of them yelled. He held a crossbow. "Stop, or I'll shoot."

But he couldn't kill her. The king wanted her brought back alive.

Smoke billowed from the bakery. Aurora swerved around the side of the building, twisting as a crossbow bolt flew toward her. Flames danced in the window. The baker was screaming.

Aurora ran onto another street, and then another, but the village was not that big. There was nowhere she could hide. She tore toward the edge of the forest, but her feet were aching and blistered, and she stumbled.

A soldier grabbed her arm. She shoved him away, fire crackling again. The man shouted in pain and let go.

The air stank of smoke. And the soldiers still ran after her, still shouted. Her head rang with the sound of their voices. They were going to catch her. There was nowhere to hide here, and they were going to *catch* her; they'd catch her, and the king would burn her, torture her, make her into nothing again.

She could not let that happen.

She sent flames across the ground, burning a line between her and the soldiers, reaching higher than the buildings around them, fed by nothing but Aurora's fear.

A house on the edge of the village caught fire. More people screamed, and the flames swelled again. They were too hot, too strong. *Stop*, she thought, but the flames swelled, as though driven by her panic.

She dove into the forest. As she ran, she dodged brambles and tree roots, racing for the stream. She leapt over the mud by the bank, the water splashing as she landed, and *ran*. Steam rose around her.

A tree with low-hanging branches stood ahead. Aurora scrambled up, the bark digging into her palms. She climbed and climbed, until the branches shuddered under her weight.

In the distance, smoke rose into the air.

The whole village was burning.

The baker had helped her, tried to protect her, and she had burned her shop to the ground.

She should keep running. Follow the flow of the stream as far as she could, before the guards caught her. But she could not move. She stared at the flames, so fierce now that they reached above the trees. She could not look away.

It had come from her. She had not decided to use magic. She had not wanted to set things alight. But the panic had taken over, and now . . .

She had done this. She did not know what else she was capable of, if she did not get her magic under control.

She stared, and she stared, as the fire burned itself out, and the sun rose and fell in the sky.

She had to go back. She *had* to. Even with the guards, she had caused this. The fire was hers. She had to help.

But it was dark before her legs agreed to climb down from the tree. She followed the stream back, each step cautious, certain the guards would snatch her at any moment.

She saw no one.

The stench of smoke and burned wood got stronger the farther she walked. And then the end of the forest was in sight. The world beyond was black, hidden by the lingering smoke that formed a blanket across the night sky.

She crept to the edge of the trees. There were no soldiers waiting. There was no one.

The village was nothing but ashes.

TWO

SMOKE STUNG AURORA'S EYES AS SHE STARED AT THE village's remains. A few buildings clung to life, with half-collapsed walls and charred beams, but otherwise, everything was destroyed. Everything was gone.

She couldn't have done this. She *couldn't* have. Her magic had always been so small before, a candle, a flash of flame. She had shattered the fountain in the square before she ran, but she couldn't burn down an entire village without a thought.

She hoped the baker had escaped. She hoped . . . she hoped many things.

Aurora stepped to the edge of the tree line. She could see no one, but surely some would have stayed behind, to salvage what they could, to mourn what they had lost. She took another step. A branch snapped under her foot.

"What was that?" a man said, from somewhere in the ruins. A survivor, or a guard? If he was a survivor, she had to help him. He could be trapped. But if it was a guard . . .

A hand clamped over her mouth. Aurora gasped, the sound swallowed by her captor's palm. She jabbed backward with her elbow, twisting, reaching for the fire. . . .

"Shh, Aurora." Her captor—a woman—murmured in her ear. "It's me. It's Nettle."

The singer from the Dancing Unicorn. She should have been miles away in Petrichor, not lurking in the forest, not grabbing Aurora in the dark.

"Do not move," she said, so quietly that Aurora barely felt the breath against her ear. "There are two guards on the other side of the village." She loosened her grip on Aurora and reached for something on the ground. Aurora could not see what she did next, but she felt Nettle's arm snap out, the air shifting as something flew past her cheek. There was a small thud, and a groan of straining wood, as one of the charred buildings shook.

Two guards came into view, torches held high. The flames illuminated the wreckage—charred fragments were falling from the wooden beam that Nettle had struck.

The beam creaked. One of the guards glanced at it and let out an exasperated huff of air, but the other continued to look around. "I know I heard something," he said.

"It was just the beams," the first said.

"We have to be sure."

Nettle's hand pressed over Aurora's mouth again, but Aurora did not need the singer to help her stay silent. She could barely breathe for fear.

The second guard looked right at them. He couldn't possibly see them, not outside the blinding glow of his torch, not when the air was thick with smoke, but for one breath, and then the next, he watched their scrap of the forest.

A crack cut through the air. The first guard had kicked the offending beam. He kicked it again, and it shuddered, more shards of wood snapping.

"What are you doing?"

"Proving a point," the first guard said. He kicked the beam a third time, releasing another burst of soot. "They creak. They snap. There's no one here but us."

The beam creaked again, as though to agree.

"I still think we should check around."

"Fine," the first guard said. "You do that. I'll be sitting over there, where it's warmer, enjoying some of that rum and giving this assignment all the attention it deserves. If you were the girl, would you come back here? No."

He strode away. The second guard gave the tree line another glance before following him.

Nettle loosened her grip on Aurora's mouth. "Quickly," she said. "Tread softly."

Aurora hesitated. She had no idea what Nettle was doing here, but she had helped her evade the guards, and Aurora had to leave. Nettle could not lead her anywhere more dangerous than this.

They crept through the forest, Nettle guiding Aurora with a hand on her wrist. They did not speak. At first, Aurora flinched every time she snapped a branch or rustled the underbrush, but the forest around them was full of noises too, owls hooting and creatures scrambling through the bracken. They heard no human voices, saw no torches or signs of pursuit.

"We have to head out into the open," Nettle said, after about an hour of silence. "We'll be harder to track across the fields. Fewer twigs to break."

Water gurgled ahead of them. The ground sloped down, and moonlight bounced off a shallow stream.

"To stop any dogs from following our trail," Nettle said, as she stepped into the water. Aurora followed her. The water soaked through her shoes, chilling her sore feet and blisters.

The stream led them out of the forest, into open hills. Flocks of sheep slept in groups on the grass, but there were no buildings, no signs of human life.

"Is it safe to talk?" Aurora asked.

Nettle let go of Aurora's wrist. "Yes," she said. "Quietly. You must have many questions."

Aurora had so many questions that for a moment she found herself unable to speak. Nettle had helped her, that was clear, but she had given no hint of why she was here, or where they were going, or what had happened in the village. When Aurora finally found her words, she said, "How did you find me?"

"You were not difficult to track. It is lucky that you evaded the guards as long as you did."

"You've been following me? Since I left Petrichor?"

"I was about a day behind. When I saw the fire in the distance, I thought I must find you nearby. I am glad that I did."

"Why?" Aurora said. "Why were you following me?"

"Prince Finnegan asked me to."

"Finnegan?" Aurora stopped. Finnegan, the prince of Vanhelm, who had helped her to escape the palace, who had encouraged her to abandon Rodric and Alyssinia altogether. Why would he ask *Nettle* to follow her? The water lapped around her ankles. "Finnegan asked you to watch me?"

"Aurora, we must keep moving."

"You work for Finnegan?"

"Yes," Nettle said. "As I said. But we must move while we talk."

Aurora did not move. Nettle worked for Finnegan. Of course she worked for Finnegan. She had been at the banquet in Aurora's honor, had been invited to perform by Finnegan himself after the previous musicians fell suddenly ill. She had sneaked into the ball; she had spoken to Aurora just before Princess Isabelle was poisoned; she had vanished soon afterward. . . . Aurora took a step back, the stream splashing around her. "Finnegan," she said. "He—was he involved in Isabelle's death? Did you kill her?"

"No," Nettle said sharply. "Of course I did not kill that little girl. And neither did Finnegan. He has flaws, but he would not include a *child* in his schemes. He certainly would not try to hurt you. I do not know who killed her."

Nettle looked sincere, unsettled by the accusation, but that did not explain why Nettle had been at the ball, or why she was here now. "And I'm supposed to believe you?"

"Yes," Nettle said. "Do you honestly think I am a murderer? That I would work with someone who was? I was at that banquet to watch, Princess. Another set of eyes and ears. Nothing more."

"Then you must know who it was," Aurora said. She was almost shouting now. She bit her lip to keep the words in, to control her anger before it gave their presence away. "If you were there to *watch*. You could have stopped it."

"Princess—" Nettle reached for Aurora's arm, but Aurora stepped out of reach.

"No," she said. "No. Have you been watching me, all this time? Is that why you were at the Dancing Unicorn when I went there? Are you supposed to be bringing me to him?"

"No, Princess," Nettle said softly. "I did not tell him any of your secrets. I was in Petrichor to watch the rebels there, before you ever awoke. And he wanted me to help you. He did not ask me to force you to go to Vanhelm, and I would not have done so if he had. He was concerned for your well-being. As was I."

"I can take care of myself." Nettle just watched Aurora, a few loose strands of hair around her face, and waited for her to speak again. "Where are you leading me?" Aurora said eventually. She should have asked more questions before she followed her. They had been going *away*, and that had been enough, but now her naïveté felt beyond foolish.

"As far from that village as we can get in one night. There is no trap, Aurora. But we cannot be caught out here when the sun rises."

"*Where?*" Aurora said. "I won't go into another village. Not now." Not until she had her magic under control.

"You won't," Nettle said. "I have somewhere safe in mind. A cave. But we must continue if we are to reach it. You do not have to trust me. You can run from me now and I will not follow you. But I want you to be safe, and I think you will be safer with me."

"Of course you think that," Aurora said. But she did not move away. Nettle had protected her from the guards. And whatever her motivations, she did not seem to want to hurt Aurora. Quite the opposite. Aurora straightened her back and started to walk along the stream again. Nettle walked beside her.

"Were you there?" Aurora said. "What happened in the village—did you see—?"

"It was already burning when I arrived," Nettle said. "But the soldiers did nothing to stop the fire. I saw them rounding up the villagers, stopping them from protecting their homes. They took them all away."

"It was me," Aurora said. "It was my fault." She had destroyed a whole village, condemned its people just by her presence.

"Your magic got out of your control?"

"You already know about that?" She did not know why she was surprised. How long had Nettle been watching her, noting details for later dissection?

"I saw you," Nettle said. "At your presentation, at your wedding. And this fire was not begun by John's men. It is not so difficult to notice."

"I destroyed that village," Aurora said. "I didn't mean to. It was an accident, but—it was me." She had grown up hearing how magic was evil, fearing the curse, knowing that it could only twist and destroy. This was her proof. Her magic was no different from any other.

"You may have begun it," Nettle said, "but the king's men were the ones who let it destroy the village. They are the ones who will use it against you."

Aurora's feet throbbed as they walked. She stumbled slightly, but she refused to slow down. The stream eventually trickled into nothing, and Nettle veered away from the path it had suggested, leading Aurora to the edge of another forest.

The sky was beginning to lighten when Nettle rested a hand

on Aurora's elbow. "There is a cave up the bank here," she said. "Hard to spot unless you know it. We should rest there."

"A cave?" Aurora couldn't see any gaps in the bank. "What if they find us? We'll have nowhere to run."

"You are safer hiding under cover than out in the open. But you may go elsewhere, if you wish."

Nettle began to climb the bank, placing each foot so that no earth was disturbed. Aurora glanced over her shoulder again, but she had nowhere else to go. She followed, careful to step in the same spots each time.

Aurora hesitated at the cave entrance, ready for some betrayal, but the singer was already spreading out her blankets. She lay a couple of water skins beside them, along with more bread and a collection of nuts. "You must be hungry," she said, as Aurora stepped inside. "Eat. Slowly."

Aurora had almost forgotten the pain in her stomach after the horror of the day. She tore off a small piece of bread and bit into it. It was slightly stale, and the effort of chewing made her jaw ache. It had to be the most delicious thing she had ever eaten.

She sank against the side of the cave, and her calves throbbed in relief. She kicked off her bloodstained shoes.

"Your feet," Nettle said. "They need attention."

"They'll be fine," Aurora said. "I'm just—I'm not used to walking."

"Certainly not in wedding shoes. May I?" Nettle gripped Aurora's ankle and studied her sole. Aurora refused to look. She knew they were a mess, from the pain with every step and the stains on the inside of her shoes. She did not want to see for herself.

If it was bad, Nettle's face did not show it. "I am going to fetch some more water to clean this," she said. "We must hope it is not infected. Be careful while I am gone."

Aurora watched her step out of the cave. Her feet throbbed, already too swollen to fit back into her shoes, and a headache pounded behind her eyes. She would fight if she needed to fight, but she could not run before she knew it was necessary.

When Nettle returned, she knelt beside Aurora again and pulled a worn dress from her pack. With one sharp motion, she tore a shred from the bottom edge.

"Your dress!" Aurora said.

"I have others," Nettle said, her expression unchanged. She swept her hair over one shoulder and dabbed the rag in the water. Aurora hissed as it touched her blisters. Nettle worked in silence, each movement gentle. When she had finished, she tilted her head, studying her handiwork. "We should bind this," she said. "To keep it clean. It will make it easier for you to walk too." She tore another strip from the dress and began to wrap it around Aurora's foot, ignoring her hiss of pain. Once she had tied it tight, she turned her attention to the other foot.

"Tell me," she said, as she wet another strip. "What is it that you plan to do now?"

"I assume you want me to go to Vanhelm."

"Finnegan would like you to," Nettle said. "I have no preference, as long as you are safe."

"And why do you care?"

"I know what it is like, Princess, to go running out here alone. Finnegan can take care of his own affairs. But am I wondering: what do *you* intend to do?"

Aurora swallowed and rested her head against the cave wall. "I don't know," she said. That was the hardest thing to admit, that she had run without any idea what running would really be like. She had rejected two offers of support, from Finnegan and from the witch Celestine, and she had run out into the world without a goal, without a destination, with *nothing* in her mind but being elsewhere. "I only know I can't stay here."

"No," Nettle said. "You cannot."

There was Falreach, across the mountains. Her mother's kingdom. The court there might have helped her, if it had not once been Queen Iris's home. Then there were the farther kingdoms, Palir or Eko or beyond, but they were thousands of miles away. Too far to walk, and although they might be a good place to hide, she would never find support.

And then Vanhelm, the dragon kingdom across the sea. Prince Finnegan had pledged his support, but could she trust him to help her? He had never been entirely honest with her.

"Why aren't you encouraging me to go to Vanhelm, if you work for Finnegan?"

"I bring him information," Nettle said, "not people.

Watching you was already an unusual task for me, although I was glad to do it. And do not doubt I will tell Finnegan what you choose to do. But I will not force you into anything."

Nettle began to bandage the second foot. Already, Aurora felt better, calmer. She pulled her necklace out from under her dress. The dragon pendant had its wings unfurled, one leg poised as though about to take flight. A blood-red jewel glinted in its eye. She twisted it between her fingertips, as though it might carry the answer. "Do you think I should trust him?"

"I could not say." Nettle tied the bandage in place. "He will always put his own concerns first, whatever that may mean. You must be careful with him. But he is honest, too. He does not act cruelly, or without reason. He is not a bad choice for an ally." She held Aurora's hand. "Test your feet," she said. "It should be easier to walk now."

Aurora winced as she put weight on her bandaged feet, but although they still ached, they were far sturdier than they had been before. She took a tentative step forward. "It's good," she said. "Thank you." She crossed the cave, each step careful, and rested a hand against the wall.

Nettle nodded and bent down to tidy her pack, hiding her expression from view.

"Nettle," Aurora said softly. "If you were watching the rebels in Petrichor . . . do you know what happened to them?"

Nettle shook her head as she folded her torn dress. "Not since I left. Their plans were always weak. But that only made them more dangerous, I thought. Their actions had consequences they did not intend. If you are thinking of asking for their help—"

"No," Aurora said. She sat and pressed her chin onto her knees. "I'm not." Even if she could find one of them, she could not trust them or their plans, not after what she had seen. A raid on the dungeons that left many prisoners dead. A foolish display that almost caused a riot and cost a guard his life. They had no strategy, no morals, no discipline. She could not work with them.

But she had one other option, a thought that had plagued her more and more as the days passed. Celestine. Every day, she felt as though the witch were watching her, like she would turn around and see her blue eyes burning through the darkness. Celestine had asked Aurora to join her the last time she had seen her, as Aurora ran from her wedding. She had hinted that Aurora would regret turning her away, that she would *beg* to join her in the end. And she had hinted that Aurora's mother had made a bargain with her. A bargain the queen failed to keep. A bargain that led to Aurora's curse.

Had she cursed Aurora with this, too? With magic she could not control, that burned and burned until it destroyed everything around her?

Celestine had answers. But Aurora could not face her. Everyone who bargained with her suffered for their naïveté. But the idea whispered to Aurora. Celestine would have all the answers she needed, if only she was willing to ask for them.

"You should rest," Nettle said. "You do not need to decide what to do yet."

"Is it safe?" Aurora asked. "To sleep?"

"It is safer than not sleeping. Go on. I will not betray you."

It was strangely soothing to hear Nettle state her fear so bluntly. Aurora wrapped herself in one of the blankets and rested her head against the wall. Nettle settled against the opposite side, her cheek pressed against the stone. And although Aurora still felt tense, although it was too soon to assume that she was safe, she was too exhausted to stay awake. The moment she closed her eyes, she was asleep.

When she awoke, it was dark outside. Nettle was gone, but her pack was still there. Aurora stretched her stiff back. She had slept better than she had for a week at least, and with the rest had come clarity.

She could not stay in Alyssinia, not when it meant hiding in the forest and doing nothing of use. But she could not abandon the kingdom entirely either. She *had* to help the people there, those like the baker, who supported her, who were relying on her to save them from the king's fury. She had to stop the king. But she also had to stop herself, to get this unpredictable magic under control.

Finnegan was her only option. She did not trust him, but he seemed to know things. He had hinted at her magic, called her "little dragon." And she had set a village alight. Was that not what dragons did?

He had helped her before, even if it had led to bloodshed. He might have an agenda of his own, but it seemed to match Aurora's own goals, at least for now. He could help her to regroup, before John cornered her again.

And he wanted her support enough to ask Nettle to follow her, enough to ensure her safety and convince her to join him again. That gave her leverage. He wanted something from her. That would make it easier to get what she wanted from him.

"Nettle," she said, when the singer reemerged with a selection of plants in her hand. "I've decided. I want to go to Vanhelm."

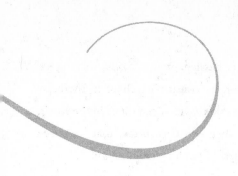

THREE

THEY TRAVELED MOSTLY BY NIGHT, AVOIDING THE roads. Aurora's feet still throbbed, but Nettle's bandages kept the blisters at bay. She borrowed some of Nettle's traveling clothes, shortening them so that she could walk. They talked little, but sometimes Nettle sang under her breath, snatches of melodies that Aurora did not recognize.

Nettle left every couple of days to visit a town and buy supplies, leaving Aurora hidden in a cave or a tree. She would return with fresh food and a carefully neutral expression.

"What's the news?" Aurora would say. "What's happened?"

The stories were never good. Guards tearing towns apart

looking for her. Merchants hassled on the roads, their stock tossed into the dirt. Rumors of continuing chaos in the capital, of rebels fighting, homes destroyed, executions in the street. And news of one village, then three, then six, that had been burned by the princess in her hatred for the kingdom.

Nettle reported it all in a steady voice, not pausing from preparing dinner or tidying her pack to give the news. Just neutral, just facts, as though the whole kingdom were not in ruins because of Aurora's actions.

"I finally received Finnegan's note," Nettle said, after she returned from one such trip. "He has agreed to send us a boat. I am glad we heard from him—we are only nearing the rendezvous point I suggested, and it would not be safe to linger there or find a boat ourselves."

"Do you think the king's men are following us?"

Nettle shook her head. "Their searches have become haphazard. They do not know where you are. But we do not want that to change."

It took them several more days to reach the coast, but one dawn they climbed over the peak of a hill, and the ocean was there. It rolled ahead of them, the water a churning, fitful gray. A ship bobbed a hundred feet offshore, surprisingly steady in the turmoil.

Aurora paused at the top of the hill to stare at it. The ocean. It was wilder than she had pictured, almost angry, as though challenging onlookers to try and cross. A chilled wind blew in from the water, and Aurora wrapped her cloak over her chest. The air tasted of salt.

It was the end of the kingdom. The end of the world, at least as Aurora had known it. Aurora took a deep breath, savoring the sharpness of the air. And then she set off down the hill, Nettle close behind.

A gruff-looking man waited beside a rowboat on the shore. He nodded at Aurora and Nettle as they approached. Nettle murmured a few words to him, and he nodded again and gestured at the boat without a word. Aurora glanced at the churning water, and then back over her shoulder at the forest.

If she got into the boat, she could not turn back. She would not be able to escape, not even if the sailors betrayed her. But she had to trust them. Finnegan had resources, knowledge about things she could only guess at. He was the best potential ally she had.

She stepped into the boat. It rocked, and she stumbled onto the bench. Nettle stepped in beside her, making the boat lurch again. Once they were both settled, the man began to row.

Aurora stared as the shore grew smaller and smaller, the trees blending into a mass of brown and green.

She let out a breath. She had wanted to travel for as long as she could remember, to see *everything*. And now the sea rocked beneath her, and the earth was falling away, and it hurt to see it go. She had not wanted to leave like this.

But she would be back. She had to come back.

★ ★ ★

The boat sailed away, and by the time the sun set, Aurora could no longer make out the Alyssinian shore. She stood on deck, leaning on the side of the ship, watching where the coast had been. Her kingdom had slipped into the mist, and another approached. Vanhelm. Finnegan's domain.

She needed to know precisely what she wanted before she arrived. She needed to stride up to his castle with her demands laid out, her offer perfectly articulated. Otherwise the sharp-tongued prince would tie her hopes in knots. She could not wait for good luck here, could not rely on his good favor.

She wanted to know everything he knew about her curse and her magic. She wanted to know why he called her "dragon girl," and why he wanted this connection so badly. She wanted him to help her to figure out her powers and stop the king. But without knowing what Finnegan wanted from her, it was difficult to predict where their negotiations would go from there.

A cold wind tossed her hair and made her shiver. The ocean and the sky all melted together, the water reflecting blurry images of the stars.

She leaned forward to glimpse the foam that bounced in the wake of the ship. The railing dug into her stomach.

Tristan once told her an elaborate tale about being a pirate. Something about being kidnapped, becoming captain of a crew. All invented, obviously, but she had thought that truth lingered behind his jokes. He was not from Petrichor. He was lighthearted, a joker, with a lively imagination. That had seemed enough to know about a person, enough to trust him. To go out into the dark with him, to hold his hand on slanting roofs and dwell in secrets together.

What a fool she had been.

Nettle emerged from belowdecks, a blanket wrapped around her shoulders, her black hair flying loose about her face. "You must be careful," she said. "The sea can be rough."

"I will be."

A shadow moved on the horizon. Another ship, perhaps.

"You are wary of me," Nettle said. "I understand that."

"I'm not wary of *you*," Aurora said. Nettle had saved her life, bandaged her injuries, walked for days beside her, slept under the same shelter. That created a connection. Aurora respected her. She appreciated her presence. Perhaps she even liked her. But she did not know if she could trust her. "I'm wary of your connection with Finnegan."

Nettle was quiet for another few moments. "I am not an extension of him, Aurora. I do not act blindly on his behalf. I help him, but only with what I wish. Only when I think it is right."

"You followed me on his orders."

"On his request. And it was something I was happy to do. I was concerned about you."

"Because I needed help."

"Yes," Nettle said. "Because I know what that is like."

Did it make a difference, whether Nettle was forced to watch her or asked to watch her? It had been Finnegan's scheme either way. Aurora stared at the water, the darkness shifting beneath them. Anything she said to Nettle could potentially be reported to Finnegan. But Nettle was also the best source of information Aurora had.

"What does Finnegan want from me?" Aurora asked. "Why did he send you?"

"I think he is fascinated by your magic."

"Fascinated? What does that mean?"

"I do not know," Nettle said. "I would not like to speculate. He must think it useful. But that is obvious, is it not? Magic in a magic-less world. Anyone would want that."

Aurora nodded. It made sense, and it was something she could use. She could not control her magic yet, but Finnegan seemed to have some knowledge about it, details he had not told her. If he wanted to use her magic himself, then he had to help her develop it. And he did not know about Celestine. He would offer many things in return for what he believed was the only magic left in the world.

"But do not think that is all," Nettle continued after a moment. "I believe he cares about you."

"*Cares* about me?"

"About your well-being, at least. He is selfish, Aurora, but he can be kind too."

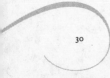

It fitted what Aurora had seen of him before she left. Finnegan had intrigued her, too, for all the ways he irritated her. But something felt slightly off about Nettle's words. "You're being very open with me."

"What do you mean?"

"Telling me about Finnegan's plans, telling me how he might feel . . . you told me you were his spy, when I doubt that is something that spies are meant to say. I don't understand it."

Nettle learned forward too, staring at the water. "I am serious about my work, Aurora," she said. "But I thought you deserved honesty. I know what it is like to be lost. I would not want to make it any harder for you than it already is."

Aurora tilted her head to look at her. "Why do you work for Finnegan?" she said. "Why him?"

Nettle was quiet for a long moment as she continued to watch the water. "I come from a place where everyone knows everybody, and where they all think they have a right to tell you what to do. And I did not want it. I did not feel like *me* there. I wanted to see everything else there was. So I turned sixteen, and I left. I did not realize how hard travel would be. One kingdom and then the next, people were cruel to me. They took advantage of me, they stole from me, and I thought, 'Oh. This is what people are like.' And I was sure that Finnegan was no different from the rest of them. But he saw my talents. How I had learned to hide, how I knew how to observe, to read people. We became friends. And he asked me to help him."

"So you did?"

"I can still travel, still observe people. But I do not go hungry. Far from it. And I have something like a friend. You will realize, Aurora, how valuable these things are."

"I know how valuable they are."

"You may recognize it, but do you *know* it? Before this week, you had never been hungry. You've never gone weeks without another person to talk to, or had people treat you like you are worthless because you dare to be from somewhere they are not. You should not judge me for accepting his alliance, or think it means I cannot care about you or want to help you."

Aurora watched the waves rise and fall. "I don't judge you," she said softly. "It's just that—" Everything was tangled in her head, her respect for Nettle, her wariness, all of the hopes and the betrayals. "Since I woke up, no one has been who they claimed to be. Everyone has had some scheme, some *motive*. Tristan wanted me in his rebellion, the king and queen wanted me as a puppet, and even Finnegan had a plan to help me run, as soon as I said the word. And now *you*. You were just supposed to be a singer. Not a puzzle, just *you*. And now—now I don't know."

"Perhaps that is the problem," Nettle said. "No one is *just* anything. Everyone will have more layers than you expect."

"More layers does not mean being a spy."

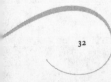

"And being a spy does not make one bad. It does not mean a person wants to use you."

"No," Aurora said. "I know." And she did. She could understand Nettle's motivation, could see the kindness in her. But she did not know what to say after that, so she turned to look at the horizon again.

When Aurora woke up the next day, she could taste smoke on the air. Nettle was not in her cabin, and Aurora could see nothing through the porthole but water, so she climbed the stairs onto the main deck. Nettle was leaning against the side of the ship, staring at the coastline.

It was a wasteland, black and red. Smoke curled from the ground, and even the sky above seemed scorched and severe. All life had been purged from the place, leaving a charred, hollow shell. It seemed wrong, for such harshness to exist so close to the roiling water.

Aurora had never imagined that anything could look like this. That *this* was what waited across the water, this was the world beyond her kingdom's borders.

Aurora crept to Nettle's side. It felt wrong, somehow, to move too quickly or speak too loudly with the desolation before them. "What is this place?"

"Vanhelm," Nettle said. "Once."

Vanhelm. When Aurora had pictured Finnegan's kingdom,

she had thought it much like her own, with forests and castles and *life*. Not these contorted ruins, smoke and ash.

"What happened?"

Nettle looked steadily across the water. "Dragons."

She spoke so matter-of-factly. But there was nothing left. *Nothing*. How could dragons have done all this?

They passed what might have been a house, close to the water. The walls had melted inward, like the building was cowering under the harsh sun.

"From the way Finnegan spoke, what Iris said . . . I did not think it would be like this."

"It does not need to be said. And this is not the kingdom now. When they say Vanhelm, they mean the island, the capital," she said. "A world in one city."

Aurora stared at the home of her ancestors, all burned away. "Only one city survived?" she said. "Just one?"

"Just one," Nettle said. "It was the only place that was surrounded by water. It was the only place that was safe." The wind caught her hair, sending black strands dancing across her face.

"Did a lot of people live outside the city? Before—before it became this?"

"Many people," Nettle said. "Most of them did not escape."

How many people had lived in this one part of Vanhelm alone? Thousands would have died. Tens of thousands. More than she could fathom.

Aurora clutched the dragon necklace that still hung around

her neck. The distant smoke scratched her throat.

Finnegan had compared her to the dragons, and they had woken up and burned his whole kingdom away. What, then, did he expect to come of *her*?

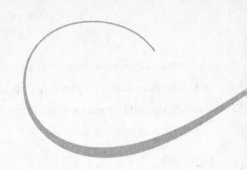

FOUR

THE CITY OF VANHELM APPEARED GRADUALLY ON THE horizon. It was a shape at first, a gray disturbance in the morning mist, but as the boat glided closer, it gained form, became buildings, towers and spires, all different heights, all reaching into the sky. Aurora had thought that Petrichor was impressive, with its higgledy-piggledy streets, sprawling from the castle in all directions, but Vanhelm was breathtaking. As intimidating as the wasteland in its own way, but gleaming too, like a city overflowing with secrets.

Their ship reached the port midafternoon. The dock heaved with people, jostling to approach the boats, holding coins aloft and shouting destinations. Traders strained against the crowd, hauling crates marked with the crests of Alyssinia, of Falreach and Eko, while fishermen sat with their feet in the water, sorting their catches for the day.

A wall separated the dockyard from the rest of the city, with an unguarded archway allowing people to pass back and forth. Finnegan leaned against it, watching Aurora and Nettle struggle through the crowd. The prince seemed even more handsome than the last time Aurora had seen him. She had forgotten the infuriating twist to his grin and the contrast between his green eyes and black hair, the way he stood like he had never been uncertain in his life. He watched her as she approached.

A couple of men waited a few paces away from him. Guards, Aurora assumed. Other people glanced at the prince as they hurried past, but they did not stop.

"You're late," Finnegan said.

"The ship was delayed," Nettle said. She stepped closer to him, but she did not curtsy. They were almost the same height. "We can hardly control that."

"Aurora might, if she tried. I've been waiting for hours." He pulled Nettle into a hug. She pressed a kiss to his cheek. Then he turned to Aurora. "Aurora," he said. He took her hand and kissed her knuckles. It reminded her of the last time he had kissed her, as he slipped a map of his city into her palm. And before that, a brush of lips against her cheekbone, late at night in the castle. "It is a pleasure to see you again."

She gave Finnegan what she hoped was a firm, fearless smile. "I am glad to see you as well."

"Are you? I was under the impression that you wouldn't come here unless you had no other choice."

She stopped smiling. "I'm sure you're used to being considered a last resort," she said. "But if you are too insulted, I will get the next ship out of the city."

"I wouldn't recommend it. Our friend King John is hunting for you. You're not fool enough to go back there now."

"No," she said, "but Vanhelm isn't the only place I can hide."

"Then it's a good thing I'm so charming. But let's not talk about it here. It's too bright a day for politics, don't you think? I'll walk you and Nettle to the palace."

Finnegan led them down the cobbled road, weaving in and out of the crowd. Petrichor had been busy, but Vanhelm was a whirlwind of people and noises and smells. The streets were cast into shadow by buildings that towered into the sky. Aurora craned her neck, trying to count the windows in the buildings as they passed. Ten, twenty . . . they stretched on forever, blocking out the light.

A man stood on the next street corner. He waved a bundle of papers, shouting at anyone who came near. "Beware your doom," he said, the words ringing above the chaos of the street. "The dragons have come to purge this land! Repent of your sins before their fires purge your flesh!" He brandished the pamphlet at Aurora as she passed.

"Do people really believe that?" Aurora asked Nettle.

"People believe what they want to believe. I have never been one for trusting in the divine."

"But they think the dragons are divine?"

"Or tools of some gods," Nettle said. "Gods that have been long forgotten or ignored. People will always come up with reasons to explain away their terror. To tell themselves that *they* will be safe."

They saw a few more men on street corners—and they were always men—shouting at passersby. No one else even looked up. It seemed like they were a common sight, seen so often that nobody noticed them anymore.

Aurora's feet were soon stinging from walking on the unrelenting stone. Her legs ached, yet her body hummed, every new street sending a thrill through her. The city was so different from Petrichor, different from anywhere she had ever been before. It had an energy to it, a drive that Alyssinia had lacked.

The palace, when they reached it, was not as tall as the buildings around it, but was wide, with columns along the front. It commanded attention, separated from the street by a large courtyard filled with stone fountains.

Finnegan led them into the courtyard. A couple of girls sat on the edge of a nearby fountain, their hands trailing in the water. Finnegan bowed to them, and they broke into giggles.

Wide marble steps swept from the courtyard to the palace itself. The building's double doors were flanked with bronze dragons. Guards bowed as Finnegan approached.

"Where's my mother today?" he asked them.

"Her Majesty is in her study," one of the guards said. "Would you like an escort?"

"No, I won't disturb her." The guard reached for the door, but Finnegan waved him away and pushed it himself. "Guests first," he said to Aurora.

She stepped inside. Two high windows beckoned in the sunlight, making the entrance hall feel bright and airy. The roof, many stories above, was a glass dome, surrounded by swirling painted designs that glittered in the sun. A huge staircase swept ahead of them, covered with a plush red carpet. The hall had only one door, to the left of the staircase, watched by another guard. The other side of the room narrowed into a corridor, but Aurora could not see where it ended.

A glass dragon stood before the staircase. The light bounced off it, making it almost appear to move. It had the same stance as the one on Aurora's necklace, wings unfurled, one front leg poised in the air, as though about to fly. Its emerald eye seemed to follow Aurora as she stepped closer. She ran her hand along its neck. Its glass spines dug into her palm.

"This is the same as the dragon on my necklace," she said.

"You don't like the design? It's the symbol of my fair kingdom. These dragons have a nasty habit of cropping up when you're not looking." He headed toward the staircase. "Come on. I'll show you to your rooms."

"No." Aurora stopped, her hand still resting on the dragon's neck. She needed to show strength now, before he gained any more of an upper hand. "We need to discuss our alliance."

"Now? Before a hot bath and a long rest?" The words were almost concerned, but Aurora heard a hint of mockery in them. "Surely diplomacy can wait."

"Now," she said. "I think we need to make some things clear before we begin, don't you agree?"

"How forward thinking of you," he said. "Don't you trust me, Aurora? I'm not trying to trap you with hospitality."

"I just think we need to be clear."

"Whatever the princess demands. Nettle, you remember the way to your usual rooms, I assume?"

"I would be a poor spy if I could not even recall that, would I not?" Nettle smiled. She glanced at Aurora, and although she only blinked, Aurora got the strong feeling the look was encouraging her. "I will speak to you both later." And with a slight nod, she swept up the stairs.

"So," Finnegan said to Aurora. "Negotiation. Are you certain you're ready for this?"

"Let's find out."

Finnegan led her up the stairs after Nettle and through another guarded door to the left. "The palace is pretty straightforward," he said. "All the rooms to the right are public state rooms and guest rooms. All the rooms to the *left*, through this door or the one below, are private. I recommend you stay in those as much as you can, if you wish to remain anonymous."

She could not see what good it would do. Someone would notice her presence. The servants, if not the court. "What should I say if someone in the court sees me? I don't know if we can trust them with the truth."

"We don't have a court," Finnegan said. "It's hard for nobility to exist when dragons unexpectedly destroy most of your kingdom."

"They all died?"

"Most," he said. "But we also do things a bit . . . *fairer* here than in Alyssinia. Guilds deal with their own affairs. And my mother manages it all, to the cost of her social life and beauty sleep."

"Your mother?" she asked. "The queen?"

"Of course. I'll introduce you to her at some point, but not today."

She frowned. "Am I supposed to be a secret?" Hiding from a nonexistent court was one thing, but hiding from the queen?

"No one has secrets from my mother," he said. "I just want to wait. Until we've settled our agreement here. We'll tell everyone else that you're a visitor from Falreach. Rose. A foreign noble visiting to use the library. No one will ask questions."

"Assuming I stay here," she said, as they approached another guarded door.

"Of course," Finnegan said. "Assuming that you stay." He nodded to the guard as he pushed the door open. "Could you find someone to bring a platter to my study, Smith? Anything will do."

"Yes, Your Highness," the guard said. "Of course."

Beyond was a bright corridor, lit by a single floor-to-ceiling window at the end. Several doors were ajar. Finnegan led her into a sitting room, with green armchairs and a book abandoned spine-up on the coffee table. *The Rushes*, the title said.

"You can borrow it if you like," Finnegan said, when he saw her looking. "But it's not very good. A bit too pretentious for my tastes."

"Too pretentious for you?" she said. "Must be unbearable." She sat on the edge of one of the armchairs.

Finnegan sat across from her. "All right, Aurora," he said. "You wanted to negotiate, so negotiate. What made you decide you need my help after all?"

She sat up straighter, considering her words. "You know the situation in Alyssinia, I assume?"

"I heard you burned a village to the ground."

"I heard I burned several villages to the ground. You should not believe all you hear."

"Not all that you hear, no. But there's a grain of truth in there somewhere. There almost always is. And I've seen what you can do."

"You've yet to see me burn down a village."

"But I've seen your magic before," he said. "I believe you're powerful enough for the rumors to be true."

"Alyssinia is in trouble," she said. "There are soldiers all over the kingdom, tearing towns apart. Homes are burning, there are riots in the capital. The king has been burning villages, just so that he can blame the destruction on me."

"And you intend to stop him?"

"I do."

"And you think I'm going to help?"

She leaned forward. "I know you want me on your side," she said. "I know there's something you need from me. You knew about my magic before I did; you came to Alyssinia because of it. You need me. So why don't you tell me what *you* want?"

"Oh, there are so many answers to that question, Aurora."

She tightened her grip on the arms of the chair. "Let's start simply, then. Why did you come to see me in Alyssinia?"

Someone knocked on the door.

"Come in," Finnegan said.

A servant appeared in the doorway, carrying a tray of cakes and a bottle of wine. He poured them both glasses before bowing his way out of the room again. Finnegan sipped his before continuing.

"I was intrigued."

She waited for him to elaborate. He didn't.

"Intrigued?" she said. "By what?"

"Wouldn't you be intrigued if someone who had been asleep for a hundred years suddenly woke up? I wanted to see what you'd be like, if only to confirm my suspicions."

"Did I meet your expectations?"

"Oh, not at all," Finnegan said. "I would have stopped talking to you long ago if you had. I figured you'd be stuck-up like Iris, or else weak and dull like Rodric. The truth was far more entertaining."

She leaned forward. "You're lying."

"About Rodric being dull? I assure you, it's true."

"About being intrigued after I awoke. You were in Alyssinia *before* I woke up. Not in the castle, not part of the ceremony, but close enough to appear within days. You wouldn't travel so far, before the ceremony even took place, on a whim."

"Perhaps I was merely traveling, Aurora. I have interests other than you."

"You weren't merely traveling," she said. "You were preparing. If you think so little of Rodric, you can't have expected his kiss to wake me. But you needed to be there, just in case. I want to know why."

"Perhaps I was a jealous suitor, hoping to whisk you away from your true love."

She stood. "We could play like this for hours, Finnegan. But I'd rather not waste our time. I'm offering you an alliance that you clearly want. So answer my questions, and then we'll see if some sort of agreement is possible between us, or whether I should head elsewhere."

He continued to sit, his face tilted to look at her. "Do you think you could keep up?"

"What?"

"If we played for hours. Do you think you'd last?"

"You wanted to cause trouble in Alyssinia," she said. "You wanted me to run from the palace, to be on your side. You knew about my magic, or at least suspected. Tell me why."

"If you sit then I will."

She stared at him for a long moment, her knees inches from the edge of his chair. Then she stepped back, still refusing to break eye contact, and sat, smoothing her skirts around her like she had seen Iris do a hundred times. "I'm listening," she said. "Tell me."

Finnegan leaned closer. "You have to understand Vanhelm first," he said. "Then I think it explains itself. You saw my kingdom on your way here, I assume? What's left of my kingdom?"

"Yes," she said. "I saw."

"The dragons appeared out of nowhere fifty years ago, and burned the whole kingdom away. Most people didn't escape. *Everything* was gone. Not good for us, I'm sure you'll agree. The only thing that keeps my city safe is the fact that dragons will not cross water. If that changed . . . it would not end well. And that's not all. This city is *small*. It feels large, but we can only build buildings so tall; we can only squeeze so many people into this space. We're running out of room."

She dug her nails into her palms, fighting to keep her voice steady. "So you want my kingdom? Or do you expect my magic to fix things somehow?"

"The former, initially. I was only teasing you at first, you know. About your magic. I didn't know about it when I came to the castle. I thought to take advantage of the unrest in Alyssinia, get the promised princess on my side . . . combined kingdoms, more space for us, more technology and advancements for you . . . not a terrible plan worth crossing the sea for, just in case you woke up. But Alyssinia is a little backward for my tastes. And then my jokes turned out to be true. How's that for accidental insight? Once I realized what you were, I knew I had it all wrong. Vanhelm needs to be free of these dragons. And I think you might be able to help."

She could not have heard him correctly. "You think *I* can rid you of the dragons?"

"You have magic," he said. "You can control fire. The first glimmer of power in Alyssinia in almost a hundred years. What else could take on a dragon, if not that?"

"*Water* magic?"

He laughed. "Good point. But there isn't much of that around. There's no magic, except for you."

She shook her head. He could not be sincere. And not just sincere, but *excited*. "You're basing all this on the fact that I can create fire, and dragons create fire too? That's *it*?"

"It was only a suspicion, in the beginning," Finnegan said. "A hope, perhaps. No one knows why the dragons returned, and if *you* awoke too, if *you* had fire . . . it was an interesting proposition. But I have more proof now." He leaned over and caught her dragon pendant between his fingertips. The red eye gleamed. "On the day of your wedding, when you made that fountain explode . . . the dragon glowed. Didn't you feel it?"

"Yes," Aurora said. She resisted the urge to clutch the necklace too. "And?"

"You have no idea what I gave you, do you? That pendant has dragon's blood in it. Why do you think the eyes glow red like that? And it responded to you. The dragon's blood magnified your power. There's a connection between them and you, Aurora. And if you learn to control your magic, to *really* control it, I think you might be the help we've been looking for."

She slid the pendant out of his grasp. The metal was warm, but that was just from Finnegan's touch. There was no connection there. "I left Alyssinia because they had impossible hopes about my magic. What makes you think I'll respond any differently to you?"

"Because I want what you want. I want you to learn how to control your powers. You can be safe in Vanhelm. You won't have to run; you won't have to keep your magic a secret. You'll have time to figure it all out. And once you've helped me, I can help *you*. I can help you get rid of King John."

"But only after I *get rid* of the dragons. You want me to kill them."

Finnegan shook his head. "Some people say the dragons can't be killed. And I can believe it. The dragons slept beneath the stones of the mountain all of these years. Perhaps you can convince them to sleep again. Or to go elsewhere, so far west that they won't trouble us."

"And you'll help me practice my magic? Tell me all you know, cooperate with me."

"Of course," he said. "And then, what? You intend to use it to take the Alyssinian throne? Kill the king, become the conquering queen?"

"Not kill him," Aurora said. "But people want magic. They are obsessed with the hope of it. If I can provide it . . . he'll lose support. I can replace him, or support a better choice."

"A better choice? Like Rodric?" Finnegan laughed. "We both know he doesn't have the guts to be king."

"Me, then," Aurora said. The words were bitter in her mouth, but she had to say them. She did not want the responsibility of ruling, she did not want more expectations weighing down on her, not when she knew so little about this time, about the kingdom's needs. But people believed in her still. That baker had believed in her. They deserved a better ruler than John. She needed to do something to help.

"You're naïve, Aurora," Finnegan said. "You will not be able to get rid of the king without killing him. He will not back down without a fight."

"We shall see."

"Yes," he said, and he almost sounded sad. "I suppose we will."

She twisted the dragon pendant in her hands, contemplating

his words. His intentions seemed good. And even if they weren't . . . well. As long as she had safety, and a space to learn how to control her magic, she could give every appearance of compliance, and take everything she needed in return. It would be easy to accept his support and then fail in her seemingly honest attempts to help him, to ensure that he did not gain any power he should not have.

But something about his words was intriguing too. Dragon magic, dragon fire. More power than she could imagine. If he was right about the connection, the blood in the necklace could have increased her strength that morning in the village, could explain why it was so out of control.

"All right," she said. She stood and took his hand to shake it. A shiver ran up her arm. "Yes. It's a deal."

"Excellent," he said. "Then we'll begin tomorrow. A trip into the waste, to see them up close."

She let go of his hand. "Are you mad?" she said. "I can't go get rid of the dragons *tomorrow*."

"I don't want you to face them tomorrow. I just want you to see them. See what you're dealing with. Consider it the first step in your research. Who knows what you might learn about your magic out there?"

She wanted to go. But the risk . . . "Is it safe?"

"Of course not. But what is?" He grabbed her hand, pulling her closer. His green eyes seemed to burn into hers, dancing with excitement. "Come on, dragon girl. Have a little sense of adventure."

"All right," she said, before she could stop herself, before doubt could take over again. "Show me."

"Until tomorrow then," he said. "Then it will all begin."

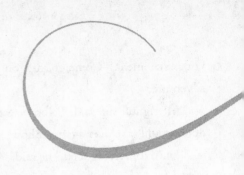

FIVE

FINNEGAN KNOCKED ON HER DOOR AT DAWN. AURORA yanked it open before he had a chance to rap more than twice. She had been awake for hours, thinking of Celestine, thinking of dragons. Anticipating the *adventure*, the danger that waited across the river.

They walked out of the palace, nodding to the guards as they passed. Only a few people were about. Some hurried down the roads, while others were already absorbed in work, unlocking shop doors and setting up stalls for the day. Finnegan led her a couple of streets away from the palace and then stopped on a large star embossed on the road.

"What are we waiting for?" Aurora asked.

"You'll see."

A few minutes passed before a bell pierced the air. People who had been walking in the middle of the road darted aside, and one of them bumped into Aurora. She grabbed Finnegan's sleeve to stop herself from falling.

"It's all right, little dragon," he said, with a grin. "I won't let it hurt you."

She released his sleeve as quickly as she had grabbed it. A strange contraption of metal and glass hurtled toward them. It was like a huge carriage, powered by its own will, its wheels rattling along.

Finnegan stuck out his arm, and the carriage stopped in front of them. Finnegan stepped aboard. With a nod at the driver, he dropped two bronze coins into a slot and gestured for Aurora to go past him.

"What *is* this?" Aurora asked, as she settled onto a hard wooden bench.

"A tram," he said. "It's the fastest way to get around the city. There's no space for horses here."

"And do princes of Vanhelm often travel like this?"

"Not always." He sat on the bench beside her. "But I like the tram. And my mother's less likely to find out what we're doing if we don't involve any guards."

"Won't your mother notice that you're gone?"

"We'll be back by the end of the day," he said. "I'm sure she'll just assume I'm doing something unsavory and think no more about it."

The wheels screeched beneath them, and Aurora's teeth rattled as the tram sped around a corner, tossing them all sideways.

"How does it move?" Aurora said. "It can't be magic."

"See how it's fastened to the cable above?" Finnegan said. "That pulls it along."

"And what pulls the cable?"

Finnegan laughed. "Magic," he said.

"Finnegan—"

"Our version of magic," he said. "We've been without your kind for a thousand years. While your kingdom relied on magic and panicked when it lost it, we actually used our brains. Figured out how to live without it. And so Vanhelm is like this, while Alyssinia . . . well. You've seen Alyssinia."

"And yet apparently you need magic from *me*."

"True." He smiled. "Perhaps there's a use for both after all."

The tram jerked to a stop. Through the window, Aurora glimpsed a mishmash of stone buildings that looked far older than the towers around them. A sign above one of the doors declared it *The Vanhelm Institute*.

Another man climbed aboard the tram. He was elderly, seventy if he was a day, with a wiry mop of white hair and dark skin that had wrinkled from an excess of expressions. When he saw them, he raised one arm in a wave.

"That's Lucas," Finnegan said. "Our guide for the day."

Lucas bowed as he approached, but Finnegan laughed and shook the man's hand instead. Then he gestured to Aurora. "This is Rose, Lucas," he said. "She's the one I was telling you about. She has quite the passion for dragons."

"It's a pleasure to meet you, miss," he said, shaking her hand. "Any dragon enthusiast is a friend of mine." He sat beside Finnegan. His weathered hand clutched the pole in front of him.

"Lucas is the best dragon expert we've got," Finnegan said. "He was on the ground when they returned, and the first to realize that water was their weakness."

"I was a bit younger back then," Lucas said with a chuckle.

"And still the man who knew the most."

"I studied dragons before anyone knew they were real," Lucas explained. "Pretty useless field of study, until suddenly it wasn't."

The tram screeched around another corner and continued along the road beside the river. The ruins across the water were obscured by the haze.

"What's the plan once we get to the waste?" Aurora said.

"Walk," Lucas said. "As far as it takes. The dragons rarely come close to the water."

"And when we find them?"

"Don't let them find us."

"We'll settle down in some ruins," Finnegan said. "And then we'll wait. But we have to get there first." He stood and gestured for the driver to stop. Once they had stepped off the tram,

Finnegan steered them along the river and onto a small dock. Only a few boats were tied up here, and most of the space was filled with stacked boxes of netting and fish. A young girl with frizzy red hair marched toward them.

"Ready to cross?" she said. "We might as well get this over with. This boat here, if you please." She gestured to a midsize wooden boat with three benches. It bobbed in the water.

Finnegan waved Aurora forward. "Ladies first." Aurora stepped into the center of the boat. It rocked underneath her, and she stumbled. Finnegan grabbed her arm. "Careful, little dragon," he said, as he squeezed past her. "Don't want you falling in."

He sat on the farthest bench and pulled Aurora down beside him. Her knees crashed into his.

Once they were all seated, the red-haired girl climbed in and cast off.

The details of the other shore became clear as they approached. It was scattered with stone that had been scorched black. Some of the buildings looked intact, worn but functional, but then the boat moved, revealing the melted roofs, the fallen walls. The town was nothing but jagged remains.

The boat came to shore in a small inlet, near a structure that might once have been a dock. Charred pillars of wood stuck out of the water. Distorted stone buildings slumped around them.

"People hid by the docks," Lucas said. His voice was rough. "Waited for rescue here. Thought they'd be safe near the water.

Wasn't near enough." He laughed, the scratchy sound of some-one too used to horror to do anything but find humor in it.

The laugh echoed off the ruins as Aurora stepped out of the boat. The mud on the shore clung to her shoe, holding her foot in place. She yanked it free. When she looked up, Finnegan was smirking.

The girl in the boat leaned forward. "Everyone have your charms?"

Aurora frowned. "Charms?"

"No one leaves my boat without one." She pulled a small packet from her pocket and tossed it to Aurora. It was a water skin, decorated with runes. Aurora moved it closer to her face, trying to recall the meanings from her books. *Protection*, one said. *Courage*. And *water, water, water*, over and over, in every color thread, over every inch of cloth. "I hope it keeps you safe," the girl said.

"Thank you."

The girl nodded. "I'll collect you when I see you raise the flag." She gestured to the building a few paces away. A red flag waited there, attached to the side of the building by ropes and pulleys. "You know where the flares are, in case the fog comes in?" Lucas nodded. "But if the fog comes in, you better race back here. I can't be responsible for you if I can't see you, right?"

"Of course, Laney," Finnegan said. "Thanks for your help once again."

"Stay safe," she said, before she sailed away.

"You never mentioned the charms," Aurora said to Finnegan, as they began to walk. "You were going to leave me unprotected?"

"They don't work," Finnegan said. "I thought you wouldn't be one for a little superstition. But wear it, if it makes you feel better. Maybe it'll balance out that dragon's blood."

She slipped it around her neck and tucked it under her shirt. It was cool against her skin, the weight grounding her. "It was a nice thought for her to give me one."

"She won't know the difference."

"I will."

Weeds grew in the gaps between bricks, weaving their way up to the roofs, but even they did not grow where the stone had burned black. One wall had graffiti near the base, a collection of names: *Anna* and *Rachel* and *Matthew*. Marks left by real people, people who may have looked up and seen the dragons descend.

Aurora closed her eyes then, feeling the remnants of the cobbles beneath her feet. She imagined she could hear the voices on the wind, the bustle of the waterside town.

She opened her eyes. "What was this place?" she asked. "Before the dragons came."

"A town," Finnegan said.

"That wasn't what I was asking."

"We call it Oldtown now," he said, "but I don't know if they called it that then."

"We did," Lucas said. "It was mostly a trading town. A place to be if you wanted to get elsewhere."

Had those names on the stone wanted to go elsewhere? Aurora hoped they had made it, before the dragons came.

"If it isn't safe to cross the river," Aurora said, as they walked between more burned-out buildings, "how did you find someone to take us so easily?" The journey had almost seemed routine to the girl on the boat.

"It's forbidden to come here," Finnegan said, "but that doesn't mean no one does. Thrill-seekers, researchers, historians, treasure hunters . . . there's always someone willing to ignore the danger. The treasure hunters are the least likely to return alive. They take big risks for whatever they think might have been left behind."

As they walked farther, the scarred buildings faded away, and the weeds along with them, leaving the Vanhelm Aurora had seen from the boat—hard, red-brown earth, with shells of buildings scattered along the horizon. It was harsh and hot, the air suffocating.

"Careful now," Lucas said. "It's dangerous, going across the open."

"It's early in the day for dragons," Finnegan said.

"They do tend to rest in the early morning," Lucas said, "when the mist is in the air. But once it burns off, they will be about, day and night."

"How many are there?" Aurora asked.

"At least fifty. All adults. But who knows how many there

are farther inland, keeping away from the shore, where there's less water."

On the horizon, Aurora could see the beginning of a small lake, or maybe a pond, shimmering in the sunlight. Grass and reeds grew around it, dipping into the water, a small splash of green.

"If they can't bear water," Aurora asked, "how do they drink?"

"They don't drink," Finnegan said. "Or we don't think so."

"I've been studying them for my whole life," Lucas said, "but still we know so little. They seem to eat stone. The charred earth they make. Meat occasionally, although they don't seem to need it. Metal too. We think the mountain they live in is full of the stuff, although no one has had the courage to check. Even before the dragons came, that mountain was considered too dangerous to enter. Too large a risk of a cave-in, you know. It was lucky, in the end, that we never tried to mine there. The mines nearer the river proved dangerous enough, until we built a moat around them to protect them."

"Yet people were still willing to work there?" Aurora asked.

"People need money," Finnegan said. "The mines pay better than anything. And people working there are rarely burned anymore."

"Rarely burned?" she said. "But it happens?"

"Only to the foolish. People who don't take the necessary precautions. Like us."

"And w

"They

burn."

"You ca

grow wher

years. Skin

straightawa

The wi

rise and fal

ears, as shar

Lucas st

horizon the

She looked away. "You don't

you do."

They walked on thro

in the sky and Aurora'

dragons flew on

after noon, t

black, mel

side,

In the distance, a long red shape burned across the sky. A dragon. It hovered for a moment, its wings held aloft, then snapped its body downward and dove out of sight.

Aurora stared at the spot where the dragon had disappeared. It should have been impossible. Impossible for her to stand here, over a hundred years after she had been born. Impossible for dragons to exist. Yet here they both were. It made her think of childhood stories, childhood dreams, that yearning for adventure. . . . Was this what others had felt, when the king announced that the sleeping princess was awake, when the dazed girl stumbled out before them? That all things were possible, now this time had come?

"See, dragon girl?" Finnegan said. "I knew you wouldn't be able to resist them."

know as much as you think

gh the waste, until the sun was high

s legs ached underneath her. A few more

he horizon, but none came close. Sometime

ey reached another abandoned settlement, with

ted buildings. A steep slope sheltered the town on one

hile a small river wove around the other.

"We should stop here," Lucas said. "Have something to eat."

They sat in what must once have been the town square. A stream trickled past, flush with greenery on either side. The grass tickled Aurora's feet, extra soft after the unyielding earth.

"Is the water safe to drink?" she asked.

Lucas nodded, so she leaned forward and cupped some in her hands. It tasted different, like it was a little charred too. It held a trace of dragon fire, as though even the things that dragons could not touch were tainted by their presence.

They ate in silence. Aurora stared at the ruins, trying to imagine that people had lived here once. And not just people, but people like her, women who had been born the year that she was born, women who might still have been alive when the dragons swooped out of the sky. Children who might have been the age of her grandchildren, if she had not fallen asleep.

The sky rumbled, and Aurora flinched and looked up, almost expecting to see a dragon descending. Instead, a large drop of rain landed in her eye, followed by another on her chin. Her shirt was soaked in seconds, sticking to her like a second skin.

"Let's get inside!" Finnegan yelled. He was barely audible above the roar of falling water. "There's got to be somewhere with a roof."

They scrambled through the streets and into a tall, lopsided building. The door was missing, but the rush of water quieted as they ducked inside.

If not for the decay of fifty years, Aurora could almost imagine that someone still lived in the house. A table stood in the center, slightly crooked, and the back wall was covered in shelves. A pile of rotting clothes waited on the table, as though someone had washed them and got distracted before the clothes could be put away.

Finnegan ran a hand through his hair, sending more droplets pattering to the floor.

Lucas sat on one of the abandoned chairs, apparently trusting it not to break, and Finnegan walked around the ruin, investigating the remains.

Aurora leaned against the doorframe, looking out at the sheets of rain. Alyssinia seemed far away. The capital, with rules and walls and Queen Iris's disapproval, seemed even farther, impossibly far, like it too had been part of another world, part of the dream while she slept, and she was finally, slowly waking up. This place was another kind of nightmare, she thought, but at least she could walk freely in it. At least she could be here to see it.

And she wanted to see more.

"I'm going to explore," she said, after ten more minutes of heavy rain.

"I don't think that's wise—" Lucas said, but she was already stepping out of the door. She turned on the balls of her feet.

"Dragons don't come out in the rain," she said. "I'll be fine."

"Want company?" Finnegan asked.

She shook her head. "I want to wander around. By myself. I'll be back soon."

The rain clung to her clothes, her hair, her skin. It pounded on the ground, drowning out all other noise. The sky was clear and blue, even as thunder rumbled across it. One of those freakish storms, the kind that should be impossible, like the dragons, like this place.

The abandoned town was a maze, and the rain blurred her vision, making it hard to even guess where to go, so she moved on instinct alone, running her hands along the stone. She could feel so much in the twists of the walls, the melted smoothness, the nicks and dimples, the occasional place where more names, more messages, had been scratched. Perhaps this town had stood when Alysse herself was born, when Aurora's ancestors set off across the sea.

Her wanderings led her to the edge of the town, where the ground sloped upward, gently at first, and then steeply, forming a hill that was almost a cliff. From this angle, it seemed to stretch up forever, blocking her path all the way to the sky. But there were a few ruined buildings on the slope too, more damaged than the rest, the ground so hard that even the rain had not yet churned it into mud. And some cracked stones remained, forming something that might once have been a path.

Aurora wanted to climb it. She wanted to stand at the top of the hill, to look over everything, to see it all for what it really was. A girl in her tower, looking out at everything she might touch one day.

She scrambled up the path, hooking her toes into the cracks between the cobbles to stop herself from falling. The rain slowed to a drizzle, quieting as quickly as it had come, but Aurora pressed onward, her knees aching with the effort. She glanced over her shoulder, and already the town was shrinking behind her. She could see the places where the roofs had bent and collapsed, the buildings that had lost their roofs altogether.

She kept climbing.

The rain faded away. The sun shone warm and bright, soothing Aurora's skin.

Above, she saw a cave.

"Aurora!" Finnegan, far below her, shouted into the space between them.

"In a moment," she said. "I just want to see."

She could hear Finnegan following, his feet pounding on the ground, and she frowned. She had told him she wanted to be left alone. How like him, how arrogant, to assume that he could interrupt her after all. And she was so close to the top now. So close. The cave loomed beside her, the inside black as night, the air around it warmer, heavy.

She paused beside the entrance for a moment, her toes clinging to the earth, and then there was a sound like a roar, like a crowd bearing down, filling her ears, echoing through the ground.

A dragon emerged from the cave. Its head appeared first, gleaming with red scales. Its deep-set eyes were red too, like the necklace, full of hunger and vengeance and rage. Black lines ran from its eyes down to its crocodile-like nose. Each tooth was the size of Aurora's hands. Before Aurora could react, the head snapped past her, revealing a long neck, and then a body that went on and on, red and terrible and burning with heat that would have made her flinch, if only she could move. The dragon unfurled its wings, so close that Aurora could see the webbing between the bones, delicate and strong as a spider's web, so large that for a moment they were all she could see. Her world turned red.

It was the most terrifying and beautiful thing she had ever seen. Heat pulsed off its skin, heat that settled within her, surging with her blood. The tail flicked past her, covered in black spikes, ending in a narrow point, so thin that she could have caught it in one hand.

Nothing existed except the dragon. She could almost taste its fire. And she knew what Finnegan meant, why his careful smile turned into genuine excitement when he spoke of these creatures. They were magnificent, uncontainable, bursting from the earth itself and refusing to sleep again.

The dragon twisted. It snapped its jaws and looked at her for no longer than a heartbeat. She looked back, her mouth slightly open, unable to breathe. Then the dragon gave its wings one powerful sweep and shot off over the top of the ridge. Aurora turned to follow its progress. A trail of fire burst into the sky, and then the creature was gone.

She could see Finnegan, waiting halfway down the slope. Her heart was still pounding, her blood hot and alive, possibility surrounding her. The waste did not seem quite so haunted now.

She began to run down the slope, slipping on the stones. "You were right!" she said. "I can feel it. We have a connection. You were right!"

"Of course I was right," he said, as though that were the only possible answer, as though he had known it all along. And for once, Aurora didn't care that he was smug, didn't care that he thought he knew everything and that nothing surprised him. Out here, the heat of the dragon still filling the air, anything else seemed laughable. And so she laughed. He grabbed her waist, and she twirled around him, dizzy with the thrill of it.

Lucas stood a few paces behind Finnegan. He gaped at her. "I've never seen anything like that," he said. "You should be dead."

"But I'm not," she said. "I'm *not*." Because Finnegan was right. Because of her *magic*. "Where can we find more?" She struggled to regain her balance. "Where are the rest? I want to see them."

"They live in the mountain," Lucas said, nodding toward the horizon. "But I really don't think—"

"We're going there," she said. "We have to go there." She spun on the spot, still laughing, joy swelling inside her. "I'm Princess Aurora, and I *command* you to take us there."

Lucas raised his eyebrows. "I wasn't aware I was in the presence of Alyssinian royalty."

Something tugged at the back of her mind, insisting that she should deny it, that she should not have said that, but she felt so *good*. So *powerful*. And if seeing a dragon felt like that, how would it be to use her magic, to connect with them? "We have to find more dragons," she said. "Go to the mountain. Right, Finnegan?"

"Right," he said. "But maybe we should do a little preparation first. Make sure we have food? And a plan?" He rested his hands on Aurora's shoulders, as though trying to keep her feet on the ground. He looked straight into her eyes. He wasn't smiling. "We should get back to the palace," he said. "Before my mother realizes anything is wrong."

The seriousness of his expression made her pause. "All right," she said.

But her heart still pounded as they walked away.

SIX

THE ADRENALINE LASTED THE ENTIRE WALK BACK TO the river. Finnegan and Lucas talked—about the dragon they had seen, about its reaction to Aurora, about the abandoned towns that they passed—but Aurora did not speak. She wanted to be alone in her wonder for as long as she could.

Vanhelm seemed even more hectic after the stillness of the waste. People hurried by on the streets, and preachers shouted at them, their promises of cleansing fire ringing more clearly in Aurora's ears now that the dragon had warmed her skin.

Yet after they bid Lucas good-bye and headed toward the

palace courtyard, Aurora began to doubt once again. The dragon had given her such a *rush*, but it seemed to have knocked away her good sense as well as her fear.

"That was foolish of me," she said, as they walked past one of the courtyard's many fountains. "I shouldn't have told Lucas who I am."

"Probably not," Finnegan said. "But I would trust Lucas with my life. He'll keep your secret."

But even if she did not worry about Lucas, she needed to worry about herself. What had possessed her to speak so freely, so recklessly? She had been almost arrogant in her joy.

They entered the entrance hall as two women swept down the central staircase. The elder one had long black hair, streaked with gray. Her pale skin was lined around the eyes and the corners of her mouth, and the crown she wore suggested that she must be the queen. She was deep in conversation with a tall girl not much younger than Aurora, with long, rust-colored hair and freckles covering her nose. Her green eyes were huge, and they were focused now on the queen, a serious expression on her face.

"Finnegan," the queen said. She paused halfway down the stairs and frowned at him. "You're late."

"I was delayed."

"You always are." She looked at Aurora. "And this, I suppose, is what delayed you. When were you going to tell me that we have Alyssinian royalty staying with us?"

"Right now," Finnegan said. "May I present to you Princess Aurora, heir to the throne of Alyssinia?"

Aurora curtsied. The queen did not curtsy back. She finished descending the stairs and looked Aurora up and down.

"Don't curtsy," she said. "You'll damage your knees."

"That isn't true," Finnegan said.

"Maybe not. But it's a waste of energy." The queen glanced at Finnegan. "Why did you not inform me of her arrival before now?"

"She only came yesterday," Finnegan said. "I did not want to concern you until we knew she intended to stay."

"Did not want to concern me?" The queen laughed. "Oh, your lies can be so pretty, Finnegan. I do not know where you learned them."

"I'm sorry, Your Majesty," Aurora said. "I didn't realize that—"

"Orla," she said. "My name is Orla, not Your Majesty. And do not apologize. It is not your fault that my son is inconsiderate." She looked Aurora up and down again. "So you're the one who's been causing so much trouble in Alyssinia."

"I did not mean to."

"A shame. If you're going to cause a fuss, you might as well be in charge of it." Orla smiled then. "I didn't expect to see you. I told Finnegan that going to Alyssinia was a fool's errand. He's not half as charming as he thinks he is."

Aurora laughed.

"When he came back empty-handed . . . well. I hoped it'd finally got through his head that he can't always control *every-thing*. But here you are." Her eyes narrowed. "And why *are* you here? Should I be planning a wedding? Because it seems awfully rushed."

"She'd never marry me," Finnegan said. "Not when dear Prince Rodric is available. I offered Aurora refuge here. She decided to take me up on it."

"And there is no refuge for you in Alyssinia? No group rallying to your cause?"

"It's not safe there at the moment, Your Majesty," Aurora said. "And Finnegan offered—"

"Oh, I'm sure Finnegan offered many things. None of which he can follow through on. But you're welcome to stay here as long as you like. King John likes us none too well as it is." Orla turned to the girl still lingering by the stairs. "I assume you have not met my daughter, either?" When Aurora shook her head, she sighed. "This is my daughter, Erin. Erin, the Princess Aurora. I'm sure you two will have much to talk about."

Erin gave Aurora a small smile and a nod, and Aurora smiled back.

"We must talk soon, Aurora," Orla said, "but I am afraid you have caught me at a bad time. Not all of us are as idle as my son." She turned to him. "Finnegan, I expect to see you in the greeting hall in five minutes. Do *not* be late." And she strode away, head tilted toward her daughter as they continued their conversation from before.

Finnegan did not move. "Well," he said. "At last you've met the current and future rulers of Vanhelm."

Aurora frowned. "I thought *you* were the future ruler of Vanhelm."

"I'm the elder sibling," he said. "But who could resist my sister's effortless charm?" His usually flawless smile looked rather forced. "I trust you can entertain yourself for the evening? We'll talk more tomorrow. Lay out our plans then."

Aurora watched him stride away. She did not think she had ever seen Finnegan unsettled before. Part of her wanted to hurry after him, to challenge him on his abrupt departure, but she sensed it would be a mistake. Better to use the time to process what she had seen in the waste and plan her next move.

But too much had happened over the past day for her to sit quietly and rest. She missed Nettle's now-familiar presence, the calming way she hummed through the quiet. Even if they did not discuss or do anything significant, she wanted to see her.

A guard directed her to Nettle's rooms, but Nettle immediately ushered Aurora out of the palace again, insisting that Aurora needed to breathe fresh air without the threat of capture or dragons pressing down on her. They ended up sitting at a round table outside a street corner café, eating a spread of breads and jam. Aurora watched the passing crowds warily at first, but nobody even glanced at them. None of them seemed to care in the slightest who she was or what she might be doing.

They talked about many things, but nothing serious. No news from Alyssinia, no strategy for the future. A breather of a conversation, after the exhaustion of the past couple of days. But Finnegan's one almost insignificant omission kept playing on Aurora's mind, demanding to be investigated.

"Finnegan never mentioned he had a sister," she said, as she spread jam on another slice of bread.

"He does not talk about her much."

Aurora lay down the knife, keeping her expression neutral. "Why not? Do they not get along?'

"They do," Nettle said. "But there is tension there. He is a little jealous of her, I think."

Aurora could not imagine Finnegan being jealous of anyone. "Why?"

"They are quite similar," Nettle said. "But they express themselves rather differently. They are both good at reading people, but Erin tends to be quieter about it. She keeps her findings to herself, while Finnegan . . ." She laughed. "You have seen Finnegan. And because of this, his mother sees those good traits in his sister, and not in him. She sees Erin as a ruler, like herself, and Finnegan as a bit of a joke. Finnegan does not like to be thought of as a joke."

"He's told you this?" Aurora said.

"It is what I have seen. I may be wrong."

Her tone implied it was unlikely. And if Nettle believed it, Aurora was inclined to believe it as well.

"Finnegan called her the future leader of Alyssinia," Aurora said carefully. "But he's her older brother, isn't he? So he will be king, however his mother feels."

"It is not unheard of for heirs to be ignored. Finnegan's grandmother was the younger sibling, I believe. Her elder brother was thought unsuitable to deal with the dragons. And the people of Vanhelm have had queens for two generations. Finnegan would be a change, and he worries that it is a change people will not accept. But for now, he is to be king."

Finnegan as king. The image did not quite fit. Aurora could not imagine Finnegan stuck on a throne, listening to complaints, dispensing laws, dealing with the minutae of Vanhelm's politics.

"So that's why he wants my help? He thinks it will make people accept him as king?"

"Perhaps," Nettle said.

Aurora sat deeper in her chair, picking at the food in front of her. It would explain his initial interest in her, his openness to the idea of her magic and her connection to the dragons. He needed her to bolster support. But so many things still did not add up.

"Finnegan was so eager for me to see the dragons today," Aurora said. "And when I saw one, it was like . . . I didn't feel like myself. But I also felt more like myself. I don't know how to describe it. But when we got back to the palace, Finnegan walked off, without talking about it. If it's so important to him—"

"It is important to him," Nettle said. "But if there is one thing that can throw him off, it is his mother. You will see. I believe—"

"Hey! Hey, lady!" Aurora and Nettle both looked up. A red-faced man strode toward them. Aurora shrunk away, but Nettle lengthened her neck to stare back at him. "We don't want your kind here."

It took Aurora a moment to realize that he was talking to Nettle, not her. The singer looked at him for a long moment, and then turned to Aurora. "I believe," she said again, "that he—"

"Hey!" the man said. "Don't ignore me. You're not welcome here."

"I live here," Nettle said evenly. "And you are disrupting my conversation."

"You think you can come here, eat our food, take up our space, and we'll accept that? You people are all the same."

"*You people?*" Aurora stood. "What exactly does that mean, *you people?*"

"People like *her*," the man spat. "Foreigners. You think we got enough to spare? She should live in her own kingdom, not take up ours."

"People like *her*?" Aurora echoed. "I'm not from Vanhelm either. Why are you not shouting at *me*?"

The man spluttered.

"She has as much right to be here as you do." Aurora could feel the anger rising within her, the burning. She took a deep breath, forcing it back. "How dare you?"

"Is there a problem here?" A thin woman in an apron approached the table. She looked at Nettle. "Miss, you're disturbing the other customers. I'm afraid I'm going to have to ask you to leave."

"This is absurd!" Aurora said, but Nettle just pushed her half-finished plate away and stood. Her expression did not change. With an upward tilt of her chin, she turned and walked off. Aurora scrambled after her.

"Nettle, what—"

"What was that?" Nettle said. "That was Vanhelm, Aurora. Such an advanced kingdom, so hardworking, so *welcoming* . . . but so low on space, so concerned about resources when they can grow little themselves. They must have priorities. And for some, that means that only certain people should be allowed to take up space here. *True* Vanhelmians. People not like me."

"But that's ridiculous," Aurora said.

"It is what it is. Do not concern yourself, Aurora. I am used to it, although it is more common in Vanhelm now than it was."

They walked in silence for a little longer. Then Aurora glanced back in the direction of the café. "We didn't pay," she said.

"I know." And finally Nettle smiled.

SEVEN

BY THE TIME FINNEGAN KNOCKED ON AURORA'S DOOR the following morning, she was prepared. She shoved a piece of paper under his nose before he had finished saying "Good morning."

"Here's my plan," she said, as he stepped through the door. "Of how we should proceed."

"It's lovely to see you too, Aurora," Finnegan said. "I *did* sleep well." He took the paper from her and read it. "This is an admirable effort, but do you really think you can plan things out this much?"

"I don't have a lot of time," Aurora said. She had been up

and dressed for the day since dawn, tossing her thoughts onto paper and honing them for the prince's inevitable appearance. "We need to know what we're doing."

"And you had to write it down?"

"I wanted to be clear." She moved closer, pointing to the scribbled words as she spoke. "I have to learn how to use my magic to help Alyssinia. You want me to use it to get rid of the dragons. So. First I learn how to control it. We practice. You help me learn more about magic in general—what it used to be, why it disappeared, what magic the dragons have—and about my curse and what happened to me."

"Because I'm the expert on the subject?"

"No," she said. "But you seem good at puzzling things out. We'll learn how my magic works, and what my connection to the dragons is."

"And hopefully figure out how to deal with them along the way?"

"Exactly. If I'm going to stop the dragons, make them sleep, we'll have to go to that mountain that Lucas mentioned—back where it all began. And once I've done that, you'll help me go back to Alyssinia, stop the violence, and replace the king."

"Simple," Finnegan said. "I can't imagine a single thing that will go wrong."

"I hope you can," Aurora said. "Then we can fix them before they happen."

Finnegan laughed. "All right, dragon girl," he said. "I'll play."

"Good." She moved to fetch her cloak. "We should go to that Institute where Lucas works," she said. "That's probably the best place to start."

Finnegan rested his hand on hers, stopping her movement. "Wait," he said. "I have a better idea."

He took her downstairs and through the door into the palace's private wing. The rooms beyond were far smaller than she would expect for royalty, but bursting with personality—books open spine-up on side tables, fluffy rugs, shelves full of knickknacks that seemed to have more character than value. Some rooms had big windows, overlooking the street or interior gardens, while some were lit only by skylights in the ceiling. There was no corridor, no sense of order, just room after room, thrown together in some unfathomable system that would break the spirit of even the most determined thief.

Finally, Finnegan opened a door and gestured for her to go ahead of him. She walked through, somewhat nervous of what she would find.

Books. Everywhere, books, covering all the walls except one. That one was floor-to-ceiling windows, letting morning light cut patterns on the wooden floor. Staircases spiraled up the sides of the bookshelves, stopping at balconies every seven feet or so, before twisting upward again. They went up, and up, and up, beyond the ceilings of the other rooms, beyond even the ceilings of the rooms above, right to the roof of the palace itself. And every shelf was full, every space bursting with paper, with stories and knowledge.

"Finnegan—"

"I know. Impressive, isn't it? Even I don't know all of what's here. There are too many books to get through in twenty-one years. Too many books to get through in two hundred years. I'm sure there's *something* in here that can help. Even the Institute's resources can't compare to this." He headed straight for one of the spiral staircases along the side of the room. The steps turned so tightly that Aurora's head spun by the time they reached the first platform. "This is the duller stuff," he said. "About plants, mostly. Edible plants, healing plants . . . useful if your kingdom's not a wasteland." He continued up the staircase, past the second balcony, and the third. "Now here is information on *creatures*. Much more interesting. Unicorn legends are somewhere over there, phoenixes, too; the lower alcove has the more mundane creatures, and *this*," he said, as they stepped onto the highest platform, "is all that we have on dragons."

"All of it?" There were only four shelves of books here, and half of them were empty. Aurora walked to the nearest one and ran her fingers along the spines. The older ones all had mystical titles—*The Legend of Dragons*, *The Day the Dragons Died*—while the newer volumes contained history, anatomy, maps of their domains.

"We know three things about dragons for certain," Finnegan said. "That they exist, that they hate water, and that they kill us. Everything else is guesswork. No one gets close enough to dragons to learn about them and lives to write a book."

Aurora twisted her dragon necklace between her fingers. "But some people must have got close," she said. "To get dragon's blood."

"But they didn't live long enough afterward to write about it. Or to do much of anything, in most cases. They might have gathered a few theories, but no facts. No proof."

"If you have dragon's blood," Aurora said, "that must mean you know how to hurt them. Why haven't you fought them before?"

"Because we can't hurt them," Finnegan said. "Not really. We tried to fight them, when they first returned. It didn't work well. First it was cannons and spears, but these things seem to eat metal. They weren't affected at all. Then some genius tried to make spears and arrows out of ice, thinking that would cut them and melt their magic. Well, they *did* cut them, but then the weapons melted, and they were left with very angry dragons irritated by minor wounds. The men gathered a little blood for further research, but that was all that they ever achieved."

"And this hard-won blood was put in a necklace?"

"It was a gift for my grandmother," Finnegan said. "They thought it would honor her. She was less than impressed."

"A gift you just happened to have with you in Alyssinia when you met me?"

He laughed. "You are far too suspicious, Aurora. I had it sent to me after your first hint of magic. I wanted to see how its magic responded to you."

She ran her finger along the rough edge of the dragon's wing. She tried to picture the blood inside it, how it had once pounded through a dragon's veins.

"But how did you see that I had magic?" she said. "You seemed to know before I did, and there were a million more reasonable explanations for what happened. What made you see?"

"I paid attention."

"And you expect me to believe that?"

"What can I say, dragon girl? You're hard to look away from."

She expected to see a mocking smile, a teasing bow, but he continued to search the shelves, all hints of smugness gone.

"I have a book," he said, as though nothing out of the ordinary had happened. "About dragons. It was my favorite when I was younger. I'll lend it to you after this. You should know the legends too."

"Oh," Aurora said. "Thank you."

They walked on to a third floor platform, halfway around the room. Most of the books there must have been over a hundred years old, their bindings falling away. Some of them did not look like they had been touched since the library had been built. But one small area was dust free.

"Here," he said, "are all the books we have on magic."

A single volume poked out a few inches, ruining the smooth line of the shelf. She slid the book free. The surrounding books clung to it, as though it didn't quite fit.

"You've been reading this one?" she said. He nodded. "Then this is the one I'm going to read first."

"You don't trust me to tell you what I've learned?"

"I just think we should start out in the same place. It'll make things easier."

"All right," he said. "I'll be back in the dragon section if you need me."

She watched him stroll away, and then sat and opened the book. The first line seemed to stare back at her, printed in a large and elaborate font.

Magic is energy, uncontrolled.

She turned the pages almost too fast for comprehension, trying to absorb the words with glances alone. Magic was energy, wildness, nature, it said. It was a part of the world, separate from any individual. Some people could tap into it, influence it, but most could not.

Yet that was not true for Aurora. At least, she did not think it was true. Her magic had always burst out of her. *You burn with it,* Celestine had said. The power came when her emotions were strongest, and it always seemed to come from *her*, from her anger or frustration or fear.

She placed the book open on the floor and seized a candle from the table. She stared at the wick.

If magic came from the air, surely she would need to draw it *in*, like breathing. She breathed in and tried to feel magic in the air, searching for a hint of fire.

Nothing. It simply felt like breathing. She closed her eyes and tried again, but still it was the same. She opened her eyes, and this time she tried pushing flames toward the wick, willing it to light.

Still nothing happened.

She wasn't entirely surprised. Her magic rarely appeared when she wanted it to. But she needed to learn how to control it, to tap into the power lingering under her skin.

She stared at the wick and willed it to burn. She thought of flames, thought of her own anger. How had it felt, the last time she had exploded with fire?

"If you burn down my library, I'll never forgive you."

She jumped. Finnegan stood by the stairs, a book tucked under his arm.

"I wasn't going to burn down the library. I wasn't doing anything at all."

"Not going well?"

She lay the candle on the ground. "The book said you have to take magic in from the air," she said. "But it feels wrong."

Finnegan bent down beside her. "You think it's more a case of directing it out?"

"Perhaps," she said. "But that goes against everything the book says about magic."

"But the author never met *you*." He picked up the book and weighed it in his hands. "You have magic in Alyssinia, but no one else does. It would make sense if you have your own source of magic. Like the dragons."

But that didn't explain why she would be different. She looked at the rows of books before them, the thick layers of dust showing just how old some of the knowledge must be. It would take forever to read them all. Her parents had never allowed her to read any books on magic during her childhood, as though even the mention of it would trigger the curse. They'd left her completely ignorant of the things that she most needed to know.

"In Alyssinia, the king said that people had stolen all the kingdom's magic. Could that be possible? Could that be why it vanished?"

"I don't know," Finnegan said. "It couldn't really be stolen, could it? It didn't belong to anyone in particular. Seems to me that it just got used up. There was magic in Vanhelm, until gradually there wasn't. And then there was magic in Alyssinia, until eventually there wasn't. Maybe it's a resource, and there's only so much."

"Then I think I got more than my fair share," Aurora said. She picked up the candle again. "How can I learn how to use my magic if no one's seen anything like it before?"

"First, you need a better place to practice," Finnegan said. "Somewhere with less chance of destroying thousands of priceless books and incurring my undying hatred."

"I'm willing to risk it," Aurora said, but she smiled.

"I have to go to some meetings," Finnegan said. "You read.

Resist the urge to burn my books. I'll see what I can do."

Aurora spent the rest of the day among the library's dustiest books, pausing only to eat. The books' pages were yellowed and fragile, some seeming on the verge of disintegrating in her hands, but their archaic language offered nothing new. They all referred to magic as an external force that only a lucky few could influence. They spoke of great deeds that had been accomplished with magic, of power channeled to grow better crops and end droughts, magic used to influence minds, magic even used to kill, but each time, the user was tapping into something in the air, helping it bloom or perverting it for their own twisted needs. No one seemed to burn with magic of their own. If they did, no one had written about them.

But then, it seemed, truly powerful users of magic were rare. Some people could use it for small tasks, and healers were common enough to deal with the day-to-day ailments of the villages, but there were few who could use it to manipulate, to control, to destroy. A few male sorcerers, who traveled to share their talents for a price. And, every now and again, a fearsome witch.

The first, the books said, had been Alysse.

Aurora leaned closer, her fingers hovering over the page. Alysse had been her hero as a child, but her own experiences since awakening had soured those stories of the beloved magical queen.

The books seemed to confirm her newfound cynicism. At first, the story was familiar—Alysse was the daughter of one of the first people to cross the sea to Alyssinia, and people thought of her as the last remnant of Vanhelmic power, a memory of what Vanhelm *could* have been, if its own magic had not faded away. She had not known about her talents until she left Vanhelm for Alyssinia, an endless forest where the magic was untouched. The land that was so forbidding to the others seemed to *whisper* to her, and she taught her people how to hear the whispers too.

Yet as Aurora turned the pages, the story changed from the version she knew. Alysse had too much power, it said. She could have made the trees bow to her if she wished it, could have changed the direction of rivers and snatched birds out of the sky. People feared her, toward the end. A girl who could talk to nature and make the land welcome them was sweet, useful. A woman with those powers, bold and fearless and unbowed by anything, was something else. They did not trust this sorceress who could make so much happen with her thoughts. And so they murdered her, a few days before her coronation. The Alyssinians had crossed the ocean for opportunity and magic, but feared it once they found it, in the hands of their once-beloved princess.

Aurora sat back on her heels. She had never heard a hint of this before, but after her experiences in Alyssinia, it made sense. And which was more likely: a beautiful queen who vanished into the mist, or a princess forced to vanish before she ascended to the throne, because other people wanted her power?

Perhaps Alysse was able to defy those trying to control her. Perhaps she ruled, and was happy, and the truth just got twisted in a myth across the sea.

Aurora was not sure she believed it. Alysse may not have been Alyssinia's first queen, but she was Alyssinia's first witch. And that, Aurora was realizing, was a dangerous thing.

EIGHT

FINNEGAN RETURNED TO THE LIBRARY AFTER DINNER, and led Aurora through a door on the second balcony. The room beyond was small and square, with a table in the center, a few boxes against one wall and an empty grate. "This is the antechamber that connects my rooms to the library. I thought it might be a good place to practice, so I cleared it out."

"*You* cleared it out?"

"My servants cleared it out," he corrected. "Either way, there are candles in the boxes, and there are no books to burn. I thought it would help."

"Yes," she said. "Thank you." She walked over to the nearest box and looked at the candles inside. They were all different sizes, all different colors, as though Finnegan thought the shade of the wax might make a difference. She picked out a solid, square-looking one and placed it on the table. Then she stepped back and stared at the wick.

"Wait!" Finnegan strode toward her. "The necklace. We should remove it first. I'd rather you didn't burn the whole palace down." He picked it up by the chain and unclicked the clasp. The metal tickled Aurora's neck as he pulled it away.

The dragon was a small thing, but she immediately missed the weight of it. She pressed her fingers to the spot where it had rested.

"Do you think the necklace is why my magic got so out of my control, in that village in Alyssinia?"

"Possibly," he said. "But I'd rather not be in my own chambers when we find out."

Finnegan stepped back into the shadows, and Aurora focused on the candle again. All she had to do was light it. She had done that before. So she stared at it, forcing her intention through the air, willing it to obey. *Burn.*

Nothing happened.

She could feel Finnegan watching her. Waiting. Anticipating her magic. "Do you have somewhere else to be?" she said.

"Trying to get rid of me, dragon girl?"

"No," she said. "But aren't you worried? I don't know anything about controlling my magic. And I'm pretty sure I once nearly set Rodric on fire. Don't you find it . . . *unnerving*? It would be safer not to be here."

"Unnerving?" Finnegan laughed. "Aurora, it's amazing. You have the power to make things *burn*, just because you want them to. You can stare a dragon in the eye and live to laugh about it. Why wouldn't I want to be there to see that?"

"Because I could set *you* on fire."

"I didn't know you were so concerned for my well-being. Don't worry, Aurora. I'll try not to incur your wrath."

Now it was her turn to laugh. "Do you think you can manage it?"

"No," he said. "But I'm willing to risk it."

She brushed her hair away from her face and stared at the candle. "The problem is that I don't know how to begin. I've tried before—standing in a room, trying to set a candle on fire. And it's never worked. Not once. It's always been accidental. Or if I meant to do it, it's as if . . . I was so caught up in the moment that I couldn't even think about it. It just happened."

"Then maybe you shouldn't try so hard," Finnegan said. "Stop focusing on lighting it."

"I should focus on *not* lighting it?"

"I mean," he said, "that you can't do anything simply by *willing* it. If you think to yourself, *walk*, you won't move anywhere. You can't *think* about moving your foot. You just have to move it."

She ran her fingers through her hair again. "That's not true," she said. "Children must have to think about walking. And how am I supposed to practice if I'm not supposed to *think* about what I'm doing?"

Finnegan stepped closer and rested a hand on her shoulder blade. "Well," he said, his voice low. "What did it feel like, the last time you used magic?"

She closed her eyes, reaching for the memory, for the traces of magic that she had not allowed herself to feel. It felt like power, like desperation, like she could no longer be contained by her bones and skin. *Dangerous.*

But as she stood in the darkened room, she only felt like herself. Flesh and blood and golden curls, too aware of the walls around her.

"It's hard," she said. "To feel something that you don't really feel."

"If you felt it once, not so long ago, you can feel it again."

She remembered the first time she had tried to light a candle, locked in her room in the castle in Petrichor. The thing that had finally caused a spark was her frustration at how useless she was. How she smiled, and curtsied, and watched as her life was crushed away. How even her parents had betrayed her, how everyone was so busy celebrating her that they never once considered her as a person of her own.

She bundled all those thoughts together, and she pushed. *Light*, she thought. *Light.*

But nothing happened. Not a breath of air moved.

She squeezed her eyes closed. She could summon fire, she had seen the proof, but there wasn't so much as a flicker now. Could she only use it in Alyssinia, where the memory of magic was fresher? Or was it *meant* to be out of her control?

Finnegan ran his hand from her shoulder to her elbow. "Did you know you had magic, before you fell asleep?"

"No," Aurora said. "I didn't."

"If using it was easy, you would have noticed before. It took a lot to bring it out the first time. Of course it's hard to control."

"But I never tried to use magic before." There was no evidence that she had even *had* magic before. She had been frustrated then, hadn't she? She'd been angry. But she had never made anything burn.

The magic could be a remnant of the curse, traces of powers used to try and awaken her. It might not even be hers.

But Celestine had told Aurora that she had been created with a spell, a bargain between Aurora's mother and the witch. Was that the reason she had magic? Was it a twist that Celestine added to the deal?

"Maybe it can't be controlled. Maybe that's part of the curse. Celestine would never let me have magic I could actually use at will, would she?"

"Maybe," Finnegan said. "But I don't think so." She could feel his breath against her ear. "Don't think about it so hard. Try *finding* the fire. Grabbing on to it. Trust that it's there."

"It's there," she said. The charred village was proof of that.

"It's like . . . it comes when I'm angry, when I'm not actually thinking about it. When I'm scared, when I'm threatened, it's there, almost without a thought. But otherwise . . ." Otherwise, she couldn't find a trace of it. How could she control something that only appeared when she stopped trying to control it?

"Well," Finnegan said slowly, "if you think about it, you're being threatened all the time right now. Considering what King John's up to."

"So I should be constantly afraid, and then I'll get stronger?" That did not sound like strength. "No," she said. "No. I should feel angry." Those were the times she had used magic. When she hated the king, hated Rodric, hated herself. When she had wanted to see things burn. "It's fire," she said. "Fire isn't afraid."

She turned back to the candle, and turned her thoughts inward. At first, she thought of her anger at herself, for how useless she had been, how she had caused so much damage in her quest to be good. Then she forced those thoughts away. Her magic needed to be her strength, and she couldn't be strong while tearing herself apart.

Instead, she dug into that lingering feeling of betrayal . . . King John threatening her at the wedding, the key clicking as Iris locked her into her room, Celestine smiling her hungry smile, Tristan staring at her from the rooftop as blood ran in the square. And then she pushed further, into those unfair thoughts she could never acknowledge—fury at Rodric, for waking her. At the people in Alyssinia, for thinking she was their savior. At her own mother, for making a deal with a witch when she knew it must go wrong. None of them had ever given her a chance. None of them had treated her like a real person. She didn't want to be their savior, didn't want to be their queen, but they did not care what she wanted, not for a moment.

The pressure built in her chest, pounding in her ears. She did not think *light,* but she grabbed the feeling and *pushed* it toward the candle.

It burst into flame.

Finnegan lunged forward to extinguish it. "Maybe a bit smaller next time," he said. "Candles do have wicks, you know."

"You want me to unleash all of my anger *and* only start a small fire?"

"Not unleash it," he said. "Embrace it. Then find the spark you need."

She stared at the deformed remains of the candle. "It's like . . . the fire, the feeling of it, rushes out of me. Maybe if I can contain it somehow, and pull out a *tendril* of it . . ."

This time, the magic came more easily. A surge of power, a spark around the wick of a candle.

By the end of the evening, several candles flickered, and a large fire burned in the grate. She was conscious of every beat of her heart. Her limbs ached, but it was a comfortable kind of tired, like she actually *fit* in her skin.

She sat on the floor, her legs tucked beneath her. Finnegan had an arm draped around her shoulder, and she didn't even mind, didn't want to shove him away. Hours of practice had made them feel closer. In tune. Hours of picking up fragments of her anger and pushing them across the room, of sharing her feelings with words, of him coaxing more out of her than she knew she had. One stubborn part of her still wanted do it alone, to have the magic be *her* power, but sharing it with Finnegan, accepting a partner, did not mean it wasn't hers. She felt . . . open.

"Well," Finnegan said. "I suppose we'd better stop for tonight."

He turned his head, his nose inches from hers. He was not grinning now. If he just shifted a couple of inches, he could kiss her.

She glanced at his lips.

It was just the dark, the candlelight, confusing her thoughts. But her heart pounded faster, and her breath hitched as he slipped almost unperceivably closer.

He was going to kiss her.

She couldn't let him kiss her. Not now, not when things were so confused, not when she needed this alliance to work. She ducked her head. "I'm exhausted," she said. "I should rest."

"You don't have to worry," he said, as he sat back. "I'm not going to kiss you."

"Why not?" She did not mean to speak, but the words rushed out before she could stop them. They were not what she would have wanted to say. *I don't want you to kiss me,* perhaps. Or *how dare you assume?* There had been something there, a moment, but that did not mean she was desperate for him to kiss her.

"I'm waiting for *you* to kiss *me*. I feel like you've been kissed enough times in your life. But if you leaned up and kissed me, if you were so overcome that you couldn't *resist* . . . well, that would be something worth seeing, wouldn't it?"

She stood up. "You'll be waiting a long time."

He stood too, utterly calm, smiling his infuriating smile. "Don't worry, Aurora," he said, as she walked away. "It'll be worth the wait."

NINE

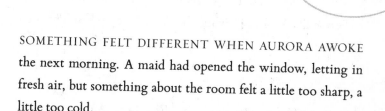

SOMETHING FELT DIFFERENT WHEN AURORA AWOKE the next morning. A maid had opened the window, letting in fresh air, but something about the room felt a little too sharp, a little too cold.

Aurora rolled onto her side and burrowed deeper into the blankets.

A rose lay on the pillow next to her. A piece of paper was wrapped around the stem. Aurora sat up, her hair tumbling around her face. Was this some joke from Finnegan, a comment on last night? She picked it up. One word had been written on the parchment.

Soon.

Aurora recognized that handwriting. She had seen it burned into the wall of her tower, taunting her for a life long lost.

Celestine.

Celestine had been here. In this city, in this palace, in her bedroom while she slept. Aurora dropped the rose and scrambled out of bed, avoiding the flower as though it might bite her.

She spun on the spot. Celestine was not there. Not in the room, not lurking in a corner, waiting to be noticed.

Aurora ripped the blankets off the bed and threw the pillow aside, hunting for another message, another clue. Nothing. Her dresser was untouched, as was her desk. Just the open window, and the rose on the pillow.

She picked up the flower again, careful to avoid its thorns. Celestine had broken in while she slept. To do what? Threaten her? Warn her?

She must know that Aurora had been practicing her magic. She must have seen her conjure fire, and this was her way of congratulating her or unsettling her. She wanted Aurora to know she was close.

Aurora ran to the entrance hall, her hair still tangled from sleep, the rose clutched in her hand. One guard stood on duty. He stood to attention as she approached, but she was too unnerved for formalities. "Did anyone come in overnight?" Aurora said. "A woman? A stranger?"

The guard frowned. "No, miss. No one unexpected."

But Celestine could bend reality, make people forget what they had seen. "Anything strange at all?" she said. "Any odd noises, *anything*?"

"I can assure you, miss. There's been nothing."

"Are you certain?" she said. "Maybe someone came in through another entrance, or—"

"There are no other entrances," the guard said. "I can promise you. You're safe enough here."

"But—"

"What's the problem?" Aurora spun around. Finnegan strode toward her. He was frowning. "Jackson, our guest is supposed to be able to move freely."

"I know that, Your Highness," the guard said with a bow. "She was asking me if I had seen anyone unusual overnight. As I told her, I've seen no one. Everything is in order."

"Then I'm certain everything is as you say." He rested a hand on Aurora's arm. "We won't disturb you any longer."

He steered Aurora through the side door and into one of the studies. Once they were alone, he dropped his hand from her arm and turned to face her. "Aurora?" he said. "Care to explain what that was about? Why are you in your nightdress? Why are you holding a rose?"

Aurora looked around the room, half expecting another hint of Celestine's presence. The witch was watching her. She could be watching her now.

"Aurora?"

"Nothing," she said. She took a steadying breath. "I just want to know how good the guards are here. If people can come and go as they please."

"Of course people can't come and go as they please. We're not going to let King John's men saunter in here."

"But there must be other ways into the palace," Aurora said. She began to pace, her limbs refusing to rest. "Servants' entrances, secret passageways. I got in and out of the castle in Petrichor without anyone seeing me. There must be passages here, too."

"This palace isn't as old as your castle. Trust me, we have all of the plans to it. There are no secret ways." He watched her pace, frowning. "Did you see something? A threat?"

"No," she said, shaking her head. "I don't know."

"Aurora." He rested a hand on her shoulder, guiding her to a halt. "What happened?"

She looked up at his face. She had told no one about Celestine, not a word about her presence or her threats, but if she was inside the palace, if she was *here* . . . Aurora had to tell someone. And Finnegan was insightful, for all his flaws. He could help her to know what to do. "Someone left this rose in my room."

"A rose?"

"Yes. Someone left it on my pillow, while I was sleeping. There was a note wrapped around the stem. It just said *soon*."

Finnegan's fingers tightened around her shoulder. "King John would never be so subtle. Ominous flora isn't exactly his style."

"No," Aurora said. "Not King John." She glanced at the window. The sun was rising, casting orange light across the floor. "It's Celestine."

"Celestine?" Finnegan's eyes were wide. "The witch who cursed you?"

"I know it sounds insane," she said, "but I've seen her. She came to me, in the castle in Petrichor, and then on the streets of the city, before I escaped. She said . . ." The words seemed too dangerous to even speak aloud. "She said she wanted me to join her. She told me that was what I was meant to do."

"But you told her no?"

"Of course I told her no. She said she would be watching me, but I didn't think . . . I thought I'd be safe, across the ocean. But she's here too. I've barely been here two days, and she's already here."

"You think she's going to attack you?"

"No," Aurora said. "I don't know." She raked her hand through her hair, her fingers catching on the knots. If Celestine wanted to attack her, she would have done it weeks ago. She'd had plenty of chances. "She's playing with me. Trying to unsettle me. She wants me to *choose* to join her, but I don't know—I don't know why she would think that I would ever do that. What does she think is going to happen? Why would she think I would want to work with the woman who cursed me?"

"What did she offer you?" Finnegan said. "If you joined her?"

"Answers. Control over my magic. Revenge."

"Those sound rather persuasive to me."

"But she cursed me. How could she think I would join her?" Celestine must imagine a terrible future, if she thought Aurora would ever want to share her power.

"Did she say what she wanted from you?"

"Only hints. But I know she wanted magic. *My* magic. She didn't seem . . . entirely *whole*." She looked up at Finnegan, struggling to find the words. "She stole magic from me. From a cut in my cheek. I think she thinks I'm key to getting her power back. But I don't know *how*. How can I have magic, when no one else does?"

"Maybe because you slept," Finnegan said. "Maybe you carried it with you."

"Yes," Aurora said again. "Maybe." That would explain Celestine's obsession with her. But if that was the case, why would Celestine not take the magic she wanted now? Why would she play with subtle threats?

"She's trying to unsettle you," Finnegan said. "You're not going to do anything that you don't want to." He let go of her shoulder. "But you could take advantage of this," he said. "She'll know more about your magic than anyone. If you pretended to accept her offer, tricked information out of her—"

"No," Aurora said. She wouldn't even consider it. "Celestine is dangerous. I don't know what she would do."

"Maybe you should ask."

"No," she said again. "I can't trust her."

"But if you learn more about her, you might find out more about your magic. The curse. The dragons. She would know."

"Then I'll research," she said. "Everything that we can find on the last hundred years, everything on Celestine before I was cursed. All of it. I can get answers without asking her." But it would be difficult to do so from across the sea. She would have to unpick secrets and rumors from over a century ago, while hundreds of miles away from where events had occurred. There might not be anything to find.

She dragged a hand through her hair. "I'll get dressed," she said. "Then I'm going back to the library. Might as well start there."

"Do you want company, going back to your rooms?"

"I can find my way."

"I thought you might be wary of being alone, considering what just happened. I can send a servant or a guard, if you like."

"Oh." It was a thoughtful thing to say. "Thank you, but I'll be fine." Celestine wanted her to be afraid. Aurora could not show any weakness now.

She returned to the deserted library as soon as she was dressed and climbed to the section on magic. There had to be *some* information there that could help.

Several books did mention Celestine, but there was little information of use. The first reported appearance of Celestine was about twenty years before Aurora was born, and the last time anyone saw her was at the banquet when she pricked baby Aurora's finger with a needle and cursed her to a near-eternal sleep. In between, she was known to live in her tower in the forest and make bargains with those who asked. Some books claimed she was vindictive, cursing the kingdom for her own pleasure, while others claimed she stayed out of affairs unless she was approached.

One author said she had been unfairly blamed for the kingdom's difficulties and the disappearance of magic, and Aurora almost threw the book to the ground. Whatever Celestine may or may not have done or been blamed for, she had cursed Aurora when she was only a few days old. She had destroyed Aurora's entire life. She wasn't a victim of anything.

"Aurora?"

Finnegan stood in the middle of the library, neck craned to peer at the balconies. "Are you in here?"

"Yes," she said, standing up. "I'm here."

There was a thud as Finnegan dropped a huge pile of paper onto the library's center table. The balcony shook. "What's all that?" Aurora said, as she descended the stairs.

"All the diplomatic records on Alyssinia I could find for the past hundred years, and a couple of decades before." He heaved a second pile onto the table. "They won't be as useful as Alyssinia's own records, I'm sure, but there might be something in there. Better to go straight to the source."

"That's fantastic," Aurora said. "How did you get these?" She

picked up the top page. It was a collection of notes and abbre-
viations, written in an almost illegible hand. The sheet below
seemed to be a list of gifts exchanged after a diplomatic mission.

"I walked into the archive and took them," Finnegan said.
"Advantage of being the prince."

She sat, pulling more pages toward her. There would be lots
of useless information to sift through, lots of pointless minutae,
but there had to be useful insight hidden in there too.

But Celestine was barely mentioned, and neither was magic.
One document dated ninety years ago questioned the value
of Alyssinia as an ally, with their magical resources seemingly
gone, and a far older paper commented on a drought that had
been blamed "on some witch often accused of blighting the
kingdom." "Evidence, it seems, is lacking," the ambassador had
noted, "but the Alyssinians are a superstitious bunch." Aurora
and Finnegan arranged every mention of magic by date, trying
to build some sort of timeline of its decline, but several hours'
work yielded few results. Celestine had been blamed for horrors,
magic had faded away—nothing they had not already known.

Finnegan held out a page to Aurora. "I think this one will
interest you," he said.

It was a letter, dated two days after Aurora's eighteenth
birthday. The princess, it said, had fallen into a cursed sleep. The
ambassador warned of potential instability to come, as the king
hunted the witch responsible, and commented that those "superstitious Alyssinians" were searching desperately for any way to

awaken her. It had been suggested that a prince's kiss might be the cure—perhaps Vanhelm could find someone to send. Waking her would be a diplomatic coup.

It was unsettling, to see her own plight described with such analytic detachment. Aurora lay the paper in its place in the timeline and reached for another one, trying to ignore the way her hand shook.

Finnegan was watching her. She refused to look up at him again.

"Why don't we go out?" he said. "Take a break?"

"We've got work to do," she said. "There are so many more pages to read."

"And they'll still be here when we get back." He gently pried the next report from her hand. "We should clear our heads a bit."

She let out a breath. Her shoulders were tense, and her head throbbed slightly, but they needed to work quickly. They couldn't just wander off now.

"I need a break, at least," Finnegan said. He stood. "Come on. I'll show you more of the city."

She knew what he was doing. He had seen the tension in her shoulders, had seen how unsettled she was, by the letter, by Celestine's rose, by everything that had occurred. There was something strangely considerate about the gesture, an attempt to distract her without insisting that *she* needed to rest.

But going out would still be risky. "Nettle showed me some of it," she said.

"Oh, but Vanhelm is always changing," he said. "Who knows if everything is still what it was yesterday?" He took her hand.

"And King John's spies?"

"If they know you're here, then they know you're here. They won't be able to do anything with me and my guards there too."

"Because you're so imposing?"

"Of course."

She did want to see the city. To escape the pressure, the *need* to understand her magic, to be as everybody hoped, for a few hours at least. Her responsibility would still be here when she returned. And there was a part of her that wanted to see where Finnegan would take her. To see his grin and hear his laugh without the pressures of courts and dragons around them.

A small break could not hurt.

"All right," she said. "Show me your city."

TEN

THE WIND BATTERED THEM AS THEY WALKED DOWN the street, flapping Aurora's cloak and tangling her hair in front of her face.

"It'll settle down," Finnegan said, shouting slightly to be heard. He grabbed Aurora's hand, his palm warm after the bite of the wind. They headed north, a few guards trailing several feet behind them. The wind stung Aurora's cheeks. She burrowed her chin under the fastening of her cloak.

"So, traveler," he said. "What would you like to do first?"

"I thought you were going to show me Vanhelm," she said. "So show me Vanhelm."

"I know just the place."

The crowds grew thicker. The preachers were out on the street corners again, shouting about the end of days to passersby, but few people even glanced at them. Finnegan's guards vanished into the crowd. Some of the people they passed seemed to recognize Finnegan—one girl elbowed another so sharply that her friend nearly fell over—but nobody tried to stop them.

They approached a square building, about ten floors high, with busts of different creatures lined up outside. A unicorn held its head midtoss, and a dragon bared its teeth near the door, nostrils flared.

One boy was attempting to clamber up the unicorn's spiked mane. He slipped, and his friends laughed.

"What is this?" Aurora asked.

"The museum," Finnegan said. "I thought you'd fit in here."

She was so surprised that she laughed. She pushed him, and he ducked away, before jerking back to her side. "Actually, Finnegan, I do believe *you're* the older one here. Maybe you belong in a museum."

"It's true," Finnegan said. "I'll never be eighteen again. But *I* don't remember last century."

She ignored him and headed for the museum's front door. Once she was inside, she found that the museum wasn't full of old relics and plaques about battles long ago, but art. From shards of pottery to lush paintings, half-crumbled stone statues and casts of bronze, every inch of space was filled with shape and color.

"This isn't a museum," she said.

"It's an art museum. Didn't you say you already knew all of your history? I didn't want to bore you."

They wandered the halls, turning wherever their fancy took them. Aurora paused in front of one oil painting that took up a whole wall. A blond girl crouched in a forest, while a fairy fluttered above her outstretched hand. The girl seemed unsure whether to be enchanted or terrified by the magic before her. Aurora knew how she felt.

Another painting somehow managed to be both dark and colorful, with purple fog twisting around a ruined tower. A girl stood in the center, a sword in hand, her face grim with defiance. Aurora rested her fingertips an inch from the paint, her breath in her throat.

"This one," she said. "It makes me think of a book I once read . . ."

"*The Dark Ones*? Rosamund Frith?"

"Yes! You've read it?"

"Only ten times or so. This painting always makes me think of it. I wanted to buy it for the palace, but *apparently*, my mother doesn't want us taking art away for our own personal use."

"That is such a good book. The bit in the tower? When all of her thoughts are coming true, so the more scared she gets, the scarier things become? I couldn't sleep after that."

"I would have thought you'd be more of one for romances, Rora."

"There's romance in *The Dark Ones*."

"Between the girl and a demon."

"It's still romance, isn't it?" She turned back to the painting, following the swirls of the paint with her eyes. "More realistic than true love and happily ever after."

"I suppose you would be the one to know."

She glanced at him, but he didn't seem to be mocking her. "Come on," she said. "I want to see the others."

Many of the paintings here had a fantastical twist. While all the pictures Aurora had ever seen in Alyssinia were portraits or landscapes, the ones here all felt like stories. The people in them seemed frozen in midaction, like everything would hurtle on the moment she looked away.

Aurora stopped as they turned the corner and then hurried toward a small painting hung on the far wall, composed of soft blues and grays. A black-haired girl stood barefoot on a stony beach, the ocean crashing around her. Her feet were half-buried by the sand, and the foam left swirling patterns as it slipped back into the water. Her hair was tossed into the air, echoing the crash of the waves.

"This one," she said. "Do you know this story?"

"I know lots of stories about the sea," he said. "None that remind me of this, though."

"I only know one." But as Aurora looked at the girl's tangled hair, she felt *certain* that this was based on the one she knew.

"Tell me."

Aurora resisted the urge to touch the foam on the canvas. "All right," she said. "Once upon a time, there was a girl who lived by the ocean. Every day, she would walk out, right to the edge of the water, so that the tide rushed over her toes, and she would stand there until she sank into the sand." It had all sounded mystical to Aurora as a child, locked in a tower with only the forest for company. She had not known what the ocean felt like, what sand really was, or how you could sink into it by *standing* there, but the image had always stuck with her. "Every day, the girl would wonder, *What's out there?* And perhaps if she stood there long enough, she would be able to see. An answer would come to her. She returned to the shore every day for years, simply *wondering*, imagining what she might find."

"And then a kind witch appeared from the air to help her?"

"No," Aurora said. "There was no witch in the story. One day, the girl thought she saw something moving in the water, right on the horizon. A creature or a vessel or *something*, she didn't know, but she could not look away from it, so she dragged her feet out of the sand and stepped closer. Perhaps one step more, and she'd be able to see what it was. She stepped, and she stepped, until the water came up to her knees, and then to her waist, her skirts whirling around her as the tide lapped in and out. And still she kept walking, because *something* was out there, and she had spent so long standing and waiting, rooted to the ground, and she had to know. Soon the girl was floating, and the land she knew so well was far behind, a line on the horizon too, but she still could not make out what was across the water."

"She swam to the other land?"

"No," Aurora said. "She drowned, trapped between the two. The current tugged at her legs, and she couldn't keep her head above water. There was nothing left of her but her footprints, sunk into the sand on the shore."

Finnegan was watching her closely. "And that's your favorite story, Rora?"

"Not my favorite," she said slowly. But she had always loved it, morbid child that she had been. Something about it had stirred her heart. "Don't go into the unknown. That's what I think it's meant to say. But it never felt that way to me. It seemed more . . . don't go unprepared. That girl spent years standing and watching. Maybe she should have spent those years learning to swim. And either way, she died where she wanted to be."

"She died on the way."

"She wanted to see what was out there, to be swallowed by the ocean. And she was. I think I'd rather be her than the girl waiting on the beach forever." She bit her lip. She had said too much. Finnegan would surely mock her for her romantic naïveté. But instead, he smoothed her hair off her shoulder. His fingers grazed her neck.

"You're not her," he said. "You're here, aren't you? And you were wise enough to take a boat."

She twisted around slightly to look at him. He was very tall, she suddenly realized. Almost a foot taller than she was.

"Shall we move on?" he said. "You haven't even seen any of the paintings of dragons yet."

The dragon art was all movement too, rushing flames and fiery eyes. Aurora stared at the creatures, hypnotized by the colors, the *power*, until she noticed the shadowed figures cowering in the corners of the canvas.

She dragged herself away.

They were walking back to the palace when Aurora saw him. Messy brown hair, a familiar walk, hurrying through the crowd. The brief glance sent a shock of recognition through her.

Tristan.

She stopped so suddenly that Finnegan half walked into her. She twisted in the direction she thought he had gone, but the boy had already vanished. And it couldn't have been Tristan. He was across the ocean, fighting his revolution. There were many boys with brown hair, and his face had hardly been distinctive. It *couldn't* have been him.

"Rora?" Finnegan said. He turned too. "What did you see? One of John's men?"

She could not tell him. How would he react, if he thought one of the rebels was in his city? "No," Aurora said. "No. I thought—I thought I saw Nettle. But it wasn't her."

Finnegan did not look like he believed her.

ELEVEN

NETTLE WAS IN HER ROOM, BRAIDING HER LONG BLACK hair in a crown around her head. She glanced up as Aurora knocked and pushed the door open.

"Aurora," she said. "What is wrong?"

"Can I trust you to keep a secret? If I ask you something . . . can you promise not to tell Finnegan?"

"It depends on what it is." Nettle's hands were bent at a painful-looking angle as she pulled the strands at the nape of her neck into the braid. "If you are planning to turn against him, you probably should not inform me. If you wish to tell me that you think he is terribly rude, then your secret is safe."

"What if I need you to find something out for me? Something that's not about Finnegan. Just something that I don't want him to know about. Yet."

Nettle paused in her braiding. "What has happened?"

"I think I saw Tristan." It felt ridiculous to say it aloud. "In Vanhelm. Today. I mean, I can't be certain, but . . . it looked like him. But he's in Petrichor. Isn't he?"

"I have heard nothing different," Nettle said. "But Petrichor is not a safe place for a rebel now. With the king crushing the rebellion . . . perhaps he left."

"But he wouldn't leave," Aurora said. "He wanted revolution. He wanted violence. He wouldn't have *left*."

"Perhaps he found that imagined rebellion and actual rebellion are two very different things. Or perhaps he wishes to find help here."

Aurora paced the space near the door. It was possible. But it did not quite make sense. "If he planned to do that, wouldn't you have heard something? You would have heard of a rebel looking for support."

"Perhaps. But I do not hear everything." She pulled more of her hair into the braid. "You wish me to find him?"

"I want to know if he's really here. Why he's here, if he is. Do you think you could find that out? Without Finnegan knowing?"

Nettle was silent for a moment as she twisted up the last of her hair. "Pass me that pin?" she said, nodding at her dresser.

Aurora fetched it for her. "Thank you. I can only say that it would be *possible*. There are many people in this city, and if he keeps quiet, it may be very hard to find him. Especially since we do not even *know* that he is here. But I will try, Aurora. I will tell you if I hear anything."

It was all Aurora could hope for, given the circumstances. She did not even know what she wanted the answer to be. Tristan had caused her such problems in Alyssinia, but he might have information. He might have news. She could not pass up the opportunity to see him. "Thank you," she said. "I just . . . I need to know."

"I can promise nothing, Aurora," Nettle said. "But I will try."

The magic was reluctant again that night. Aurora could barely summon a single spark, and she went to bed exhausted and irritated. No roses waited for her when she awoke the next day, but their absence wasn't comforting. Celestine must still be watching her.

Aurora was already in the library, shuffling through the diplomatic papers, when Finnegan appeared.

"I've received the most curious thing," he said, in lieu of a greeting. She turned in time to see him walking down the stairs from his antechamber, holding a roll of parchment. "Dear Queen Iris wrote me a letter. Don't you think that's odd?"

"You were her guest," Aurora said. "She's nothing if not polite."

He approached the table. "You'd think she'd have other things to worry about, with the death of her daughter and the kingdom practically breaking into civil war. Yet she wrote me the politest, most pointless note I've ever received. Lots of pleasantries, thanks for attending the wedding, apologies for the turmoil, all the usual things you would expect, and then this: *I hope that I will be able to visit Vanhelm soon and see its legendary fire for myself. My daughter was always fascinated with the idea, but my husband has never been fond of traveling overseas. He would certainly not consider it safe without a heavy guard, and with so many of our guards searching for the imposter princess, it would not be possible.* Strange, isn't it, that Iris is yearning for a holiday, at such a time?"

"It could just be pleasantries," Aurora said. "An empty offer to return the favor."

"Perhaps," Finnegan said. "But listen to the rest of it. *It feels we are all in danger here, after the death of my daughter, Isabelle. Trouble can strike so unexpectedly, precisely when we think we are safe. Please write back to assure me of your safe return to Vanhelm, and do be careful of the dangers across the sea. The threat now seems greater than ever.*" Finnegan looked at Aurora over the paper. "The dragons aren't across the sea from here, but King John and his men certainly are."

"You think he's going to threaten Vanhelm?"

"I think that Iris knows you're here. She can be clever, despite how insufferable she is. And if *she* knows, John may know too. So she's warning you."

"He isn't as clever as she is," Aurora said. She reached out and took the piece of paper, reading through it herself. "So unless she told him . . ."

"He is always suspecting Vanhelm of some betrayal," Finnegan said. "The possibility of you coming here must have been one of the first thoughts in John's head. And Iris is not entirely horrid. She may want to protect you."

Iris had always seemed far more concerned about protecting her son and her throne than about Aurora's well-being. But she had tried to speak out in Aurora's defense in those final days, when the king threatened her. She had done what she thought was right.

And she would want to protect Rodric, whatever that would mean.

"Can you get a message back to Alyssinia?" Aurora said. "Without anyone knowing of it?"

"You want to write to Iris?"

"No," she said. "To Rodric. He doesn't know what happened to me. And I don't know what happened to him. If there was a way to let him know I'm all right, and for me to know that *he's* all right, without anyone else knowing I'd contacted him . . . well, I would appreciate it."

"I'll send a message," he said. "It'll get the job done."

"Thank you." Aurora read through the letter again. "They're calling me an imposter now."

"Well, the real promised princess would never defy them."

"Does that mean they claim to have the *real* Aurora hidden somewhere?"

"I haven't heard it said yet," Finnegan said. "But I don't doubt they'll try it, if it turns out to be useful. Get someone else to be you."

They could find another girl, someone willing to be their silent figurehead in return for a comfortable life in the palace. The king would regain control, his reign would continue, and the real Aurora would be hunted as the pretender who used her position to burn half the kingdom away.

"He won't just stand down, will he?" she said. "He's going to fight."

"Of course he's going to fight, Aurora. You knew that."

"I know," Aurora said. "I just—I *hoped*—" The words would not come. "I don't want to fight," she said. "The bloodshed at the wedding, the fire in that village . . . I never want to do anything like that again. I never want to *see* anything like that again. But he's going to force me. He's going to make sure it happens."

"Unless you back down," Finnegan said. "Unless you let him have what he wants."

The idea was almost appealing. She could run far, far away, never worry about responsibility again. But the way that baker had looked at her, the *hope* people had for her . . . "I can't do that," she said. "I don't want that either. I just wish my magic was strong enough to convince him not to fight. If I could intimidate him, or look so powerful that he backed down out of self-preservation . . . but I don't see how I could do that without killing a lot of people along the way."

Finnegan was quiet for a long moment, watching her. He had that glint in his eyes again, the excitement that meant he was about to suggest something dangerous.

"What is it?" she said.

"What about the dragons?"

She frowned. "What about them?"

"You have a connection with them," he said. "What if you can use them? What if you could add their power to yours? If you appeared in Alyssinia with dragons behind you, no one would dare challenge you."

"Because they'd be terrified of me."

"But you wouldn't have to hurt them."

She shook her head. "Perhaps I have some connection with the dragons, but that doesn't mean I can bring them across an ocean and use them to threaten Alyssinia without destroying it. We both know what Vanhelm looks like, Finnegan. We both know the river is the only thing protecting the city."

"If you could control them enough to make them cross the water, you could control them enough to stop them from attacking anyone. Or to direct their attacks. Think about it, Aurora. No one would dare to challenge you then."

"I am thinking about it," Aurora said. "It's impossible."

But it would be power. She could not turn away from that, not when Celestine was watching her, not when the need to do *something* grew every minute she was away.

And she had to admit, something about the idea was appealing. The heat of the dragons, the rush of their magic behind her. No one would challenge her or dismiss her then. No one would think her less than she was.

"Someone must have been able to control them, once," Finnegan said. "People lived in Vanhelm for thousands of years. There must have been some way they coexisted with dragons. And we don't know much about Vanhelmian magic, before it faded away. What if it was like yours?"

"How would I have *Vanhelmian* magic?" Aurora said.

"Your ancestors were from Vanhelm, weren't they? You're a descendent of the princess Alysse. And they said she had magic like no one had ever seen."

"Not a descendent," Aurora said. "Related, maybe. I don't know. But if she was the source of my magic, someone else in my family would have had it too. And if it's Vanhelmian magic, someone *here* would have that power. It doesn't add up, Finnegan." She leaned forward, her hands pressed flat on the desk. "Even Alysse didn't have magic like mine, did she?" she said. "That's what the stories say. She didn't know she could use magic until she went to Alyssinia and felt all the power there."

"But it's a legend," Finnegan said. "And you've proved they're not always true."

The end of Alysse's story was misleading, wasn't it? Aurora

had learned that she was beloved, but the books here suggested that she had been murdered for her power, that people had not loved her after all. Who could say whether the other parts of the story were true?

"She might have showed hints of her magic in Vanhelm," Finnegan said. "And that's why she left."

"To find a place she could use it properly?"

"Or to escape. Perhaps that's why they ran across the sea. People in Vanhelm didn't *need* magic. Everyone else would have followed the settlers if we did. They must have had a good reason to risk traveling so far and starting anew."

Aurora tapped the pen on the desk, feeling the reverberations in her hand. No one in her family had had magic for generations, as far as she knew, but it was possible that she was related to Alysse. Aurora had never heard any suggestion that Alysse had any children, but some stories claimed that her cousin took the throne after her death. The scanty records made it difficult to be certain.

A distant family connection from hundreds of years ago was not enough to explain her powers. But Celestine's bargain with Aurora's mother might. Celestine had told Aurora she was made of magic. And if Celestine's power combined with that dormant connection to dragons . . . could Aurora's fire be the result?

Yet something stopped her from sharing this theory with Finnegan. The secret of her mother's bargain, the thought of what Aurora's true nature might be . . . they felt too personal, like speaking them aloud would allow Finnegan to see beneath her skin.

"I need to know more about Alysse," she said. "Do you have records of when her people left Vanhelm? Reports from that time?"

"Perhaps," Finnegan said, "but they'd be much harder to get hold of than these ones, especially if they have any secrets. And people have been studying that story for hundreds of years. Someone would have spotted something like that in the records, especially considering how much Alyssinia wants magic now." He stood. "I have a better idea," he said, "risky as it might be."

"Tell me."

"Alysse's family lived in a small town in Vanhelm," he said, "downriver from here. Her house was turned into a museum. It's in the waste now, almost certainly destroyed, but—"

"But you think there might be answers there," Aurora finished. "Answers not in books?"

"You have magic," Finnegan said. "And you have that connection to Alysse. Maybe you'll be able to uncover secrets that other people missed."

There were threats to consider. The dragons, for one. The need to travel there unseen. The possibility that it was just a ruined museum, with no answers at all. But the idea was thrilling nonetheless. A chance to travel across the river again, to see where Alysse had grown up, to glimpse the dragon fire up close . . . .

"When can we go?" she said. "Today?"

Finnegan grabbed her hand and pulled her to her feet. "I'll make the arrangements," he said.

TWELVE

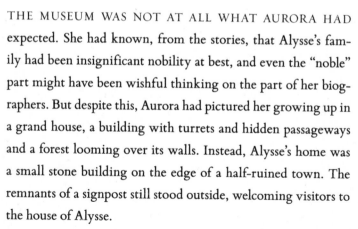

THE MUSEUM WAS NOT AT ALL WHAT AURORA HAD expected. She had known, from the stories, that Alysse's family had been insignificant nobility at best, and even the "noble" part might have been wishful thinking on the part of her biographers. But despite this, Aurora had pictured her growing up in a grand house, a building with turrets and hidden passageways and a forest looming over its walls. Instead, Alysse's home was a small stone building on the edge of a half-ruined town. The remnants of a signpost still stood outside, welcoming visitors to the house of Alysse.

The house's front door had burned away, and the stone around it had distorted, leaving a narrow space. Aurora ducked through ahead of Finnegan, and found herself in a larger-than-expected entrance hall. There was a stone desk in the center, and a few rotting scraps of paper lay atop it, advertising the museum. Aurora tried to pick one up, and it fell apart in her hands.

The room beyond must have once been a "step into history" experience, preserved as it would have been during Alysse's time. Fake food on the dining table, iron tongs by the hearth, even the remnants of soft furnishing on the chairs. A desk against one wall was almost perfectly preserved, its display under a sheet of glass. Notes believed to have been written in Alysse's own hand, according to the sign. Her childish handwriting overemphasized the spikes of the letters as she recorded her day.

Aurora pressed her hand on the glass. Proof that even Alysse had been a real person, hundreds of years ago. A famous queen, growing up and concerned with the most mundane things.

No one would stop Aurora if she removed the glass and stole the papers. But if she touched them, they too might vanish into ash.

"Can you feel anything?" Finnegan said. "Any traces of magic?"

She shook her head.

There was a staircase in the far corner of the room, spiraling both up and down. Half of the steps up were missing, and Aurora wouldn't trust the damaged floor above to support her, so she tested the strength of the first downward step. It held firm, so with a glance back at Finnegan, she began to descend.

There were no cobwebs, and very little dust. Aurora followed the stairs around, the light fading away until she could see nothing more than the gray outlines of the walls on either side.

She could see nothing at all in the room below. The air here was cold and clammy.

Finnegan handed her a candle, and she concentrated on the wick, shaping her curiosity into fire. The candle lit a small circle around Aurora's feet, revealing a cracked stone floor.

Aurora stepped fully into the room, and her foot caught on something soft on the ground. A blanket. She bent down to look closer. It was in almost perfect condition, the fleece soft under her fingertips. Too new to be from before the dragons came.

Finnegan descended the stairs behind her. "What is this place?"

"I don't know," Aurora said. "I thought just the basement, but . . ." She held the flame higher. "Someone's been living here."

A few books were piled on the table. Novels, mostly, adventures, but one was the story of Alysse that Aurora knew so well. The cover was ripped in half. Beneath it lay *The Tale of Sleeping Beauty.*

Most of the pages had been torn away.

She looked through what remained between the jagged edges. Someone had slashed across the paintings that remained, marring the faces of Aurora's parents, of the prince, of Aurora herself. Only one page had survived intact. The final words still read the same as they always did. *And we will all live happily ever after.*

Aurora raised the candle higher. It finally illuminated the walls.

They were covered in writing. Every inch of space had been marked, some words scratched into the stone, even more painted with ink that looked like blood. There was a crude map of Vanhelm, but the artist's attempts had been covered with more repetitions of the same words: *burn them burn them burn them.* A few childhood nursery rhymes covered a second wall, and at the bottom, four words in a weak attempt at a poem.

Fire, stone, bone, blood.

On the far side, two huge words had been gorged in the wall. *Only her,* it said.

"Celestine," Aurora breathed. They had stumbled across Celestine's nest. Not from before the return of the dragons—she could not have hidden here unnoticed. But sometime since the destruction of Vanhelm, Celestine had lived here. She might be living here still.

"You're sure?" Finnegan said.

"I've seen her writing before. That note." Aurora moved closer, running her fingers along the scorched letters. "This was her."

Why would Celestine have come *here*? It was too clear a landmark to have been a coincidence. Aurora glanced at the books on the table again. The story of Alysse, and the tale of Sleeping Beauty. The girl with the ancient power of Vanhelm, and a princess with the magic of fire.

Only her.

"Well," Finnegan said, "this is the most disturbing thing I've seen in a good year at least, Rodric kissing you included."

Aurora took a step back, eyes fixed on the wall. Paper crunched underfoot, and she bent down to pick it up.

It was an illustration from her storybook. The painted Aurora's finger hovered over the spindle, but the spindle point and her fingertip were already specked with blood.

In fact, the whole painting was a lot redder than Aurora remembered. Red on the spinning wheel, red on the ground, red smeared on her dress.

Aurora yelped and dropped the page. Celestine had added the blood herself. Or the red paint. Aurora hoped it was red paint.

"Blood," she said. "Look at this. She was obsessed with blood. Was that why she cursed me with the spindle? Did she want some of my blood?"

But why would Celestine want her blood? Why would she get it in such a roundabout way, with a curse, with magic? Why would Celestine hide in the ruins of Alysse's house and scratch frantic words about burning and blood on the walls?

She must have had plans in Vanhelm. Plans that had gone wrong, plans that had driven her to this.

Aurora traced the words, *only her*, again and again. "Look at these books. She's talking about *me*. She wanted to use me. *Burn them all.*"

"Burn who all?"

"I don't know. Everybody."

"But she cursed you," Finnegan said. "If she wanted to use you, why would she make you sleep?"

"I don't know," she said again. Her thoughts were moving so fast that she felt dizzy. The *only her* was almost like a scream, words of desperation. "What if I am connected to the dragons waking up? What if that was Celestine?" She was talking faster now, driven on by the writing whirling around her. "What if she was involved in waking up the dragons? What if all she needed was my blood, the blood from the spindle? What if she used my blood to wake them?"

"Aurora." Finnegan grabbed her arms, holding her steady. "You're not making sense."

"Look here," she said, wrenching herself away and thrusting her hand at the wall. *Fire, stone, bone, blood.* "She needed blood for something. Her curse took my blood. What if that's what she wanted it for? To wake the dragons, for some twisted part of her plan? What if that's why I have a connection to them? And then something went wrong." *Only her.* "What if she wanted to control them? But she can't. Only I can control them." She swayed, the force of her words hitting her. If she was right, Celestine had created her for destruction. That was why Celestine wanted her by her side.

She was meant to burn.

She stumbled back, and Finnegan caught her with a firm hand in the small of her back. "Rora," he said softly. "You're just guessing. You don't know."

"No," she said. "No, I suppose I don't." But her blood seemed to burn inside her, telling her that she was right, she was *right*, this was what Celestine intended, this was why she'd cursed her, why she was watching her. She could hold all that fire in her hand and bend it to her will.

"Note down what she's written here," Aurora said eventually. "We need to leave before dark."

Finnegan did not protest. They searched the rest of the room, and the rooms above, but they found nothing else of interest. No more hints of what Celestine might have planned.

They were about to step back onto the street when a shadow fell over them, heat filling the air. A dragon. The ground shook as it landed.

Aurora hurried to peer through the ruined window. The dragon was directly outside, so close that she could see nothing but the blue scales on its side, shimmering in the sunlight.

Finnegan grabbed her hand, tugging her down out of sight. The dragon shrieked. It beat its wings, crashing against the roof of the museum, and screamed again. The air hissed, and the dragon let out a stream of fire.

The words on the wall still raced through Aurora's thoughts, *burn them* and *only her, only her,* a princess made by Celestine's will, a princess with magic in her blood, with a connection to Vanhelm, to the dragons. Aurora could not hide from it. There was a dragon, here, outside, *now*. She had to see what it would do.

She wrenched her hand out of Finnegan's grasp and darted out of the door before he could stop her. Flames danced across the roof of a building across the street, and the cobbles around the dragon were cracked and black.

The dragon whipped its head around to look at Aurora, and the world seemed to still. She stared straight into those black eyes, and she could feel the pump of her blood, feel magic rushing to her fingertips.

"Go," she said to the dragon. "Go."

It tilted its head, considering her for a long moment. Then it beat its wings and launched itself into the air and away, sending a streak of flame across the sky.

THIRTEEN

SHE HAD BEEN RIGHT. THE DRAGON HAD OBEYED HER.
They were meant to be hers.

The magic came easily that night, flames whirling around
the practice room and then vanishing as quickly as they had
come. She thought of the dragon, of the gleam of its scales,
and the fire summoned itself, as natural as breathing. And she
thought she could feel the dragons, too, feel the pound of their
blood and the tremor of their hearts.

This was the answer she had been looking for, the key to
stopping the king.

But the magic was almost too strong. She paused to regain her breath, and the world seemed to sway around her.

This magic had been designed by Celestine. It was meant for destruction. And as helpful as it might be, as powerful as it might seem, it intoxicated her. If she mastered her magic, would she really control it? Or would it control her?

She sank onto the practice room floor. Scorch marks surrounded her.

"Aurora?" Finnegan said. He stepped closer, frowning. "What's wrong?"

"I just . . . I need to rest. I need to think."

He looked at her for a long moment. "Want me to go?"

"No," she said, and she was surprised to realize she meant it. "No, don't go." She traced the black mark on the floor.

"I controlled a dragon today," she said. "A dragon." A creature that should not even exist, and she had controlled it. She had told it to leave, and it had flown away. She twisted the pendant between her fingers. "The research, my magic . . . it's working."

"Is that bad?"

"No," she said. "I don't know. If Celestine woke them using my blood, my magic, that must mean I can make them sleep again. I can stop them from hurting anyone again. That's *good*."

"But you're not happy."

"I'm worried," she said. "I'm worried that I'm right, that this is all part of some plan of Celestine's. If I learn how to control my magic, I could end up making things worse."

"We don't have any proof that Celestine meant any of this," Finnegan said. "And even if you are right . . . you're still you. The magic isn't bad, just because Celestine decided it would be. It depends on how you use it."

"I almost burned down a village," she said. "All by myself. And King John is telling people I burned more. If I use my magic to fight him . . . I'm going to hurt so many more people."

"You might," Finnegan said. He sat beside her, scattering soot across the ground.

"Then how can I do it?"

"By knowing that more people will be hurt if you don't. By trusting yourself."

But if she did nothing, they wouldn't be hurt by *her*. Not directly. She would not have spilled their blood.

"After I saw the dragon . . ." she said, "after it saw me . . . I didn't feel entirely like myself."

"Then how did you feel?"

It felt wicked to even whisper it. "Powerful," she said. "Like I could do anything. Like I didn't have a fear in the world."

Finnegan shifted closer. "How is that a bad thing?"

"It made me reckless, too."

"Sometimes," Finnegan said, "I think reckless people are the only ones who get anything done. All the safe and sane ones are too busy thinking through every possible outcome to even *start* making a difference."

She made a vague noise of agreement. This had to be a good

thing. Real power of her own. Perhaps that intoxication was only the first step. But something about it itched under her skin. She did not want this magic if it meant burning, too.

She looked at Finnegan through trailing strands of hair. "Nettle said that you were worried you wouldn't get your throne," she said. "Because you were too reckless. Do you really think your sister will become queen?"

Aurora did not expect he would let her get away with changing the subject, but then he shrugged. "It's possible."

"Does that upset you?"

He looked back at her, one eyebrow raised. "That I could lose my inheritance because my sister is more likable than I am?"

"I mean . . ." She tucked her feet underneath herself. "If you had the choice, would you *want* to be king?"

He stared at the fire in the grate, his brows furrowed. When he finally answered, he spoke slowly, as though considering every word. "There are things I like about being a prince," he said, "and I assume I'd like them about being king as well."

"Such as?"

"I like the power," he said. "I like that people like Iris have to be polite to me, even though they loathe me. I like all the resources I have, all the influence. But I'm not sure I'd want to be responsible for the well-being of everyone in this kingdom. I like making decisions for *me*. I'm not sure I want to make decisions for everybody."

"And that's the truth?" she said.

"And that's the truth."

She ran her fingers along the ground, leaving swirling patterns in the soot. She could see Finnegan out of the corner of her eye, watching her.

He leaned closer. She imagined she could feel every millimeter of space between them, the air vibrating. "Care to tell me a secret in return?"

"I thought I didn't have secrets from you," she said. "I thought you knew everything about me."

"Prove me wrong."

She turned to face him. Even sitting, she had to tilt her head back to look him in the eye. She wanted to be honest, she realized. She wanted to share some part of herself with him, whatever that might mean. "I don't understand you," she said. "That's my secret."

"That's not much of a secret."

"But it's the truth. I can't make my mind up about you. About what you're doing."

"Because I'm so charming?"

"Something like that."

He still smelled of heat and ashes. And he was so close again, close enough to touch her with just the slightest shift.

When he'd said that he was waiting for her to kiss him, she should have done it before he finished speaking, if only to see the look on his face. She could have stopped any knowing remark that followed by kissing him again. He would have laughed, and she would have felt the chuckle rumble through his throat. But then . . . then he wouldn't have been laughing. Then he would have put his hands on her waist, or maybe one at the back of her head, tangling in her hair. He would have to bend down to kiss her . . . or maybe he would hoist her up, pulling her onto her tiptoes, onto the table. Making bold moves to put himself back in control.

She glanced at his lips. She could do it now. Take the rush of the dragon, the rush of her magic, and finally *act* for once in her life. Take something that she wanted.

The corners of his lips ticked upward. Lips that had kissed her before, in the dust of her tower, although she could not remember it. Because his attempt to build an alliance had failed. Because he was not her love, if the curse was true.

She could not kiss him. She needed to leave, before she did something she regretted. "I should rest," she said. "It's been a long day."

Finnegan's laugh told her everything she needed to know. He knew what she had thinking. He knew why she was leaving.

She stood up and strode away without another word.

"I want to kiss Finnegan."

Nettle raised her eyebrows at her. The singer stood in the doorway of her room, dressed to attend a ball. Her red silk gown clung to her skin, and her light makeup made her eyes seem brighter, deeper. A small dragon pin kept her hair away from her face. The dragon's scales glittered with rubies.

"This is a surprise to you?" Nettle said.

"No," Aurora said. "I don't know. Can I come in?"

"Of course." Nettle stepped aside. "What has happened?"

"Nothing has happened," Aurora said. "That's half of the problem. We were talking, and I—I wanted to kiss him. It was all I could think about."

"Then you should have kissed him, should you not? I find that helps satisfy that particular impulse, at least for a while."

Aurora laughed. "You know I can't do that."

"And why not? You want to. He wants to. I do not see the issue."

Aurora sank onto the bed. "I'm not certain if I should trust him," she said.

Nettle turned back to her mirror, adding a few more touches to her lips. "And you have to trust him to kiss him?"

"No," Aurora said. "I don't know. But I am starting to. Trust him."

"Sounds like all the more reason to kiss him."

"But I can't." How could she explain it? She could barely understand the feeling herself. "I need to be sensible. I need to do what's best for Alyssinia."

"And what about what is best for you?"

"Kissing him is not what's best for me, either."

Nettle looked at Aurora in the mirror. "It would only be a kiss."

But it wouldn't *only* be a kiss. Her kisses with Rodric had been *only* kisses, a detached display that she had to perform. If she kissed Finnegan, it would mean something else. It would mean tasting something that she longed for, going against what destiny had dictated. If she kissed Finnegan, it would not stop with a kiss.

Nettle sighed at her escaping hair and pulled the dragon pin loose, sending her hair falling back across her face. Then she grasped the strands in a twist to fasten up again.

Aurora looked down at the blanket. Blue swirls had been embroidered into the cloth. "We traveled to the waste today," she said. "I think—I think I might be able to control the dragons."

"That is a bold theory."

Aurora nodded.

"I have seen many strange things in my travels, but nothing quite so strange as that."

"Finnegan said I could use them to regain Alyssinia. To frighten King John away. But . . . I don't know."

Nettle was quiet for a long moment. "I do not think that Alyssinia will achieve peace without violence now. But it does not matter what I think. It matters what *you* think."

"I don't know what I think."

"Then perhaps do nothing until you decide."

"I don't have time to do nothing," Aurora said. That was the worst part of all this, the need for time to process things, to research, when everything was already falling apart. "Alyssinia needs help *now*."

"And rushing into things without a plan will not make things better."

"You said I should rush into kissing Finnegan."

"It is not rushing if it is what you want to do."

Aurora traced the pattern on the quilt. Her hair fell in front of her eyes. "I was wrong before," she said finally. "When I thought I liked somebody."

"You're speaking of Tristan?"

She nodded. "I suppose I did like him," she said. "For a time. I thought—how *romantic*. Meeting a boy at an inn, watching the city from the roofs . . . how *exciting*. But it wasn't at all like that."

The mattress sank as Nettle sat beside her. "But Finnegan is not like that," Nettle said.

"He's not?"

"You wanted Tristan to be romantic, did you not? You wanted him to be the answer to your problems. But Finnegan . . . you did not like him. You did not want his help. And yet now you have spent time with him, you have these feelings for him. It is different, do you not think?"

"I suppose it is," Aurora said. But she still could not let herself give in to it. She needed to help Alyssinia. *That* was her first priority. She could not get distracted with another boy, after the trouble caused by true loves and rebels and her own mixed-up fate.

"Have you heard anything about Tristan?" she said. "Any hints that he's here?"

"I've seen nothing, Aurora. If he is here, I do not think he wishes to be found."

Aurora let her head fall against Nettle's shoulder. Would she prefer for Tristan to be here, safe, or fighting in Petrichor? She did not know. And the day had been too exhausting to figure it out now. "What have you seen?" she said instead. "On your travels? What was the strangest thing?"

"Well," Nettle said. "In one kingdom, there was a princess who slept for over a hundred years before being awoken with a kiss. That was rather strange." Aurora laughed, and Nettle leaned back, resting her head against the wall. "Let me see," she said. "There is a city-state in the northeast where all disputes are settled with games of chess. There are people who live in the mountains who believe that they are at risk of suffocating if they go near the sea, because the air will be too thick and heavy. There is a deadly desert near Palir, and people run across it for days, for *fun*. Just to say that they have done so. But still, Princess. I believe that your story is by far the strangest."

"I would like to see them someday," Aurora said. "The things in the other stories."

"You will," Nettle said. "You already are." She combed the ends of Aurora's hair with her hands. "Shall I pin your hair up for you?"

"Please."

Nettle ran her fingers along the curve of Aurora's face, separating strands. Then she twisted them back, one by one, layering them and leaving the ends flowing free.

"So," Nettle said. "Are you going to kiss him?"

Aurora closed her eyes. "I don't know what I'm going to do."

"What would you like to do?"

It should have been such a simple question to answer, and yet . . . "I don't know."

"You do," Nettle said. "You just do not want to accept it."

"Do I have to accept it?"

"You do not have to do anything," Nettle said. "But it will help, I think. It does not have to change what you do, but lying to yourself . . . it is not worth it in the end."

FOURTEEN

ANOTHER ROSE WAITED ON AURORA'S PILLOW WHEN she returned to her room. This one was as red as blood, with a single thorn on its stem. Half of the petals had been torn away.

There was no note.

Was this a message, a comment that she was getting closer to the truth? Or was it a mockery of Aurora's attempts? The last rose had appeared once Aurora began to control her magic. Had this one appeared because Aurora was beginning to figure out what Celestine wanted her to do?

Aurora shredded the petals, letting them flutter to the ground. She stepped on them as she strode to the window and threw the bare stem into the breeze.

If Celestine wished to frighten her, she would have to try harder than that.

But Aurora tossed in bed that night, her heart pounding with fire. She imagined she could feel a heartbeat inside the necklace as well, a whisper just for her. She imagined Finnegan beside her in the dark, his hand on her hip, his lips so close that she could feel him exhale.

She imagined, and the dragon pendant was warm against her skin.

Aurora awoke in the morning to a knock on the door. "Yes?" she said, before she had time to think. She shoved her tangled hair from her face and sat up.

Finnegan stepped through the doorway. "Good morning, Sleeping Beauty. I trust you're well."

She glared at him, pulling the blankets tighter around herself. "It's early, Finnegan," she said. "What are you doing in my rooms?"

"My dear mother has summoned us. She has some news, I assume, or else wants to be sure we haven't caused chaos yet."

Aurora climbed out of bed, raking her fingers through her hair. "And you couldn't send a servant to fetch me?"

"And miss this delightful sight? I would never do such a thing. Get dressed quickly, though. My mother is casual, but not quite that casual."

"And what does she want to see us about, so early in the morning?' she asked, as she walked over to the wardrobe and pulled out the first day dress she could see.

"I told you. I don't know."

"Now that's something I don't often hear from you." She turned back to face him, dress held against her chest. "Go outside while I change."

"If you insist."

She waited until the door clicked shut before she moved again. She tried to throw together a polished early-morning look, but even dressed, her hair brushed with an actual brush, she looked like someone who had just woken up. She pressed the heels of her hands against her eyes, as though that would make them less puffy. What could the queen be summoning them for? She could not have learned about Aurora's connection to the dragons. Could she know about their trips across the waste, and be planning to berate them for that?

Finnegan waited on the other side of the door, looking as collected as always. He held out his arm to Aurora, and together they walked through the palace.

Orla's study was messier than the rest of the palace, with books piled high on a huge oak desk. Several tomes held down the corners of a huge map, and quills of various lengths were strewn across the surface. Erin sat between the desk and the door, while Orla sat behind it, her black hair tumbling out of a bun.

"Ah, Aurora," she said. "And Finnegan. I'm glad to see you. Do sit. I have been meaning to speak with you, Aurora, but with things as they are . . . the dragons coming closer, the threat to Alyssinian trade . . . I have not found the time. But now a more pressing matter has arisen, and we must turn to business. Tell me. What was your opinion of Prince Rodric when you met him?"

Her opinion of Rodric was pressing business? Aurora looked at Orla for a long moment, hoping to decipher something from her expression, some hint of what the queen wanted to hear, but her expression gave nothing away. "He's nice," Aurora said slowly. "A good person. Nothing like his father."

"Yes, I'm sure he's wonderful," Orla said. "But did you think he would make a good leader?"

A good *leader*? Was Orla intending to interfere with Alyssinia? Or had something already happened? "He cares about people," she said. "And he wants to do good. I think people would be loyal to him, if they knew him. Why? What's going on?"

Orla ignored the question. "Any ruthlessness?"

"No," Aurora said. "Not ruthless at all."

"Not one to make harsh decisions, then," Orla said. "And what about his subtlety? What are his political abilities?"

"What is this about?" Aurora said. "Surely you have met Rodric yourself."

"I have," Orla said, "although not for many years. I wanted

your opinion on him. You seem in the position to know him best."

"But why?" Aurora said. "How is my opinion on his *subtlety* useful to anything?"

"His subtlety is everything," Orla said. "If you give me your opinion, honestly, then I will answer your questions."

Aurora stared back at her. If something bad had happened, if Orla was planning to interfere, then she had to say the right thing. "He can keep a secret," she said. "I would trust him with my life."

"And yet you left him."

"It wasn't him I was worried about."

Orla nodded. "Very well," she said. "I have received reports from Alyssinia, regarding your prince. They say that Prince Rodric is working against his father. I wanted some insight as to whether it might be true."

Rodric, working against the *king*? "It's possible," she said. People dying because of unrest, homes burned, not enough food . . . he would want to help. He had always complained of being so *useless*, just as she had. And he was in a position to do good. He had the money, the influence. He could be trying to help.

But it was as Finnegan had said, forever ago in Petrichor . . . his was not a heart for this place, for this time. It was a heart for when peace had already been won.

"What do the rumors say he has been doing?" If the king

found out he was involved in the rebellion, in any way, the punishment would be swift. King John would not bear any betrayal, and Aurora could not believe that he would forgive Rodric simply because he was his son.

"Distributing food, mostly, I believe. Helping people to leave the city who need to."

It could be true. Rodric was kind enough, selfless enough. But would he brave enough to face his father like that? Aurora did not know.

"Where did you learn this?" Aurora said. If Orla had heard these rumors, all the way across an ocean, then surely the king would have heard them too.

"I have sources," she said. "Different ones from King John, I assume. He may be too distracted to check constantly on his son."

"Then what shall we do? How can we help him?"

Orla pursed her lips. "Nothing, for the time being. We cannot interfere."

"You interfered with *me*."

"My *son* interfered with you. I told him not to go. And we certainly will not be putting ourselves at risk for a foreign prince who may or may not be doing things his father disapproves of."

"Then why did you bring me here?" Aurora said. "Why ask me about him?"

"I was not entirely decided," Orla said. "On whether it was true, or on how to respond. I am still not entirely decided. But as you implied, he is loyal, but not a schemer. Not a leader. Not *subtle*. His attempts will probably fail, and it would be too great a risk for us to interfere. We will watch the situation, and if things change . . . perhaps we could consider it. But for now, no."

"He's a good person," Aurora said softly. "A good prince. If you wish for someone to support in Alyssinia, he is a good choice."

"But Aurora," Orla said. "It is quite clear that we have already put our support behind *you*." She sighed. "I will have it investigated further. There may be something in it. But for now, I expect you to have patience." She waved her hand. "I wish to speak to my children, in private. Excuse us."

Aurora stood. She wanted to argue, wanted to scream in protest, but Orla was her host. She was only here because of her goodwill. "He deserves to be safe," she said eventually. "He deserves your support."

Orla nodded, her expression almost understanding. "If only I could make all my decisions based on what people deserved," she said.

Aurora tried to practice magic again that day, but her thoughts would not settle. She could not stop thinking of Rodric, of what he might be doing now. Rodric captured, Rodric arrested, Rodric hurt by the rebels he wanted to help. Rodric, still in the middle of it all, while she ran far away.

She had left him there, to deal with his father and the fighting

alone. He had wanted to help people, together, and she had run and taken that hope away from him.

Worst of all, she had barely thought of him since. She hadn't imagined him in danger or putting himself at risk. A few moments of concern, perhaps, a request for Finnegan to write to him, but that had been it. She had not even penned the letter herself.

How could she have been so selfish?

Flames burst around the candle, growing larger and larger. She tried to pull the fire back, to make it dim. It only grew brighter.

So much practice, so much effort, and she still could not fully control it. Meanwhile, Rodric was actually helping. He was actually making a difference.

If the reports were true.

She knocked on Nettle's door a little while later, too frustrated to practice any longer. "Aurora," Nettle said, as she opened the door. "Are you all right?"

"Did you hear?" Aurora said. "They think Rodric is working against the king."

"I have heard," Nettle said. She guided Aurora into the room and closed the door.

"Tell me everything you've heard," Aurora said. "Every detail. I have to know if it's true."

"I doubt I know any more than you."

Aurora paced across the room. "If *Orla* has learned of it, then the king must have learned of it too." And the king's reaction would not be pleasant. "I don't understand. Is he working with the rebels? They seemed to hate him. Or is he working alone? How would he know where to begin?"

"I do not know, Aurora. I wish I could tell you."

Aurora suddenly noticed that the room was half-bare. Most of the pots of color had been cleared from the dresser, and the gowns were tidied away. Nettle's pack leaned against one wall.

Aurora stopped pacing. "You're leaving."

Nettle nodded.

"You're going to find out more about Rodric?"

"To find out if these stories are true."

"When?"

"Tomorrow morning."

Tomorrow morning? It was so soon. Aurora sank onto the bed. "Were you going to tell me?"

"Yes," Nettle said. She sat beside Aurora. "Of course. I only found out recently myself."

"Won't it be dangerous?" Aurora said. "If Petrichor isn't safe—"

"Nowhere I go is ever safe, Princess. Do not worry about me." Nettle combed Aurora's hair with her fingers. "Such lovely hair," she said. "Do you mind if I braid it?" Aurora shook her head, and Nettle began to braid, her hands moving as quick as spiders.

"Take care of Rodric," Aurora said. "If you can."

"I will try," Nettle said softly. "But I am a spy, not a fighter. I do not know what I can do."

"Then stay safe. Promise to stay safe."

"Only if you promise me the same."

"I promise."

Nettle tugged lightly on her hair. "Liar."

She was braiding it into a crown, Aurora realized. Aurora reached up to touch the spiral of hair that stood out from her head, but Nettle pushed the hand away. "Not yet," she said. "I haven't finished."

Aurora closed her eyes. A shiver ran along her scalp. Nettle's very presence was soothing. And she had done so much. She had saved Aurora, in her own way. "Thank you," she said softly. "For helping me, in Alyssinia. I don't know what I would have done if you hadn't come along."

"You would have survived, Aurora. You are good at surviving."

"I don't just mean that. You were my friend, too. I have not had many of those, but you . . . you made things easier. So thank you." She wanted to say more, but she could not think of the words. She could sense Nettle smiling behind her, but the singer did not reply.

Nettle tied off the end of the braid and tucked it in. "There we are," she said. "You look beautiful."

"Like a princess?"

"Oh," Nettle said. "Much more beautiful than that." She

hesitated, and then moved to pick up a folded piece of paper from her dresser. "Here," she said. "You should have this."

Aurora unfolded it. An address had been written there in precise letters, followed by a time.

"What is this?"

"I found Tristan."

Aurora stared at her. "You *found* him?"

"Perhaps. I have not seen him myself. But he should be there, at that time, at that address, tomorrow. It may have been better if I did not tell you, but as I can no longer go . . . I know the address, and it is as safe as one could hope, but that does not mean it is actually safe. Still. I believe I should let you decide what you wish to do with this information now."

"Thank you," Aurora said. Her voice wavered. This was trust. Information given, without distortion or agenda. "How did you find him?"

"An Alyssinian, matching his description, new in the city. It was far from my most challenging assignment." Nettle looked at the piece of paper again, and her voice took on a note of warning. "I cannot be certain it is him, and I cannot be certain meeting him will be safe. Be careful. But if you wish to know why he is here, you may find your answer there."

Aurora looked at the address again. She had to go. "What will I say to him?"

"Whatever you wish." Nettle leaned forward and tucked a loose strand of hair behind Aurora's ear. "You do not need to go, if you do not wish to. But if you do . . ."

"Yes," Aurora said. She refolded the parchment and placed it in her lap. "Thank you."

Nettle smiled at her. "You will be fine, Aurora," she said. "I know that you will. Trust your instincts. They're stronger than you believe."

When Aurora returned the next morning to bid her good-bye, Nettle had already gone.

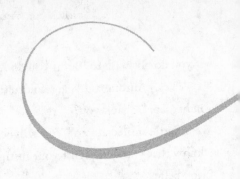

FIFTEEN

THE ADDRESS LED HER TO THE EAST SIDE OF THE island. The ocean stretched out ahead of her, the sea breeze tangling her hair. She could just make out the foam on the crashing waves. Some people strolled along the pier, friends with their arms looped together, couples walking a few awkward inches apart, the occasional individual staring at the water in thought.

A row of buildings overlooked the water, tall and so thin that they could barely have a single room per floor. They did not look threatening, but it would most likely be risky to enter any of them alone.

Aurora walked along the street, checking the numbers above

each door. She was looking for number 33, but the buildings stopped with number 29. After a gap, they leapt to number 50 without any explanation.

Aurora turned back to look at the ocean, at the people walking there. It was peaceful, after the pounding energy of the rest of the city. A boy was sitting on a stone bench nearby, a few feet from the drop into the water. He had messy brown hair.

Aurora stared at the back of his head. She couldn't be sure it was Tristan. She couldn't know she was safe even if it *was* Tristan. But she had not come here to shy away from him now.

She crossed the street. As though sensing her gaze, the boy turned around. His eyes widened in shock, and he stood.

"Mouse?"

He looked gaunter than Aurora remembered, and his brown hair was longer. Something about him seemed *wilted*, his exuberance dimmed. She walked slowly toward him, keeping a few feet between herself and the bench.

"Yes," she said. "It's me." She was not sure what else to say.

"What are you doing here?"

The breeze tossed her hair across her face. She pushed it away. "I could ask you the same thing. Why aren't you in Alyssinia?"

She couldn't quite believe she was seeing him, in daylight, against the backdrop of the ocean. She had forgotten so much about him since she last saw him, her memory reducing him to the tiniest details: his knowing smile, the anger in his eyes when he spoke of the king, the sickness she felt when she realized people had been executed because of him. And yet he was here.

"I thought I was meeting Nettle," he said. "I had some things I wanted to say to her, now I know who she works for."

"She had to leave. And it was always me who wanted to talk to you." She let herself take another step closer. She would not be a fool with him, not this time.

A small group of people walked past them. Aurora and Tristan stood in silence until they were out of earshot again.

"Why are you here, Tristan? What happened to the rebellion?"

He sank onto the bench. After a moment's hesitation, Aurora sat beside him. "There is no rebellion. Not anymore."

"What do you mean, there is no rebellion?" That couldn't be right.

"How do you think the king reacted to what happened on your wedding day? *We* weren't the ones who started that, but the king blamed us anyway. He was so desperate to crush us that more people fought, for a bit. Guess they didn't like him destroying *their* homes and killing *their* friends for no reason."

"But it didn't work?"

"He responded hard, and ended it all in one night. One night, after everything. The king attacked people in their homes and rounded up anyone even suspected of rebel sympathies. They're all dead now. He couldn't have your wedding on those castle steps, so I guess a mass execution had to do."

Aurora gripped the back of the bench to stop herself from

swaying. "How many?" she said.

Tristan shrugged. "I couldn't exactly count."

But then, Tristan didn't care much for incidental lives, did he? He had been involved in a scheme that led to many deaths, *innocent* deaths. Aurora had seen it herself. He could not play the victim entirely.

"How did you escape?" Aurora said. "If you're here . . . how did you get out?"

"I wasn't home," he said. "I was out on the roofs; I saw them coming . . ."

Aurora gripped his arm. "The inn," she said. "Your cousin . . . Nell . . ."

"I don't know," he said. "By the time I got back, the inn was on fire. Trudy and Nell weren't at the executions, so maybe they escaped . . . but I couldn't find them. I couldn't do anything."

"So you left?"

"I couldn't *find* them," he said. "They're dead, or they're hiding, but I couldn't find them. And I couldn't lead the king to them, if they were alive. So I left. There was no hope anymore. There was no point in staying."

"I'm sorry," Aurora said. The words felt so inadequate, but she did not know what else to say.

"Yeah, Mouse," he said. "So am I."

She stared out at the crashing water. "It's not over," she said. "I'm going to go back. I'm going to do something about this."

He laughed. Actually laughed, a single gasp of amusement.

"You don't believe me?"

"What can you do? You're hiding here. You don't even know what's happening. And it's your fault, isn't it? You helped to start all this, and then you ran off. You left us with your mess."

"*My* mess?" She fought the urge to stand, to leave now. She had not asked for any of this. She had woken up and had this whole mess thrust at her. She had not reacted perfectly, but who would? Who *could*? "You were as involved in this as I was, Tristan. You left too. There are still people to help, but you left too."

"I guess we're the same after all."

She looked at the water, her blond hair falling about her face. She had so many questions, about Rodric, about Alyssinia, but they stuck in her throat. "Why did you come here?" she asked eventually.

"Easiest place to get to. And what about you? You don't look like you're on the run anymore. Enjoying Prince Finnegan's protection? Or are you a spy like Nettle now?"

Aurora pushed her hair behind her ear and straightened her back. "He's helping me," she said eventually. "I'm going back. But I can't do it alone."

"If you wait much longer, there won't be anything to go back to."

A ship bobbed on the horizon, breaking up the endless blue. "How did you leave?" she said. "Did Rodric help you?"

"Prince Rodric?" Tristan sounded genuinely confused.

"Why would he have helped me?"

"I've heard rumors," she said. "That Rodric has been working against his father. Helping people get out of the city. I thought perhaps he was helping the rebellion, but . . ."

"No," Tristan said. "I never saw him. And there's no rebellion now to help. If he's doing anything, he's doing it alone."

Aurora could not see Rodric acting alone. But then, he had always cared about people. He had always wanted to help. Maybe he had finally figured out how.

What would Rodric think of her plan now? More destruction, more horror, in the name of peace. Dragons and magic and fire. She did not think he would approve.

She could ask Tristan what he thought of her plan, whether he thought the risk was worthwhile. He cared about Alyssinia, for all of his flaws. But she swallowed the words at the last moment. She had seen Tristan's methods before, had *hated* them. His approval would not be reassuring.

And he had left. After all of his impassioned words, all the sacrifices he wanted her to make, the risks he had taken . . . he had run away to save himself. He had lost his right to an opinion on her actions long ago. "What are you going to do now?" she said instead. "Are you going to stay in Vanhelm?"

"I don't know," he said. "I don't know what I'm going to do."

She turned to look at him again. He looked so diminished. He no longer seemed like *Tristan*. "You should go back," she said. "You should help."

"And do what? What could I possibly do?"

"I don't know," she said. "Try."

Another laugh, a slight shake of his head. "You didn't like it when I tried. Why would things be any different now?"

And there it was, the truth neither of them had wanted to mention before. They both wanted the king gone, and they had a history, but that was all, in the end. She could not see him as anything other than rash and blind, and he could not stop seeing her as closed-minded, too privileged to possibly understand. They could sit on a bench by the ocean and talk for hours, but that would never change.

"And you?" he said. "What is Vanhelm doing for you?"

"We're figuring out how I can win," Aurora said.

"So then you can be queen?"

"So I can help. Whatever that means." She stood. "I should go," she said. "I shouldn't stay here. But it was good to see you. It's good to know you're alive."

"You too," he said. "Princess."

She looked at him for a long moment. She doubted she would ever see him again. He would return to Alyssinia, or run farther, find some other life for himself. And she had already learned the dangers of associating with rebels. She'd learned all about the ruthlessness behind their idealism.

But he had still been *something* to her, once. He had still helped her feel less lost, in those first days after she awoke, when everything felt wrong. This was still a good-bye, whatever had occurred between them.

There were no words to express that. Nothing to bridge that gap. So she stepped back, giving him one last look, memorizing his features. And then she left him behind.

It took her a few minutes to realize that she was being followed. Three men, falling into step behind her as she left the ocean-side road, and taking all the same streets afterward, always about twenty feet away. The city was crowded with people heading in every direction, so the fact that they were following her could mean nothing. But one of the men was a pale blond, a rare enough sight in Vanhelm, and there was something off about the way they walked. They weren't talking to one another, Aurora noticed, as they followed her around another corner, but they stuck together.

She paused outside a tailor, looking at the bright cloth and sample dresses through the window.

A few paces back, the men stopped to look in a different store.

Aurora ducked into the shop and browsed for several minutes, pretending to be fascinated with the different fabrics.

When she emerged, the men were still there.

She walked faster, using her shoulders and her small height to squeeze through gaps in the crowd. The space between her and the men grew slightly, but they were still there, still pursuing her.

Another turning, another busy street. People's elbows bumped into her sides. The crowd engulfed her, so close that Aurora could barely breathe, but she struggled her way through, dodging onto a smaller side street at the last moment and running as quickly as she could.

Another turn, a leap around a street preacher, and she found herself on a narrow road with shops on either side. Cloth awnings hung over the entrances, embroidered with store names, and people stood outside the doorways, passing out free samples of bread and brandishing trays of earrings and bracelets.

Aurora glanced over her shoulder. The men were still behind her, closer than before.

Were they working with Tristan? She did not think so. If he had wanted to corner her, he would not have waited until their conversation was over. So either Finnegan was having her followed, or they were working for King John.

She needed to know. And a busy shopping street would be a better place than most to confront them.

She stopped in front of another shop window and waited for the men to pause as well. Then she turned to face them.

"Why are you following me?"

She expected them to deny it, but the man nearest to her bowed his head. "We're here to take you home, Princess. If you cooperate, it'll be easier for all of us."

"Princess?" she said. "I don't know what you mean."

"I think you do. We're been watching you awhile, Princess.

Staying in the palace. Traveling with the prince. So don't try and lie to us now."

Aurora stepped sideways, toward the shop.

"You'll get no help from in there," the man said. "People mind their own business here. So come quietly. Walk off with us now, Princess, and there'll be no trouble, right?"

"If Queen Orla finds out you're here, trying to force one of her people to leave, it'll be taken as a declaration of war." She didn't know that, not for certain, but it seemed a credible threat. She had Finnegan's support, and no ruler would abide foreign threats in her kingdom uninvited.

"That's the king's problem," he said. "All I know is there's a damn good reward for your return. No one said anything about when and where we can grab you."

Some of the shoppers were watching them now, but as many were pointedly *not* watching them. They stood with stiff backs, their eyes focused elsewhere, or their voices grew louder as they riffled through the stores' wares. No one moved to intervene.

She glared back at her pursuers, hoping she looked defiant. "You will stop following me," she said.

The man laughed. "I don't think we will, darling." He reached for her arm. The moment his hand clutched her skin, something in Aurora snapped. She jerked away, and fire cracked along the cobbles, sending the men flinching backward. Red marks scorched the spot where they had stood, and the man's hand burned red as well, his fingers blistering.

The dragon flared around her neck.

"It's true," he gasped. "You witch." He lunged for her again, but she was already running, darting around his outstretched arm. The world blurred. She elbowed her way through the crowd, then swerved onto another hectic street, then another. Running footsteps pounded behind her, and someone shouted, but she did not pause to look.

She reached an even wider street. A wire hung in the air along the center, marking the path of a tram, so she ran beneath it, searching the ground for the stars that marked its stops, hoping that a car would rattle down the street so she could ride it to safety.

She turned a corner, and a tram waited ahead. It was stuffed full of people, and one last person was trying to squeeze aboard.

"Wait!" she shouted, waving her arm in the air. "Wait, please!" She forced her legs to move faster. The driver gave her a weary expression through the window, but the tram did not move. She swung herself aboard, crashed into another traveler, and dropped a bronze coin into the slot.

"Thank you," she gasped.

The man shook his head. "You kids," he said, "always rushing about. Try to be on time next time, all right?"

"Yes," she said. "Thank you."

Her pursuers watched them as the tram hurtled away.

SIXTEEN

AURORA HURRIED TO THE LIBRARY. THE ANGER, THE fear of what might have been, was so strong that it nearly choked her.

Had Tristan known those men? Had he had been the bait to distract her? No. He couldn't have been. He did not even know she would be there. And those men hadn't seemed like rebels. But the meeting with Tristan had thrown off her balance, and those men had grabbed her in the middle of the day, like they were invincible, like no one would stop them.

An old candle sat on the center table, and she grabbed it,

holding it up to her eyes. *Light*, she thought. She shoved her anger forward, and the wick burst into flame. Grim with triumph, she blew it out and lit it again, then again, all her anger and frustration burning outward.

Yet as she calmed down, as the adrenaline slipped out of her, the fire faded too. The attack had unsettled her, infuriated her, and the urge to burn had overwhelmed her, swallowing her thoughts.

She wasn't controlling the magic. The magic was controlling her.

She threw the candle to the ground. It landed with an unsatisfying thud.

"Oh!"

Aurora spun around. Erin stood in the doorway, a pile of books under her arm.

"I am sorry to disturb you," Erin said. She paused in the door another moment, and then crept farther into the room. "I was coming to return some books."

"No," Aurora said. "No, you're not disturbing me. I was just—"

"Just getting revenge on the candle?" Erin smiled. "I hope it is not my fool of a brother who has made you so angry. I assure you, he's not worth the effort."

"No," Aurora said again. "No, I just—I'm sorry. I shouldn't lose my temper like that."

"Who am I to tell you what you should and shouldn't do?

And if you *were* angry at my brother, I would not be surprised. He often deserves it."

Erin began arranging the books on the table. She had lugged four of them with her, all tomes with Alyssinia in the titles.

"History books?" Aurora asked. "On Alyssinia?"

"Yes. My mother wanted me to study Alyssinian history in more detail . . . I presume because you are here."

"I've been trying to research too," Aurora said. "I missed so much while I slept."

"None of these books are that modern, I'm afraid. It's mostly older history. Alysse, Queen Desdemona, the Golden Age . . ." Erin fidgeted with her books. "They are my favorites, I think," she said. "The hated queens. Driven out for having too much power. It's fascinating."

"Yes," Aurora said. "Fascinating."

Erin pulled one of the books toward her, and then paused. "Actually, there is something I wanted to ask you. The other day, you spoke of Prince Rodric as if you liked him well."

"Yes," Aurora said. "He's a good person. Why?"

"I had wondered, with you running here. . . . People always say good things about princes, but you were still reluctant to marry him."

"That was not why I ran."

Erin nodded. "There were discussions about a marriage alliance between us, you see. I think my mother was more interested in pursuing one farther away, in Palir perhaps . . . but after the tragedy with Princess Isabelle, she may pursue it again. If Finnegan cannot cement the alliance, then it might fall to me. And so I was curious."

Aurora looked at the younger princess, the way even the curl of her long red hair was elegant. She was the sort of girl Iris had expected, the sort who could have taken everyone's adoration and spoken wisely and used it for good. Perhaps Aurora should have been jealous, to hear that Erin might marry Rodric one day. But Rodric deserved happiness, and it would not come with Aurora. She had no claim to him, except as a friend. She didn't *want* any claim to him beyond that. "Rodric is wonderful," she said. "He would make a good husband, I think."

"Yet you did not marry him."

Aurora opened the book in front of her and began to turn the pages, without really looking at the words. Her hands could not keep still. "I could not stay," she said. "I could not support John like that . . ."

"That is the only reason?"

Aurora looked back up at her. Erin was watching her, lips apart. Intrigued. "It was strange," Aurora said. "At first, I thought Rodric was rather . . . awkward. That we didn't fit together. But I don't think I've ever met a kinder person. It was as though . . . he seemed exactly like the sort of person I *should* love. That I would be a fool not to see the value in him."

"You did see the value in him," Erin said. "From what you've said."

"But I didn't feel for him that way," Aurora said. "I liked him as a friend, and we might have been happy enough together, but—I didn't feel what I should."

"You felt what you felt," Erin said. "And if you did not love him, and the marriage could only hurt the kingdom, it is better that you ran, don't you think? A sweet person like that deserves someone who will not resent him."

"I don't resent him."

"Then you are a better person than most, if that is true."

Aurora turned another page. "And you think you will resent whoever you marry?"

"No," Erin said softly. "No, of course not. I think there is a difference between making a diplomatic alliance you've expected your whole life, and waking up in a future to find out that your throne is no longer yours and you are expected to marry the new heir. It is a strange sort of coup. If you do not mind my saying so." She let out a little huff of impatience. "Besides, the sooner I'm marked to be queen of *another* kingdom, the sooner Finnegan will realize that I do not intend to usurp *him*."

"I do not think he thinks you plan to overthrow him," Aurora said carefully. "But he thinks people would prefer you as queen."

"Finnegan is ridiculous," Erin said, and for the first time, her voice was harsh. "He is the elder sibling; he is next in line to the throne. That is how it works. Maybe if he allowed people to see his serious side occasionally, he would not worry about this so much." She stopped and looked at Aurora again. Then she blushed. "I should not have said that," she said. "It does not matter. He is next in line to the throne. My mother may get irritated with him, but that changes nothing."

Erin's cheeks were still red, the first hint of awkwardness Aurora had ever seen in her. But even her blush looked lovely somehow. She looked like someone who was meant to rule. "Would you want to be queen?"

"If it was my right," Erin said. "But if I were queen of Vanhelm, that would mean Finnegan was either dead or disinherited. I would not wish for either. And . . . well. Queenship never seems to end well in the histories, does it?"

"It seems to work for your mother."

"Perhaps," Erin said. "But I am not like my mother."

Aurora could not entirely agree. "Do you think you would make a good queen?"

Erin raised her chin. "I do."

"I do too."

"You barely know me," Erin said. "And surely your loyalties should be with Finnegan. Or do you have other hopes for him?"

"Other hopes?"

Erin tilted her head, still watching her. Aurora could see Finnegan in her, in the curve of her lips and the green of her eyes. They were the exact same shade, and shone with the same understanding. Erin's expression was much softer, though, with some of the steel of her mother. "I'm sorry," she said. "That was presumptuous of me." She glanced at the door. "Thank you for letting me intrude. I'll leave you to your day."

When Erin had gone, Aurora turned back to her slightly dented candle. But Erin's comment lingered. Did she not want him to be king? She wanted Finnegan to be happy, yes; she had assumed that he would be king, but the idea of him *not* inheriting the throne held an appeal that she had not acknowledged before. She enjoyed flirting with Finnegan the irreverent prince, the one who schemed and dreamed and shoved rules aside, but a king would be very different. So weighed down by responsibility, so concerned with things other than himself. His actions dictated by the diplomatic needs of the kingdom. Prince Finnegan was appealing, but *King* Finnegan . . .

It shouldn't matter what Finnegan's future held. They had a temporary alliance; that was all. But this thought of a different future unsettled her. There was a part of her, a voice that she fought to ignore, that wanted Finnegan to be hers. That wanted all other responsibilities, all other allegiances, to disappear.

She wanted Finnegan to be part of *her* future, not his own. And that thought worried her most of all.

SEVENTEEN

"IT MUST BE AMAZING," FINNEGAN SAID, AS THEY ATE dinner that evening.

Aurora looked across the table at him. She had been so lost in thought that she barely heard him speak. "What must be amazing?"

"Whatever you're thinking of. It's distracted you for the last half an hour at least."

She could not stop thinking of Erin's words, of this new insight into herself. She wished she could ask Nettle for her thoughts. Nettle would be clear, and she would not judge. She pushed a piece of fish across her plate with her fork. "I'm sorry," she said. "I guess I miss Nettle. I hope she's doing all right."

"She'll be fine, Rora. She's an expert at this stuff." He laid down his knife. "Now tell me what's really bothering you. Did Celestine threaten you again?"

"No," Aurora said. "Not that." But she couldn't tell him the real reason for her distraction, and she wasn't certain that she should mention Tristan, either. She could not know how he would respond. "Some men cornered me in the city today," she said instead. "They wanted to capture me, trade me in for King John's reward. But I'm fine. I just didn't expect his men to find me so soon."

"He sent guards after you?"

"No," she said. "I'm sure he needs all his loyal men to protect *him*, if what I've heard about events in Petrichor is true. But plenty of other people seem to be willing to do his dirty work for him."

Finnegan frowned, and suddenly he looked much older, much more tired than he had before. "People are getting reckless," he said, "if they'll try to capture you on the street in daylight."

"A thousand gold coins is a pretty big reward."

"I'll have more soldiers patrol the city and watch the docks." He looked at her for a long moment, as though considering, and then pushed back his chair. "Let's go see a play," he said. "I know of a good one. Lots of drama, epic romance. You'll love it. There's no point sitting inside and worrying about this."

"It isn't safe," she said slowly. "King John's men—"

"Nothing is safe," he said. "And you survived, didn't you?" He walked around to her side of the table and grabbed her hand, pulling her to her feet. "Come on, Rora," he said. "What's the fun without a little risk?"

The play was everything Finnegan promised: a star-crossed romance, mistaken identities, the enemy disguised as a friend. The songs stuck in Aurora's head, the death scene put tears in her eyes, and when the curtain fell, she leapt to her feet to applaud.

"See?" Finnegan said, as they walked out onto the street. "That wasn't so terrible, was it?"

"It was passable," Aurora teased. "Your tastes are not as bad as I thought."

"Such a compliment." He held out his arm. "Shall we return to the safety of the palace then, my lady?"

Aurora hesitated. The night was unseasonably warm, and the stars were bright. She felt safer, out in the darkness. She was not ready to return to her worries yet.

"Maybe we could walk around," she said. "For a little while."

Finnegan smiled. "I know just the place."

She rested her hand in the crook of his arm, and they stepped down the street together. Streetlamps sent light flickering across the stone roads, and a tram bell rang in the distance.

They walked in silence. Aurora could hear the distant hum of conversation behind some of the doors, but they saw very few people once they left the theater behind. It was so different from Petrichor, with its night festivals and crowded inns.

Ahead of them, the press of buildings fell away, leaving an expanse of grass and trees. After the crush of the city, it felt as wide and peaceful as a forest. A low metal fence ran around the edge.

"It's . . . a garden?" she said.

"A park. *The* park. We need a little green amid all the steel and smoke."

A sign hung over the fence. *Coppergate Park. Closed from sunset to sunrise.* A padlock held the gate in place.

"It's closed, Finnegan," she said. "We can't go in."

"I'm the prince," he said. "And you're a princess. I think they'll waive the rules."

"It seems rude."

"No one will know. No one will care." They reached the gate. Finnegan stepped over it with ease. He held out his hand. "Or are you afraid?"

She ignored his hand and placed her left foot on the bottom rung of the fence. Her legs were barely long enough to reach over the bars. She stretched on tiptoe, her skirts tangling on the spikes, and stumbled as she dragged her other leg over. Finnegan caught her, laughing.

He tugged her deeper into the park. A couple of trees rustled in the breeze above them.

It was so peaceful, so freeing. She stepped away from

Finnegan and cupped her hands in front of her. For a moment, she let her thoughts turn to fire. Her anger that those men had tried to kidnap her, her fear for Tristan and Rodric. But no. She did not want to think of those things now. Instead, she closed her eyes and tried to pull out other feelings. The indignation that raced through her when Finnegan grinned and told her that he was waiting for *her* to kiss *him*, and then the curiosity, the sensation that tugged at her stomach and made her regret walking away.

There. She snatched the spark inside her, the little tendril of magic she had discovered before, and tried to tease it out. To coax it into her cupped hands. To let it *burn*.

Warmth licked her palms, and light burst before her eyelids. She opened her eyes. A small ball of flames floated above her hands.

"Impressive," Finnegan said.

The light flickered, then grew stronger. She held it out to Finnegan. "Here," she said. "Take it."

"If you want to set me on fire, you'll have to be more subtle than that."

"Take it," she said again. She tilted her hands, and the fire slid out of them, floating a few inches away from Finnegan's chest. It cast light and shade across his face. His eyes glinted.

"Thank you."

She sank into a mock curtsy, and he laughed.

"Can you create more?"

She could. Her chest swelled with something beyond anger and fear, an excitement that could not be touched by the world outside the park. She tugged another tendril loose, letting a second ball of flame form over her fingertips. She slid that one free as well, then another, and another, until the air glimmered with light, like she had summoned a hundred fairies to dance around them.

One spun past Finnegan's head, and he ducked, laughing. "Careful," he said. "I really *don't* want to be set on fire, if you can avoid it."

She laughed too. Another light slid from her fingers, green this time, like the light that Celestine had used to enchant her, all those years ago. It floated through the air, dancing around Finnegan's hair.

"Stop, stop, stop," Finnegan said, running forward to grab her hands, but he was laughing as he spoke. "It's still *fire*, Rora."

"You don't trust me?"

"Oh, about as much as you trust me." He tugged her toward him. "How about some fireworks?" he said. "Up in the sky."

Fireworks. The explosion on the castle steps, the screams of the crowd as they tried to escape, the blood that stained her fingers as she shoved Rodric away. So much pain, even then. She pulled her hands free of Finnegan and threw her head back. Then she tossed the memories into the air, a golden, swirling ball of flame. It rushed up and up, past the trees, over the rooftops, up to the stars. Then she gave it one final push, and it exploded.

Tiny streaks of flame rained down.

"If anyone sees this, they'll think it's proof the end is coming," Aurora said.

"Let them," Finnegan said. "What do they know?"

Aurora tilted her head farther back, taking in the stars. It was a dark night, the moon almost covered, but the stars still glowed.

She tumbled back onto the grass. Lights floated around her, bobbing as though uncertain where to turn. She grabbed Finnegan's arm and tugged him down beside her. He landed with a thump, and she giggled.

"You're drunk, Rora."

"How can I be drunk?" She wriggled in the grass, letting it prickle her back. "I haven't had anything to drink."

"Drunk on magic," he said. "Drunk on yourself."

She turned her head to look at him. Her hair fell over her cheek.

"Do you really think I can do this? Control the dragons, stop King John?"

"I think you could do anything. Anything at all."

"That isn't true," she said. "There are many things I can't do."

"Name one."

"I couldn't marry Rodric," she whispered. "I couldn't help Alyssinia when I was there. I couldn't stop the king from doing all the things he did."

"Those things don't matter."

"Of course they matter."

"Why do they have to be your responsibility? Why can't you do what *you* want to do?"

"Because," she said. She closed her eyes, feeling the grass against her cheek. "I can't."

"You can do anything that you want to, Aurora," he said. "Anything that *you* want to."

"And if I don't know what that is?"

"Then you'd better try everything at least once," he said. "Just to be sure." She could hear the smirk in his voice, and she laughed. It was good to laugh. To be *here*.

"You wanted to know my secret?" she whispered. When she opened her eyes, she could see his, inches from hers, the green sharp in the dark. "Sometimes I'm glad that King John turned out to be so awful. Because it gave me an excuse to leave. Otherwise, I would have married Rodric, and then . . ."

"Then you'd never have been able to be here with me?"

"Yes," she said. "My life would have been theirs forever. I needed a good reason to leave. To figure out my magic. My wanting to wasn't reason enough."

"And what do you think now?" he said, his voice low. "Do you think wanting something is reason enough?"

"I don't know." The words were barely audible above the breeze. Every hair on her arm prickled.

He won't kiss me, she thought. *I have to be the one to kiss* him.

The tension was too much. She turned her head away,

looking at the stars again. "Why do you think the dragons disappeared?"

"Because the world couldn't keep them," Finnegan said. "Dragons are magic, aren't they? So when the magic faded here, they faded too. Or, at least, they went to sleep, until their time came again. And that just happened to be thousands of years later, when we had forgotten all about them."

"So you don't think a courageous slayer saved the day?"

"What's one hero against a dragon? Trust me, Rora. It was the world that got rid of them."

"But you think I can make them sleep again?"

"I think your magic can. Don't you?"

Aurora rubbed the edges of her pendant, letting the roughness of the wings scrape against her thumb.

"And what about Celestine?" she said. "She's the one who made me sleep. She's planned all of this. Is she part of the *world's* work too?"

"Perhaps," Finnegan said. "She had to become the way she is for a reason, don't you think?"

She felt the sudden urge to tell him the truth. She had carried Celestine's secrets alone for too long, letting them worm their way inside her and unsettle her thoughts. She wanted Finnegan to know too. "She said that my mother made a bargain with her," she said. "And when my mother failed to keep it, she cursed me."

She refused to turn and look at Finnegan, but she could feel him watching her. "What was the bargain?" he said.

Now she let her head tilt to the side. He was close, his expression curious, undemanding. "Me," she said. "She wanted me."

"Celestine? Or your mother?"

"My mother. I don't know what Celestine wanted in return."

She almost expected Finnegan to leap in with a theory, to pull the conversation into schemes and insights once more. But he continued to watch her, almost gentle. "So that's why you have this magic," he said. "That's why you think Celestine wanted to use you to control the dragons."

"Yes," Aurora said. She closed her eyes. "Perhaps. But then what could my mother have offered?" she murmured. "How did she think she could outsmart Celestine?"

"Maybe she offered her power," Finnegan said. "People always want power."

"But why would that tempt Celestine? She had more than enough."

"Maybe she saw her power was fading. Maybe she wanted more."

Was the curse what she had wanted all along? Perhaps her mother had never been meant to honor her bargain. Perhaps the bargain had been designed to be impossible to keep.

"So she used me to wake up the dragons," Aurora said. "So she could have their power too."

"Yes," Finnegan said. "Perhaps."

She pushed herself into a sitting position. There was

something of the dragon in her. And she was not sure she wanted to know exactly what it was. If her magic was like theirs, if it was destructive, if nothing could live where her fire had been . . .

She pressed her hand to the grass and urged it to grow. To twist around her hand, to prove that she could create as well as burn. To show that she was more than she suspected.

The grass did not move. She tugged it with her fingers, as though that would make it respond. The strands tore from the ground.

"Rora?"

She shifted around to face Finnegan, close in the dark. "She told me that I was like *her*. What if my magic can only destroy things, like she does, no matter what I intend? What will happen to *me* if I keep trying to use it?"

"I don't know," Finnegan said slowly. "I guess you have to insist on being yourself."

"But I don't even know who that *is*."

"Not Celestine. Not like her."

Loose strands of grass floated from her hands. She turned away, staring at the outline of nearby buildings against the night sky. "It feels like my choices are do nothing, and allow awful things to happen, or try and fight, and do awful things myself. And sometimes . . . I don't know which is worse."

"Waiting," he said. "Not being able to do anything. Always that."

"To you, perhaps," Aurora said. "I'm not so sure."

She leaned her head against Finnegan's shoulder and closed her eyes. He wrapped his arms around her, and they settled into silence, her magic still flickering around them.

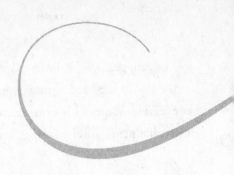

EIGHTEEN

AURORA STRUGGLED TO SLEEP THAT NIGHT.

It wasn't only a question of good versus evil, of fighting or waiting, of who she wanted to be. Rodric was helping. He had to be. And if she did nothing, if she left him to fight alone . . . she did not see how he could last, not with his father so close. But if she fought for him, if she challenged the king, if she did so with *dragons* . . . would Rodric want her help, if it meant causing more destruction along the way? He would not want her to burn the kingdom in his name.

But people believed in her. People were relying on her. She

could not just leave them. But neither could she betray them with fire.

She needed advice, the thoughts of someone she could trust. And although she had talked in the dark with Finnegan, telling him things she wanted to hide even from herself, he did not really know war. For all of his bravado, he had little more experience than Aurora herself.

But Orla might know. Aurora could not tell her about their plans with the dragons, but she could reveal more about her magic and about the king's state of mind to gain her trust, and the queen could tell her more about whether violence could ever really lead to peace. Orla had a no-nonsense attitude that suggested she had tackled many difficult decisions before. She seemed as fair as she was practical, and Aurora could not imagine her letting her feelings get in the way of the right decision.

As soon as the sun rose, Aurora wrote a note to the queen, requesting that they have lunch, and sent it off with a servant. Half an hour later, the servant returned with another piece of paper, fastened with the royal seal of Vanhelm. The parchment was littered with inkblots. Among them, Orla had scribbled an invitation to join her in her study.

"I'm glad you wrote to me," Orla said, after Aurora sat and a servant had gone to fetch food. "I have been wishing to speak to you alone for some time. Things are tense, as I am sure you know. And with Vanhelm between Alyssinia and the dragons . . ."

every day, discussions, every day, strategy. But that is the role of a queen, is it not?"

She watched Aurora as though expecting some reply. Aurora nodded.

"So tell me," Orla said. "What is it that you wished to speak with me about? I am certain that you did not simply wish for my company."

"Oh." Aurora said. She could not think how to respond without being rude. "I wanted your advice."

"You want advice from me? I am your kingdom's enemy, am I not?"

"I don't believe so," Aurora said. "And even if you were, that doesn't mean your perspective isn't worth listening to."

"And what is it you want advice on?"

Aurora smoothed her skirt to stop herself from fiddling with her hair. "It seems," she said carefully, "that the only way I can possibly stop King John is by challenging him. Whether I get people there to support me or find outside help . . . I'm going to have to fight."

"You do not *have* to fight," Orla said. "You could leave things as they are."

"I could," Aurora said. "But if I wish to change anything, then I have to fight. But I can't stop thinking that my interference could make it worse. I could be responsible for awful things that *wouldn't* have happened if I hadn't interfered. But if it's to do good . . . is that good?"

"Aurora." Orla rested her elbows on the desk and clasped her hands in front of her lips. She watched Aurora thoughtfully for a moment. "Such questions have disturbed our greatest minds for about as long as we have existed. If you wish for me to give you a solid, undisputable answer, I am afraid you will be disappointed. No one can answer that but yourself. But perhaps you are asking the wrong question here. It is not about what is 'right,' but what is practical. What is the best course of action, assuming that *all* of them will have some bad ends? So the first question, perhaps, is whether you intend to return to Alyssinia."

"I have to return," Aurora said. "Eventually."

"Why? Alyssinia already has a queen. A king, too, and a prince, and plenty of people fighting for the throne. If you can make a difference for the better, then you should go. But can you do that?"

"I have to," Aurora said. "It's what I'm meant to do."

"*Meant* to do? Oh, my poor girl. No one is meant to do anything. According to your country, no woman is *meant* to rule on her own, and I am sure they'd see our dragons as punishment for our audacity. But I believe I am where I am best suited, and I believe I do good work for my kingdom. I barely sleep, but I have found I am good at these things, Aurora. At strategizing, at working hard, at getting people to compromise. You must figure out what you can do best with the skill you have, and then tell everyone else that that is what you are *meant* to do. If you are convincing enough, they will believe you."

Orla was watching Aurora carefully. "I put little stock in rumors," she continued. "Gossip is my son's distasteful domain. But there are whispers that you have magic. I do not believe they are baseless superstition. Am I right?"

Something about Orla's bluntness compelled Aurora to trust her, at least in this. "Yes," she said. "I have some magic. Although I do not understand it."

"And that may be for the best. You can't rely on magic when making plans." Orla tapped her fingers against the desk. "Here is the truth about magic, Aurora. It makes people weak. They do not study, they do not *strive*, because they expect magic to save them. And when that magic fails . . . well. You have seen what Alyssinia has become. What it was, even in your own time. A backward little kingdom, unable to survive. I do not see how magic will help."

But Orla was wrong, in that at least. Magic was the only chance that Aurora had. It might not work by itself, perhaps, but she had seen what magic could do, how it had torn her own life apart. If one person had magic and the other did not, the person with magic would be the one to succeed.

"You do not believe me," Orla said. "That is the Alyssinia in you, I suppose. But consider this, then. Consider what happened to your kingdom in your absence. Even after your curse, they were complacent. They had mountains, and they had the memory of magic, so they had no proper defenses, no city walls, no *advancements*, nothing to protect them when Falreach attacked."

"But they survived."

"Yes," Orla said. "They survived. Because my kingdom helped them. Alyssinia was our neighbor and trade partner, not Falreach, and it had more to offer us. They could promise aid in return if *we* ever ran into difficulty. They could give us access to the sleeping princess, in case her *true love* came from our kingdom. The kingdom would have fallen without Vanhelm's aid. That was not something we wanted."

Aurora had seen a similar opinion in the diplomatic documents Finnegan had shown her. "So you saved my kingdom," she said carefully. "Is that why John and Iris are nervous of you now? They think you're waiting for the debt to be repaid?"

"Not precisely. You must know that the years after the war were not good for Alyssinia. Drought and famine, kings changing as rapidly as the seasons, and each ruler more distant from the royal bloodline . . . and then Falreach attacked again. And once again, Vanhelm offered assistance, for one simple price. We wished to be included in the line to the Alyssinian throne. My mother would marry the current king's son. The children were four and seven at the time, but a treaty was drawn up, and we saved them once again."

"But the marriage didn't happen?"

"No, it did not. We had not foreseen that *dragons* would return. They destroyed our kingdom, and while we struggled to rebuild, Alyssinia denied us aid. They claimed they were still too weak themselves. And then when the old king of Alyssinia died, a council of nobles disinherited his son, staged a coup of their own, and threw Vanhelm aside. Considering the state Vanhelm was in, we could hardly retaliate. Both kingdoms had to fight to survive . . . but Vanhelm has always been the stronger side of the sea, and while Alyssinia grew weaker, we recovered. So now Alyssinia fears that we will pursue revenge. That we want our promised throne."

"And do you?" Aurora said. "Do you want the throne?"

"Revenge is a waste of energy," Orla said. "We have more productive things to be doing than fighting over fifty-year-old slights. I renewed the trade treaties between the two kingdoms myself, when I became queen. Finnegan would have the chance to wake you, although he was only one year old when we made the agreement, and eventually we decided that young Princess Isabelle would marry him when she was grown. We have no interest in revenge."

Yet Aurora could not help noting that wanting revenge and wanting the throne were not the same thing.

"So you see," Orla said. "Magic is not the boon you believe it will be. Your fears are misplaced. Fighting will not be your greatest mistake. It will be believing that magic will not hurt far more than it helps."

Aurora had never believed that magic would not hurt. But Orla's words had not had their intended effect. Magic was dangerous, yes. But it was Aurora's only advantage here. She couldn't proceed without it now.

"So," Orla said. "How do you find the truths of Alyssinia's enemy?"

"Enlightening," Aurora said.

"A diplomatic answer if I ever heard one. Iris has trained you well."

The door creaked open, and the servant returned, carrying a plate piled with different breads and fruit.

"But come," Orla said, as the plates clattered onto the table between them. "This is getting too serious for a lunchtime chat. Why don't you tell me of my son's behavior in Petrichor? I need some entertainment."

After that, they only talked about light and humorous things. Orla told Aurora stories from her own past, and tales of Finnegan when he was younger, and Aurora told the queen all her impressions of Vanhelm, how overwhelming and inspiring she found its streets.

Yet when Aurora left Orla's study, with promises to meet again once the queen had a free moment, all she could think of was how different Orla was from Iris. She was so self-assured, so fond of the truth, so *powerful*, yet no one appeared ready to knock her aside or fight for her claim. She ruled alone.

And she was supposed to rule Alyssinia as well. Both kingdoms were meant to be her heritage. Both kingdoms were meant to be *Finnegan's*.

Aurora found Finnegan bent over a chessboard in one of the palace's many studies. He held a rook in one hand, a few inches above the board. Erin sat on the other side of the table, her hands folded in her lap.

"Don't think I'll bend the rules for you," she said, as Aurora slipped in through the door. "Once you've touched a piece, you must move it. I am not to blame if you did not think ahead. Am I right, Aurora?" The younger girl turned her head and smiled. "He cannot cheat, just because he is losing."

"It wouldn't be very gentlemanly," Aurora said.

"Fine." Finnegan placed the rook, knocking one of the white pawns out of the way. "Slaughter me if you must."

Erin leaned forward, as though reaching for her queen, and then laughed. "Surely, after sixteen years, you do not think I'm that easily fooled, do you, brother? I'm not going to allow you to pantomime me into checkmate." And, ignoring his rook, she moved a pawn instead.

"Good move," Finnegan said.

"I know."

"Well, you did learn from the best."

"And when they weren't available, I picked up a few tips on how *not* to play from you." She looked at Aurora. "Do you play chess?" she asked her.

"A little. I have not had many people to practice with."

Erin stood. "Did you wish to speak to my brother?"

Aurora glanced at Finnegan. "Yes," she said. "Just for a moment."

"Of course," Erin said. "Please make sure he doesn't move

anything on the board while I'm gone. He never has been above cheating to gain the advantage."

"Oh, I didn't mean you had to leave—" Aurora said, but Erin waved her words away.

"It is fine," Erin said. "I wish to speak to my mother about something anyway. I'll be back soon."

Her footsteps echoed as she walked away.

Finnegan did not move from his chair. His black hair fell about his eyes, and a little stubble lined his jaw. Aurora's stomach tightened at the sight of him. She had been so close to him last night. She had told him secrets that might have been better left unsaid.

"You wanted something?" Finnegan said. "Or can you just not go a day without the pleasure of my company?"

She stepped closer. "You never told me you're supposed to be *entitled* to my throne."

"I'm entitled to many things," he said. "I wasn't aware your throne was one of them."

"Your mother told me," she said. "About your treaty. She said that the thrones of Alyssinia and Vanhelm were *both* supposed to belong to Vanhelm."

"Well, it looks like I'm not getting either of them, doesn't it?" Finnegan said. "So what does it matter?"

"It matters," she said, "because you didn't tell me. You brought me all the diplomatic reports on Alyssinia over the past hundred years, and you didn't show me any of this."

"I brought you everything I could find, Rora. And we still haven't gone through them all. I didn't hide this from you."

"You must have known, though. You told me that we had a shared heritage, that we *belong* together. But you didn't say one word about this."

"If you thought I thought I was *entitled* to you, you'd never have trusted me. You'd never have even pretended to trust me. You have enough of that whole entitlement thing with Rodric, don't you think? And I'd much rather get what I want on my own terms. Do you think I care at all about history or about what I'm supposed to do? When has that ever figured into anything I've done?"

"I don't know," she said. "I'm still trying to figure you out."

"Well, be sure to let me know when you do." He picked up a rook and twisted it between his fingers.

It sounded like a dismissal, so Aurora turned away. But she paused when she reached the door, her hand on the doorknob. "I want to believe you," she said. "I do. But everything you say seems too good to be true."

She stepped out of the room before he could reply. But that night, a piece of paper slid under her door. *The truth is what you make it*, Finnegan had written. *So why not make it something good?*

NINETEEN

THE DEATH KNELL WAS SO INNOCUOUS WHEN IT CAME.
A letter in Finnegan's hand. Concern that even he could not
hide. And a mud-splattered poster, shipped across the sea.

"I received a letter from Nettle," he said, marching unan-
nounced and unexpected into the library. "You'll want to see it."

Aurora looked up. She had been searching through the diplomatic documents, hunting for evidence of what Orla had told
her. She had found nothing so far. "What is it?" she asked, as
Finnegan approached. "Has she found out more about Rodric?"

"No," Finnegan said. "She has no news about him; she wrote
before she reached the capital. But she sent this."

He held out a worn sheet of paper, and Aurora took it from him. It was surprisingly thick, the edges contorted by rain. Aurora unfolded it.

It was a wanted poster, like many Aurora had seen before. Aurora's likeness stared back at her, regal and commanding. The king now promised two thousand gold coins for her capture.

It was covered in graffiti. Several different hands had scrawled insults across the paper, over her forehead, filling every spare inch. *Traitor*, one said. *Murderer. Whore.* And across the bottom, underlined several times, *witch.*

She tightened her grip on the paper, contorting the words. *Murderer. Witch.*

"This is what they think of me?"

She shouldn't have been surprised. She knew the lies that the king had spread about her. But to see it there so baldly, to see people's hatred of her, their words thrown out like truths, like *nothing* . . .

She had thought they needed her. She had thought they were waiting for her support. She had not thought this.

"Was there a letter, too? An explanation?"

Finnegan held up two smaller sheets of paper. She took them from him, but the words were all in code. "What does it say?"

"Things have gotten worse since you left. No one wants to be in the capital. Nettle says that there are rumors that magic will return if you're killed. She doesn't say if the king started them, but it's what they're all saying now. That that's what the prophecy meant after all."

Aurora closed her eyes. "Of course they're saying that," she said. "Of course." They had believed that Aurora was their savior, woken by a magic kiss. After that, any story would be easy to believe.

She crumpled the wanted poster into a ball in her fist.

"Not everyone will believe it," Finnegan said.

"But enough do," she said. "Enough to write those things about me."

"Did you expect them all to be on your side?"

"I don't know." She threw the crumpled poster onto the table. Perhaps she had. She had spent so much time worrying about them, planning for them, sacrificing herself for them. Surely they should want her help in return. But no. While she had been worrying, they had been *hating* her. "They'll think whatever they want to think."

Finnegan rested a hand on her arm. "It's good that you came here," he said, so quietly that she almost couldn't hear him. "They would have torn you apart if you'd stayed."

She stared at the ball of paper. She could not even call the accusations lies. She was here with Alyssinia's enemies, wasn't she? She was a witch, for whatever that was worth.

"They're right," she said. "They're right about me."

"They're not."

"They are." She thought of Petrichor, of Tristan, of Iris, of curtsies and smiles and accusations of betrayal, of a little girl choking on a cherry eaten from Aurora's own hand. Of stiff kisses with promised princes as hundreds looked on. People cheering for her, and then turning against her as soon as they could. And the anger that burned inside her, the way the fire sparked out of her control. She swallowed. "You don't understand. If I let out everything I felt, I'd burn the whole city to the ground."

"Why don't you?"

"Why *don't* I? Why don't I destroy a city, kill the people in it?"

"Destroy the king," Finnegan said. "Raze that castle and that curse. Or ignore them all and do what *you* want to do. Use your magic for whatever you want. Nothing is stopping you, except yourself."

"No," she said. "That's not who I am."

"Aurora," Finnegan said, softly, firmly. He held her by the shoulders, his face inches from hers. He swept the hair away from her face. "I know we've been talking about Alyssinia, about how you can help, but you don't *have* to do this. You don't have to ever go back. You're too good for those people. You're too good for all of them. Why don't you let them go?"

"Because," she said. "I *can't*."

But as she lay in bed that night, staring at the canopy, she began to doubt. She could not stop picturing that wanted poster, all its hateful words in different handwriting, how despised she must be. She had spent so long trying to please the people in her kingdom, and this was how they reacted when she failed to meet their expectations. She had worried about her magic, worried about the harm she might do, and they called her a murderer either way.

She had tried to marry Rodric, for *them*, for *their* hope, and they called her a whore.

They had praised her and loved her, hoping she would bring magic back into the world, and she had recoiled at the idea, so afraid of what magic had done to her, so certain that she could never do what they dreamed. But now she had magic, and they recoiled from *her*, insulted her, blamed her for all of their ills.

The story of Alysse came to her again. *They did not trust this sorceress who could make so much happen with her thoughts.* She would never be enough for them. She clenched her hands, her fingernails digging into her palms.

She had never been anything to them but a story.

She slipped out of bed and crept back to the practice room. Defiance filled every breath, a furious, desperate, proud determination to be exactly who she could be, regardless of what anyone else wanted or expected. She balled it in her chest, the power of it, and she teased out strands, bit by bit, until candles and fireplaces burned, until she could cup fire in her hands and make it vanish with a breath, until flames whirled around her without scorching a single hair on her head. The power had a madness to it. It was indestructible. She sent it out and pulled it back in, the anger, the sadness, the magic filling every inch of her, until it felt as much a part of her as breathing, as the blood pounding around her veins.

And as the magic burned, she realized what she needed to be. How she could use her magic, how she could help them, how she could be *free*.

Nothing but a story.

She marched into Finnegan's room as the sun began to peek over the horizon. He lay in bed, shirtless, his chest rising and falling in sleep. "Finnegan," she said, softly, clearly, and he startled awake. "I'm ready."

He blinked at her, still half-asleep, his hair tousled around his eyes. "You're ready?"

"Let's go and find some dragons."

TWENTY

FINNEGAN'S HAIR STUCK UP IN FIVE DIFFERENT DIRECtions. He ran his hand through the spikes, pushing them back, and continued to stare at her. "What?"

"You were right," she said. "About the dragons, about Alyssinia. I need to use them to attack them, attack the king. And they'll hate me for it. But I have to do it. I have to make them hate me."

"Rora," he said. "What are you talking about?"

"They hate me," she said. "They hate me already. They want my power, but they're afraid of it too. They're afraid of being unable to control me. And I can't change that. Not ever." Not if the story of Alysse was true. "So I'll get the dragons," she said. "I'll rid you of them. And then I'll take them to Alyssinia, and I'll stop this violence. I'll stop the king."

"And become a queen they're all afraid of?"

"No," Aurora said. "Then nothing will have changed. *Rodric*. Rodric is helping already. If he's king for another time, then I'll create another time. They can hate me, and he can be the hero."

"And what?" Finnegan said. "Let them kill you?" He climbed out of bed and moved to stand in front of her.

"I can vanish," Aurora said, and the smile as she said it seemed to fill her whole body. "Like Alysse. Rodric wouldn't chase me. I'll stop being their Sleeping Beauty; I'll stop having this responsibility; I'll be able to do what *I* want."

Finnegan raked his hand through his hair again. "What about Celestine?" he said. "The plan that she had?"

"She wanted me to turn on them," Aurora said. "She wanted some of this. But you were right. Even if she made me, even if she's the reason I have a connection with the dragons, she can't control what I do. I'll use the magic to do good, even if people hate me for it. It's all that I can do."

Finnegan darted forward, clutching her face with his hands. For a giddy moment, Aurora thought he was about to kiss her, but instead he laughed. "You're amazing, Rora." And then he picked her up, whirling her around, and she laughed in delight too, gripping his arms to hold herself steady.

"You're pretty amazing yourself," she said, as he placed her back on the ground, and it felt like the moment, the point where everything would change, the time when he would kiss her, or she would kiss him, and they would laugh, and things would hurtle on.

But then Finnegan stepped away and grabbed a shirt off a chair. "I'll contact Lucas," he said. "We'll go to that mountain, today. Deal with the dragons at the source." He pulled on the shirt. "Give me a couple of hours, dragon girl. Then we'll go see what you can do."

They left that afternoon. Preparing for a multiple-day expedition in the waste could not have been easy, especially while concealing it from Orla, but Finnegan had clearly been planning for days. He already had lies prepared, about spending time in a library on the far north of the island to research Aurora's magic. The excuse would give them a couple of days before they were missed.

Lucas provided them each with packs, filled with water skins and nonperishable food, kindling for lighting fires in the desolate waste, blankets for the cold nights, maps and compasses for navigation. The packs themselves were waterproof, he told her, coated inside with tar in case they had to swim to safety on the journey. Each one was designed to sustain the carrier if they were separated from the group, but Aurora's was smaller and lighter than the rest. She had not been given kindling. "Can't weigh you down too much," Lucas said with a smile. "You still need to be able to walk."

"I've had some experience in walking," she said, "these past few weeks."

"Good," Lucas said. "You'll need it. But no point in making it harder than it needs to be."

Lucas could not have forgotten who Aurora was, but his attitude toward her did not change at all. He spoke to her now as half-girl, half-fascination, an exciting addition to his dragon research. According to Finnegan, it had not taken much to persuade him to travel into the waste with them again. He wanted to see if the dragons could be controlled as much as they did.

This time, Finnegan had bought his own boat, using Lucas as intermediary to keep the transaction secret. They sailed across the river and hid the boat in a hollowed-out building on the shore.

"What if someone sees it?" Aurora asked. "What if it gets burned?"

"Then we'll need you to send some flares," Finnegan said. "So try not to die on the way."

They soon left the ruined port behind, trudging out into the waste. The baked earth beneath their feet might once have been a road, but any markers had long been lost. No trees, no scrub, no weeds growing between the occasional piles of stones. Nothing but dust, and ash, and death. A few hills and cliffs broke up the landscape, and the corpses of towns were scattered about, their unburned fragments gleaming white in the sun.

In the distance, a mountain loomed. Aurora saw a flicker

of movement around the summit, like a dragon was circling, but perhaps that was her imagination. Soon, she would be there herself.

The journey would take about two days by Lucas's reckoning. They planned to walk for most of the afternoon, until they met another wide, slow-moving river. Then they would follow the river north, sticking close to the bank, until they reached the point where it swerved southwest. North of this river, Lucas said, was dragon territory. The dragons lived south of the river now too—they lived everywhere in the waste—but they were concentrated near the mountain where legend said they had slumbered and in the dry land stretching into the west.

If their group walked directly across the waste, they would reach the dragons in almost half the time. But without the river to guide and protect them, any explorers were unlikely to make it through alive. Despite the dangers of their eventual destination, Lucas insisted that they stick to common sense and take the river path.

Lucas would get them safely to the mountain, avoiding the dragons as much as they could. Then it would be Aurora's turn. No one knew precisely what the inside of the mountain was like, but Aurora pictured some kind of cavern, where she could walk to the center, command the dragons' attention, and then . . . then she did not know. She did not know how many she could control at once.

Perhaps it would be safer to start at the edge, to control one first, and then two, until she felt herself reaching her limit. She would soothe those dragons back to sleep, and then more, until only the ones she needed for Alyssinia remained.

It was not a strong plan, but how could she predict what would happen when dealing with dragons? She would trust her instincts, as she had with them before. When she saw them, she would know what to do.

They reached the river as the sun began to set. It was wider than a city street, and the water rushed past, leaping over rocks and splashing the bank. Reeds grew along the sides, bending inward as though bowing to their river god.

"There's an abandoned house a little way up here," Lucas said. "We'll rest there tonight, give ourselves time to regroup. It'll be the last relatively safe spot for a while."

House was a generous word for the small pile of rubble that waited ahead of them, but one wall stood right against the bank, sturdy and unburned. The other walls had not fared so well, but it would shelter them from sight, and Aurora doubted they would find anything better so far into the wild.

They stepped through a space that might once have been a front door. The ground floor was all one room, and although the walls leaned inward and rubble dusted the ground, it looked stable enough. Pots hung above the fireplace, and a table had been knocked over in the middle of the room.

"We should check upstairs," Finnegan said. "Make sure it's safe."

"A dragon couldn't fit in here," Aurora said.

"A dragon couldn't, but an outlaw might. Who knows who else might think this a good place to rest?"

The stairs led to an attic room that was half-destroyed by fire and time. Rubble and tiles had fallen from the roof, and the remnants of the bed frame were still littered with ash. Something sat by the end of the bed, low to the ground, impossible to make out in the gloom. Heart pounding, Aurora gathered a small ball of fire in her hand, casting a dancing light across the room.

It was a skeleton. It slumped against the ruined wall. Aurora stared at it. It stared back at her with empty sockets, reproaching her for some unknown crime.

"The people here didn't want to leave," Finnegan said. She jumped, and the fire flickered out. "They thought they'd be safe, so close to the water, and so they stayed. No one was safe."

She had never seen a skeleton before. Her life over the past few weeks had been full of death, of family members long gone and friends choking out their lives before her, but she had never seen how it left them, how time had torn everything away.

"It looks safe up here," Finnegan said. "Come light a fire downstairs. I think it's going to be cold tonight."

They all huddled around the grate, Aurora's fire warming their faces and knees as the cold of the night crept steadily across their backs. Lucas prepared them a quick meal of salted meat and bread that they had packed from the city, but Aurora barely tasted it. Her skin prickled, like the skeleton was still watching her from the shadows.

Finnegan sat close by her side, and his elbow bumped hers every time he moved. Aurora did not move closer, but she did not move away.

His sleeve grazed her bare arm, and the urge to kiss him rushed through her.

Lucas leaned close to the fire. The flames lit the hollows of his eyes. He had seen so much, she realized, out here in the waste. He had seen it before the dragons came. He had watched it change.

"Lucas," she said. "Could you tell me what happened, when the dragons came back? What you remember of it?"

Lucas shifted closer to the fire. "They appeared out of nowhere," he said, "and we had no defenses against them. Most people didn't think they'd ever existed, and suddenly they were burning everything to ash. No one believed the tales of those who survived the attacks. A dragon burned the city? More likely a fire got out of control, and the survivor has been driven mad by grief. Or guilt. It was a while before people accepted them as real."

"When did you accept it?" Aurora asked.

"I suspected it from the beginning. From the things I had read, the things I heard—I knew they'd existed, and I believed they were back. I must have been one of the first people to see them and live to speak of it. I was young and foolish, so I went out to find them. To prove the rumors true. And I did."

Aurora watched the flames, trying to picture it. Creatures descending out of myth and burning your world away. "What did it feel like," she said, looking at him again, "when you first saw one?"

Lucas stared into the fire. The light darted across his face, highlighting the lines there, the whites of his eyes. "It was terrifying," Lucas said. "Of course it was terrifying." But the way he spoke, it was almost as though he were convincing himself.

Had he felt like she felt when she'd first glimpsed one, captivated and alive, like nothing existed in the world beyond this?

"Are you ever glad?" she asked. "Do you ever think . . . at least I got to see them?"

"No." He spoke so sharply that Aurora almost jumped, her hands tightening on her knees. Lucas still stared at the fire, but he was frowning now, the lines deepening around his eyes. "Never. The death, the screaming . . . what would be worth that?"

"I'm sorry," she said. "I didn't think."

"No," Lucas murmured. "Neither did I." He let out a deep sigh. "I'm going to rest. Put out the fire before you two sleep."

The fire flickered even as he spoke. Lucas stretched out a few feet away, his back to them.

"That was thoughtless of me," Aurora said to Finnegan, in a low voice. "I just wondered . . ."

"Wonder away," Finnegan said. "I've wondered the same."

She fidgeted with the corner of her tunic, twisting the material between her fingers.

"Not regretting coming out here?" Finnegan said.

She thought of the bones above her head, the bones she would become herself, tomorrow or one hundred years from now or someday. The bones she should have already been, if the world was just.

Perhaps her curse had given her a gift. She had the chance to live in a time she should never have seen, to become friends with Rodric and flirt with Finnegan and hunt down dragons across a waste that had been full of life before she closed her eyes. She had so much opportunity, here across the sea, even while her kingdom threatened to tear her apart. She wouldn't give that up now, not for all the security in the world.

"No," she said. "No. Right now, it's exactly where I want to be."

But as they settled down to sleep, she imagined that she could *feel* the dragons, their heartbeats pounding against her skin.

She ached to slip outside, to see them glow in the dark sky, but she did not dare to leave. A sliver of common sense remained, telling her *no*, she must stay. She must wait.

But they called to her, long after she closed her eyes. And all she could think was *tomorrow*. Tomorrow she would see them again.

TWENTY-ONE

FINNEGAN WOKE HER EARLY THE NEXT MORNING, with one gentle hand on her shoulder. She sat up, stretching her stiff back muscles. "Up the river today," Lucas said.

"Hope you enjoyed the shelter," Finnegan said. "I doubt we'll find anything like it once we get close to dragon territory."

"Then how will we sleep tonight?"

"With caution," Finnegan said. "We'll keep watch. If the dragons get close, we'll have to have a sudden swim."

Aurora had never swum in her life. "All right," she said. She hauled her pack onto her shoulders.

The walk north proved exhausting, the mountain growing

so slowly on the horizon that they seemed to be walking in place. Aurora slipped her hands through the reeds as they passed them. They prickled against her skin.

The dragons were large in the sky now. Aurora could make out the points where their wings met their bodies, the claws on their legs. She watched as they soared through the air.

One of the dragons landed close enough to make the ground rumble, almost throwing Aurora off her feet. She looked east, where the dragon shook its wings, its tail thrashing from side to side. It stared back at her. Even from a distance, she could feel its eyes, cutting down to her heart.

Aurora gripped the dragon necklace, imagining she could feel the heat of the dragon's blood glowing inside it.

As they walked, Aurora kept thinking back to that tattered wanted poster, to the words scrawled across the paper. *Witch*, they had called her. They would see how witchlike she was now.

Their group settled on the riverbank as night fell, sitting as close to the water as they could without falling into the mud. Aurora lit a fire.

"I'll keep watch," Aurora said, after they had eaten a scanty meal. "I don't think I'll sleep anyway."

She half expected someone to argue, but Finnegan nodded. "Wake us the moment you hear anything," he said. With the prince in agreement, Lucas could do little to protest. He and Finnegan lay on the hard ground, blankets wrapped around them, and Aurora urged the fire out. They did not want to alert the dragons to their presence overnight.

Aurora hugged herself with her own blanket, waiting for her eyes to adjust to the darkness. Hundreds of stars blinked above her, never-ending spatters of light as far as she could see, and she tilted her head back, taking in every one. She had expected the night to be eerily quiet, for the stillness to creep into her bones, but even this desolate place bristled with sound, once she got quiet enough to listen. The wind tickled her ear, and she could hear the soft splashing of the river as it tumbled over stones, Lucas's soft breathing, the way Finnegan shifted on the ground. This was a different kind of sleeplessness, she found, as she curled her legs beneath her and stared across the river. It was stillness that wasn't really still at all. The world was breathing around her.

The river reflected the moon, creating a second sky, blurred and distorted. She clutched her necklace, running her finger along the ridges of her dragon's wings. Finnegan shifted again, his blanket falling to rest against her side. Even though he did not speak, she knew he wasn't asleep.

"Can dragons see in the dark?" she whispered.

"I don't know," Finnegan said. "No one's ever tested it." The blankets rustled, and he sat up. "They can create their own light though."

"Yes," Aurora said. "That's true." She pressed her thumb against the dragon's feet, as though it were perched on her hand, about to fly. "You're not sleeping."

"Couldn't," he said. "I can take watch if you like."

She laughed softly. "Not afraid, are you?"

"What's there to be afraid of? Man-eating dragons? Not me." He shifted closer. His hand rested on hers, fingers sliding into the gaps between her knuckles. She didn't know how he had found it in the dark. She could make out the outline of his face, the shape of his nose. She couldn't tell if he was smiling.

Aurora looked away, staring back up at the stars, searching the horizon for any hint of a dragon. Red streaked across the sky.

"There's one thing I still don't understand," she said. "About any of this. Why did Rodric wake me up? I don't love him, not the way true love should mean. He doesn't love me. And even if it was true love . . . why would Celestine give me that? Why would she make that the thing that woke me?"

"Maybe she was lying," Finnegan said. "Maybe it was something else."

"But then what was it? Luck?" She rested her chin on her knees. "I guess it fits. It makes things seem so *simple*. The good savior, awoken by true love, letting everyone live happily ever after. People can imagine I will save them without imagining me *doing* anything at all. And then when it isn't true love, when it doesn't all fit together, it's so easy to imagine me as the villain instead. Because I'm not really a person to them. I'm just a piece of the story." She twisted her body so that she half faced him, her knees colliding with his. She strained to make out his expression in the dark. "Do you remember that rebel in the dungeons, back in Petrichor?" she said. "Tristan. I'm sure Nettle told you all about him." Still Finnegan did not speak. "I thought I liked him," she said. "I thought he was my friend, because . . . because he was kind to me, and joked with me, and was far from the castle and all that I was supposed to be. But it's like . . . it's like I made him up inside my head. In reality, he was quite different from what I thought. He wanted to use me, like all the rest."

"Is that what you think of me?"

"No," she said. "I hated you when I met you." So arrogant, so confident, so certain he knew everything about her. "It's nicer, thinking you hate someone and then realizing they're not so bad after all."

"Not so bad?" he said. "You're too kind to me, Rora."

She knocked him with her shoulder, making him sway backward. "I'm being serious, Finnegan," she said. "I don't—I know you. There are no illusions there." It was too easy to be honest, here in the dark, where she couldn't see his expression, where her knee pressed against his and their hands clutched together.

Finnegan was not her true love. He had climbed those dusty, winding stairs, and he had pressed his lips against hers while she slept, hoping that their future love would awaken her. And Fate had rejected him. He was not her hero, not the man to rescue her.

But that didn't mean she couldn't choose *him*. The thought shivered through her, all the possibilities that Finnegan presented. Nothing promised, nothing fated. Just them.

Now Finnegan looked away, staring out into the sky. Was he looking at the redness too? Could he make out the dragons, right on the edge of the world?

Tomorrow, those dragons would come under her control. A betrayal of Alyssinia, perhaps, to help their enemy . . . or a betrayal of King John, the man she hated anyway. That power, that fire, would be hers. If she wanted, she could take the kingdom for her own.

Until someone came to overthrow her. Until their distrust burned into rebellion again.

"I'm glad I get to be the enemy," she said. Her voice scratched her throat. "I never wanted the throne. I don't want to rule them."

Finnegan looked back at her, and she could feel his eyes burning into hers, despite the dark. "Then what do you want?"

This, she thought, but that was one truth too far, one simple word that could not escape, even in the darkness. "I don't know," she said instead. "I just know—I've spent my whole life letting people tell me who I have to be. And they hate me anyway. I want space to be *myself*. To do things for me."

"You'll have it," Finnegan said. "When this is over, you'll do whatever *you* want to do."

She found herself nodding. Her free hand clutched the dragon pendant, that simple, unexpected gift. "Finnegan . . ." She lingered on the word, uncertain what she wanted to say next, uncertain if there was anything to say. She shifted on the ground and found her thigh pressing against his. She dropped the necklace, dropped her hand onto his leg.

Everything she wanted was so impossible, so indistinct, fire and life and adventure, dreams half-formed and always far away. That, and Finnegan. Impossible, wonderful, untrustworthy Finnegan, someone she knew so little about but couldn't avoid, couldn't stop thinking about or being near, someone who made thrills run across her skin every time he looked at her. She shouldn't like him, she knew that. She shouldn't want anything to do with him. But should and shouldn't had become so tangled over the past few weeks, and all she knew for certain were her instincts, the part of her that wanted to whisper secrets to him in the dark, the part that screamed at her to move closer and closer still, to tangle herself in him and let him swallow her whole.

Her heart beat so strongly that she could feel it in the back of her throat.

Everyone else had always said *stop*, but Finnegan said *go*. Fight. Rage. Think. Cry. Kiss. Be free.

Why should the one place she stopped be around him?

She leaned closer. His hair tickled her nose, and another strand caught the corner of her lip. She hesitated, lingering millimeters from his ear. His free hand shifted too, resting on her knee, pulling it closer.

She shifted again, her hand sliding upward to steady herself against his neck. The new wisps of hair there tickled her skin, hidden under the longer strands at the back, and she wrapped her fingers around them, barely daring to breathe.

Finnegan shifted his head toward her, so that his nose almost touched hers, his fingers digging into her knee possessively, but he did not move to kiss her.

Her lips brushed the corner of his, missing her target slightly in the dark. She giggled, unable to help herself, and shifted forward again, fingers pulling his head to meet hers. One kiss, quick and light. Undemanding. She pulled back. His breath warmed her lips. Her other hand wrapped around his shoulders, and she kissed him again, deeper, firmer, until one of his hands found her hair and the other pressed into the small of her back and she was clambering closer still, the certainty burning within her that any distance was too much, that she would combust if she stopped. She had never kissed anyone like this, her desperation and inexperience growing into something that was hot and clumsy and fierce and forever.

Around her neck, the dragon burned red.

TWENTY-TWO

THE DAWN SENT TENDRILS OF FIRE ACROSS THE SKY.
Aurora had barely slept, not for the hours that she kissed Finnegan, the whole world forgotten, and not when Finnegan finally smiled and said that she should sleep. He kept watch, and she let him think that she slept, but eyes open or closed, all she could do was relive their conversation, all she could see were Finnegan's eyes in the dark. Memories of the kiss blurred together, so that she could feel it on every inch of her skin. She never wanted to leave this moment, even if it meant never sleeping again. She had slept enough for several lifetimes.

But she didn't let Finnegan know that she was awake. She

wanted time to remember as well as to act, to relive every sensation and scorch it into her memory. The watch changed, and when she finally sat up and balanced her chin on her knees, Lucas did not comment.

She stood, stretching her legs. With a nod to Lucas, she strode away, back along the bank of the river. She needed a moment of privacy, at least. A moment to catch her breath.

They would face the dragons today, but she wasn't afraid. It felt right to be out here, to plunge into dragon territory with little more than conviction, like those kisses in the dark. Ill-advised, but *right*.

She dipped her toes into the water, savoring the chill.

When she returned to the camp, Finnegan was awake, and all trace of their presence had already been packed away. Finnegan and Lucas were talking together in low voices, but when Finnegan saw her approach, he smiled. It was a mix between the softer look he had given her that last day in the library and the excitement that shone in his eyes every time he spoke of dragons. Aurora looked away. It was harder to face him and their kiss with the sunlight growing around them. It felt like it should belong to her now, to her memory and to the dark, and seeing Finnegan reminded her that it was his as well. It made her feel self-conscious, like her bones were too big for her skin.

She swung her pack onto her shoulders. "Let's go, before the day gets too late."

They walked in silence, for an hour, and then another, no

one commenting on the death in the air.

The noon sun blazed overhead by the time the ground started to slope upward, loose stones skidding under their feet. Every breath burned now.

They climbed the mountain in silence. Aurora's legs ached with exhaustion, but she forced herself to stay quiet, taking step after painful step. The waste spread out below her.

Then the ground started sloping downward again, falling away under their feet, a steep plunge into the heart of the mountain. "Well," Lucas said, as they paused on the edge of the descent, peering into the darkness. "This is it."

"Have you ever been here before?" Aurora said.

"Once," Lucas said. "Only once."

She took a deep breath, letting the hot air fill her lungs. She could still feel the heat of the night before, of Finnegan's hands on her waist, the way the necklace burned against her skin. *Dragon girl,* he had called her, over and over again, whispering it into her ear, letting it loose under her skin. She would not be afraid.

"Maybe you two should wait out here," she said. "It'll be safer for me alone."

Finnegan laughed. "Since when has splitting up *ever* been a good idea? If something went wrong when you were alone, you'd be dead. We're coming with you."

"Then remember," she said. "Leave the dragons to me."

Her walk turned into a clumsy run as she gained momentum.

The men's footsteps followed.

The cave grew darker and darker as they descended. Sunlight peeked through the entrance, but Aurora could see nothing in the cave itself, hear nothing, as though the rocks were absorbing all hints of light.

Aurora held out her hand, thinking of kisses in the dark, of lives betrayed. She summoned a small ball of flame, casting orange light across the walls. She could see the features of the rock now, the contours of Finnegan's face as he moved to walk beside her, but the area beyond seemed darker as a result. More threatening. The flames flickered with uncertainty, but she frowned, forcing the magic to hold.

"Seems risky," Lucas said, "bringing a light here."

"It's risky anyway," Aurora said. "At least we can see if anything approaches."

They picked their way over more sliding stones, down and down and down. Then the path twisted and split. She could not see the bottom of either tunnel, so she chose the one on the left, the one that was less steep.

"Think you can send the light ahead?" Finnegan asked, his voice barely above a whisper.

As soon as she tried to nudge the light away, it flickered and weakened, the burning in her chest slipping. In the park, it had all been so easy, but she could not sustain it under the oppressive stone. She shook her head. "I'll go first," she said.

Finnegan clutched her free wrist, but he did not stop her.

Heat rushed toward them. Aurora flinched as a dragon catapulted up the tunnel, its scales shimmering red, its eyes glowing like smoldering coals. It stopped a few feet from Aurora. It had to hold its wings tight to its body to fit in the cavern, but Aurora knew that it was small, nothing compared to the beasts they had seen. Its head wove back and forth as it stared at them, mouth half-open. Aurora's light glittered off its razor teeth.

It could destroy them all in an instant, burn them away so that no trace of their existence remained, but for one heartbeat, and then two, it simply looked at them, as though curious why they had come into its domain.

"Girl . . ." Lucas said.

The dragon snapped its head at the sound of Lucas's voice, and its lips curled back.

"Hello," Aurora said, her voice soft, soothing. She stepped forward, holding the fire aloft. "Hello. Look at me."

The dragon looked back at her, and it paused, as though trying to puzzle her out. Aurora met its gaze, and a shiver of terror and excitement ran through her. The fire grew.

Finnegan tightened his grip on her arm, but Aurora pulled away. The dragon looked at him, its tail smacking against the wall, but Aurora stepped forward again, her free hand outstretched. "Hello there," she said. "Hello. We're no harm. We're not going to hurt you." The dragon lowered its head, inch by inch, until Aurora could feel its hot breath on her skin. The light in her hand fizzled out. She barely noticed. She had no thought for anything but this creature, the majesty of it. She knew, she *knew*, deep in her bones, that it would not hurt her. It was as fascinated with her as she was with it.

She trailed her fingers across the dragon's nose. The scales were smooth and cool to the touch, as though the dragon gave off so much heat that it had none left for its own skin.

And Finnegan didn't matter. Lucas didn't matter. The chaos in Alyssinia, all the hatred, the expectations . . . none of it mattered, as she ran her hand along this impossible creature's snout, hypnotized by the feel of it, the lines of every scale.

"Hello," she said.

The dragon watched her.

"Careful, Aurora," Finnegan said.

The dragon shifted again, eyes settling on Finnegan. Aurora's hands stroked its nose, trying to pull its attention back to her, but it was focused on Finnegan now, on the intruder in its domain.

"Steady," she said, but this one did not listen. Its muscles rippled with agitation. The pendant around her neck burned. She stepped back.

"Aurora——" Finnegan said.

The dragon screamed.

"Aurora!"

Fingernails scraped against her throat. Aurora twisted around in shock as Lucas grabbed the dragon pendant and tugged.

"What—" The chain snapped. Lucas threw it through the air.

Aurora snatched for it, seconds behind its fall. It hit the ground with a rattle, and she landed moments later, grasping it out of the dust.

The dragon roared again. Its scream shook the walls of the cavern, making the ground roll like water. It snapped its head up, eyes still fixed on Finnegan. Its tail crashed against stone.

"Finnegan, look out!" Aurora yelled, all magic forgotten. Finnegan dove to the ground, as a gust of fire burst across the wall where he had stood. The whole cavern blazed.

"Finnegan!" She leaped forward and grabbed his arm. He winced, and his skin was too hot under hers, hot and red and scorched by fire.

Water flew through the air, and the dragon flinched. Lucas stood before it, an empty water skin in his left hand. He scrambled through his pack for another.

Aurora couldn't find her magic, couldn't gather a thread, couldn't even *think* about what was happening or what she should do. She clutched Finnegan's hand and pulled him up the slope, away from the thrashing creature. Lucas stared at the dragon, his face pale.

"Run!" she said. She pushed Finnegan to Lucas's side. "Get him out of here."

Lucas didn't need to be told twice. With a strength Aurora

wouldn't have believed the old man possessed, he hauled Finnegan upward and began to run toward the cave entrance.

"Aurora," Finnegan said, half mumble, half shout, but she turned her back to him, facing the dragon again. She couldn't think, couldn't breathe, her heart stuttering and racing, but the dragon had been fascinated by her before, had been calm and tame, and all she could think to do was to pull its attention on her again. She had lost her focus, and now Finnegan was burned, and Finnegan could die, they all could die, unless she regained control.

"Stop!" she shouted. "Stop. I won't hurt you!"

The dragon continued to roar, continued to writhe, but it did not snap its jaws, and it did not breathe fire again.

She had to control it. Calm it, and they'd all be safe. But she didn't know *how*. It would not listen to her, and she couldn't move. She couldn't do anything except stare at the dragon, forcing herself to breathe.

It was too much, all too much, her fear for Finnegan, the dragon staring her down, her own failure, all rushing together and making it impossible to think, impossible to grab a single idea, a single feeling, to pull it into magic.

She took one step backward, her foot shaking beneath her. Then another step, and another, never taking her eyes off the dragon, certain that any moment she would fall, any moment she would crumple away.

The dragon shifted backward, its wings squeezing together above its head.

Aurora ran. She ran faster than she had ever imagined she could, feet springing off the ground, racing to where Finnegan and Lucas stumbled ahead. She ran, and behind her, the dragon began to fly, its tail crashing against the walls, its wings propelling it upward with one big sweep. Aurora barreled into Finnegan and Lucas, using her momentum to flatten them to the ground as the dragon rushed above them, its jaws unleashing fire into the open sky.

They all lay still. Aurora's heart felt like it was trying to force its way out of her mouth. She sat up, the pendant still clenched in her fist, and stared down at Finnegan in the dark. She could see nothing, now that the dragon was gone, but she couldn't find the strength to summon a light. Panic was rising and rising within her, that Finnegan was hurt, Finnegan was burned, she had failed them all.

"Aurora," Finnegan said. "Aurora, are you all right?" His voice was laced with pain.

"I'm fine," she said. "I'm fine. Finnegan, we need to get you out of here. We need to move, we need to go, we need to—"

"Panicking, little dragon?" Finnegan coughed. "Now's not really the time."

"Can you stand?" she said.

"I think so."

She and Lucas hauled him to his feet and staggered toward the mouth of the cave. Finnegan leaned heavily on Aurora, his hand clutching her shoulder. The light ahead seemed impossibly far away.

When they emerged from the cave, the sudden brightness of the sun made Aurora's eyes sting. She forced herself to keep looking forward, to not even glance at Finnegan, until they had scrambled onto the outer slope, collapsing behind a pile of rocks to breathe.

Then she looked. One side of Finnegan, the side she had been supporting, looked fine. Dusty and scraped from their climb and their fall, but healthy enough. But the right side of his face was blackened, and the burns ran down his arm, his shirt melted and molded to his stomach.

"Finnegan—"

Lucas lay Finnegan on the ground, sheltered by the rocks. He ran his fingers around the edge of the burn. "Get the cream," Lucas said. "In my pack."

Aurora untied the flap of his bag and rummaged inside. Her hands shook. "This will cure him?"

"No," Lucas said. He snatched the jar from her as soon as she pulled it out and scooped the cream into his palm. Finnegan hissed in pain as Lucas rubbed it onto his burns. "But it'll help. We have to get him back to Vanhelm. Now."

"It's almost two days' walk from here!"

"We might be able to do it in a day," Lucas said. "If we go

directly there. Leave the river behind. But it won't be as safe, without the water. If a dragon finds us—"

"I don't care," Aurora said. "We don't have a choice."

Nothing lived where dragon fire touched. That was what they said, that was what the waste screamed to her as she slid down the mountain toward it.

The sun scorched the skin on the back of Aurora's neck, but they stumbled on, step after step after step, ignoring the screams of the dragons, ignoring everything except one foot, and then the other, through burned villages, through the bleak emptiness, through looming shadows and the whisper of the wind. And slowly, Vanhelm took form in the distance, a collection of faint buildings, stretching to the sky.

TWENTY-THREE

IT WAS DARK BEFORE FINNEGAN SPOKE AGAIN. "STOP," he said, through gritted teeth. "I need to rest. For a minute." They sank to the ground, backs pressed against a half-melted wall.

"How far are we from Vanhelm?" Aurora asked.

"We should reach it about midday," Lucas said.

Midday. The sun had barely set. They could not drag Finnegan along for another sixteen hours or more. He couldn't keep walking, his skin black and burning. They would never make it back to the palace.

But they did not have a choice. They *had* to succeed.

"Are you hurt, Aurora?" Finnegan asked.

Every inch of her hurt, but she shook her head, forcing herself to smile. "I'm fine," she said. "Perfectly healthy. I'm just worried about you."

"You're holding your hand strangely."

The dragon pendant sat in the center of her fist. It had worn grooves into her skin.

"My necklace," she said. "I forgot." She had forgotten everything in the panic. She looked up at Lucas, moving so suddenly that the muscles in her neck snapped. "You broke it," she said. "You threw it on the ground."

"I did," he said. "That dragon was getting out of control. I thought it was going to kill you."

"So you broke my necklace?"

"It has dragon's blood in it," he said. "I thought if I threw it aside, the dragon would follow, and we could get away."

She stared at the pendant. The silver chain had snapped, the two threads hanging uselessly from her palm. She did not believe him. His words sounded reasonable, but something about the shake in his voice, the way he spoke a little too quickly, suggested he was lying. Whatever his reasoning, it had not been to protect her.

"I'm going to need a new chain," she said. "When we get back." She couldn't think of anything else to say.

Finnegan laughed, but it came out as more of a groan. "I'll get you a new one," he said. "You deserve it after today's rousing success."

"Now who's a bad liar?"

"Still you, Aurora. That's still you." Finnegan wrenched himself to his feet, wincing in pain. "Better get going," he said. "Don't want to miss lunch when we arrive."

The sky was vast and dark, lit by a few stars and the slightest sliver of the moon, but Aurora could see the outline of Vanhelm, growing with every step as they approached.

She did not dare create a light.

"If only you had water magic," Finnegan said. "Might help around now."

She forced herself to smile. "I could have put out that dragon," she said. But his words lingered, and she tried to imagine what water magic would involve. Calmness, tranquility, a sense of utter control. Everything she was supposed to be.

They reached Oldtown a few hours before noon. Aurora's feet shook underneath her as they picked their way through the rubble. The boat was still tucked safely away, and Aurora and Lucas carried it to the river together. Aurora was certain that her strength would fail at any moment, that she would crash to her knees and never move again, but her resolve held. They placed Finnegan in the boat and began to sail to the city.

She tried not to look at his wounds, tried not to think about how long it had been since he received them, how even his attempts to laugh and joke had worn away now. She stared at the city instead, at the skyline that had stolen her breath the first time she saw it.

The boat crashed against the dock, and Aurora sprang out, already shouting, waving her arms with the last energy she had. "The prince," she said. "The prince has been burned. You have to help him!" People appeared from everywhere after that, as though they had been waiting for her cry. They took up the yell as well, until royal guards came running.

They hurried him away, and she was left standing on the pavement, dusty and exhausted, staring at the space where he had been.

A crowd pressed around the palace.

Yes, the prince. I heard he's injured. I heard he's dead. I heard it was dragons.

Aurora pushed through and limped up the steps. The guard on the left opened the door without a word to her.

"Finnegan," she said, her throat burning. "Is he—"

"He is inside," the guard said. He did not elaborate. He did not even look at her.

She stumbled through the door. Maids and guards were running through the entrance hall, shouts echoing from the maze of rooms to her left.

She grabbed a maid by the arm, a little more forcefully than she meant to, swaying on her feet. "Where's Finnegan?" she said.

"You have to take me to him."

"He's in his rooms," the maid said. "This way, my lady." She led her up the stairs and along the upper corridor. Aurora's feet had moved past pain and into numbness. She felt like she was floating above the ground.

Two guards stood outside Finnegan's door.

"No one can enter without the queen's permission," one said.

Aurora would not be stopped by guards now. "I have to see Finnegan," she said. "I have to see if he's all right."

"Not without the queen's permission."

"Then where's the queen?" she said. "Take me to her. I have to see him. I have to—"

"I'm here." Orla walked out of Finnegan's rooms. Her face was white, her hair half-tumbled around her face, her lips worried red.

Aurora wanted to move closer to her, to push through the door, but her feet would no longer cooperate. "Finnegan," she said again. "Will he be okay? Will he—"

"I don't know. It is unlikely."

Aurora swayed. She put a hand against the wall to steady herself. "What do you mean?" she said. "Is he going to die?"

"He was burned by a dragon, Aurora. Do you think he is going to be fine? No one who is burned by a dragon fully recovers."

"But—"

"But what? You thought you were both immortal? You

thought that running off into the waste would be *safe*?"

Not exactly. She had known it was risky, but Finnegan had always seemed so confident, so *present*, that the idea of him being in true danger seemed impossible. It could only be a romantic kind of danger, the sort that sent her heart racing, that gave them thrilling stories but ultimately left them unscathed.

"I cannot believe the foolishness of you both. How could you have been so senseless?"

"I'm sorry," Aurora said. "I'm so sorry. I didn't mean—" She could not get the words out. She did not know what she could say.

"Sorry means nothing, unless you can help. I assume your magic is no use for this, or you would have already healed him."

"No," Aurora said. Her voice shook. "I don't know how to help him."

"Then get out of my sight."

Aurora did not move. "Will you let me know?" she said. "If he—if there's any change?"

Orla stared at her. "I will send someone," she said eventually.

"Thank you." Aurora did not want to leave, but she could not stand in the corridor forever, staring at a locked door. She turned to walk away and then paused. "He thought he was doing the right thing," she said. "He thought he was helping Vanhelm."

"Then he was more of an idiot than I had believed," Orla said. "Go."

Aurora's footsteps were too loud as she walked away.

She could sneak into Finnegan's rooms through the library door. Bribe any guards that stood there and see him that way. She stopped, almost ready to turn for the stairs, but what would be the point? She could not help him. As Finnegan had said, her magic was all *fire*. She didn't know how to heal.

But Celestine did.

Celestine would know what to do. She had saved lives before, hadn't she? She would have a cure.

Aurora pushed her way into her rooms and fell back against the door. She needed a solution, a way to help Finnegan without invoking the witch. But it had taken her weeks to master fire. She did not even know if she had any other powers beyond burning and light. And Finnegan could not wait. Finnegan was dying *now*.

He had trusted her, he had trusted her magic, and she could do nothing for him.

Was this the madness that had driven others to Celestine, over a hundred years ago? The thought that at least Celestine could help. At least she could do *something*.

No one made a deal with Celestine and won. Aurora was living proof of that. And Aurora already knew what Celestine's price would be. An alliance. Aurora, working by her side.

But at least Finnegan would live. He was the only person who had ever really *seen* her, strengths and anger and all, and liked her for it. He made her feel more like *herself*. Like she fit.

And if he died, people would say it was his own fault, that he had died from his selfishness and recklessness. They wouldn't recognize his genuine desire to help.

Aurora stumbled over her swollen feet. Celestine was weak, crazed by a century of dwindling magic. If Aurora could strike a careful deal, if she could outsmart her, take what she needed and then run, as she'd run before . . .

She could offer Celestine one favor, one more taste of her magic, something small and specific. And she could get more from the arrangement than Finnegan's life. If she spoke to Celestine, appeared to bargain with her, the witch might let slip something she could use. Celestine would think that Aurora was weak, but Aurora would be listening, Aurora would be strong.

And what should she care, if she *did* help Celestine? The people of Alyssinia hated her. They despised her. All of her allies were gone, or dying, and her kingdom was burning, and they called her a traitor. Called her a whore.

Why should she sacrifice one of the few good things in her life, for their sake? They would not do the same for her.

She could not allow Finnegan to die. Celestine was the only answer she had.

And she knew she was close.

The library was deserted. Aurora yanked the curtains closed, blocking out the glare of the afternoon sun and the bustle of the street. Then she summoned flames, casting light and shadow across the cavernous room.

"Celestine," she said. The heavy curtains swallowed all sound. "Celestine!" she said again, louder this time. "I know you can hear me. I want to make a deal with you."

Nothing happened. Self-consciousness prickled the back of Aurora's neck. But Celestine *wanted* her to ask for help. She would be watching. She would not ignore her.

"Celestine!"

"You've been practicing." Aurora spun around. Celestine stood behind her, her fingers dancing around one of Aurora's lights. She looked stronger than the last time Aurora had seen her, a little taller, her blond hair thicker. It curled around her heart-shaped face, and her red-lipped smile was like a wound. "Impressive. But you'd have learned more with me." She raised her hand, and Aurora's lights died. "Poor girl. I did warn you, my dear. I said you would regret turning from me. But you would not believe me, and now we are here." She stepped closer and traced her fingers along Aurora's neck. "Finnegan is going to die if magic does not intervene. You know he will."

"What do I need to do?"

"You know that is not how deals work, my dear. Tell me your desires, tell me precisely what you wish, and then we shall see."

"Save him," Aurora said. "Cure him of his burns, make it as though he had not been burned at all. *Please.*"

Celestine tilted her head. "And in return? What will you offer me?"

"Another taste of my magic," Aurora said. "Like the one you had before."

Celestine laughed. The sound was sweet and sharp. "Come, Aurora. You think your prince's life is worth as little as that?"

"An alliance then."

"Why would I need to bargain for that? You are already mine. If Finnegan dies, you'll lose your last friend. Queen Orla will not keep you here, when she can blame you for her son's death. King John will not let you live, and Rodric cannot protect you. If Finnegan dies, you will come crawling to me, crying for revenge against them all. And I do not bargain for things that I can have if I do not intervene."

"Then what do you want?"

"It is only a little thing. I want you to return to the mountain and face one of the dragons there. I want you to take its heart and bring it to me."

Aurora struggled to catch her breath. She had been right. All of her theories about Celestine, her bringing back the dragons, her plans . . . she had been *right*.

"Bring me a dragon heart, Princess. Place it in my hands, and I'll save your precious prince." She stroked Aurora's jaw line with one long finger. "What is it? Are you afraid to take the heart of a creature that has killed tens of thousands of people, to save your prince? Are you too *good*?"

No. She was not *too good*. She was already bargaining with Celestine. But if she did this, then she would be giving Celestine what she wanted. The ability to control the dragons, like Aurora could.

But Celestine had only asked her to *place it in her hands*. Wording mattered in these deals. As long as Aurora placed the heart in Celestine's hands, her part of the deal would be fulfilled. Celestine had said nothing about letting her *keep* the heart. "Why not get it yourself," Aurora said, "if you are so much stronger than me?"

"I cannot," Celestine said. "It must be you."

The words on the wall of that room. *Only her.* She had been right. She had been *right*.

"And if I do, Finnegan will live?"

"He will live."

"Not just live," Aurora said. "He'll be as healthy as he was before. He'll be completely unchanged by the dragon."

"He will be unchanged, although he will remember."

If Aurora put a dragon heart into Celestine's hands, the witch would control them. But Finnegan would live.

And Aurora could trick Celestine. She could keep the bargain, and then snatch the heart away. She could use it herself. She could use her connection with the dragons, the connection she did not have, to burn Celestine away. The heart might not even *work* for Celestine. The witch had been wrong about the dragons before, when she had assumed that she could take one of their hearts herself. She might not be able to use the heart, even if it was placed in her hands.

But Aurora could not be certain.

"What do you plan to do with it?" she said.

"That is not part of our deal, nor any of your concern."

"I want more. If I get you the heart, I want answers, too. Honest ones."

"You already named your price," Celestine said, "but I am in a generous mood. I will answer three questions. That is a good number, don't you think? Three questions, and the life of your precious prince for a dragon heart. Do we have a deal?"

Aurora closed her eyes. In the darkness, she could almost smell Finnegan's charred skin. She could feel his hands on her waist, his lips against hers, every cell inside her sparking alive. A choice for herself. She would burn down Petrichor herself before she let one of the few good things in her life die.

"Yes," Aurora said. "We have a deal."

Celestine's snatched Aurora's wrist, yanking her so close that Aurora could feel the witch's breath on her cheek. "Good choice," she said.

TWENTY-FOUR

AURORA WANTED TO LEAVE IMMEDIATELY, BUT exhaustion weighed her down, and she needed her strength if she was going to survive. She had to use this day to rest, and to prepare.

Her pack still had plenty of supplies, especially for two days of nonstop travel, and a quick message to the kitchens furnished her with fresh bread and water. Her feet were blistered and bleeding, so she wrapped them in bandages, trying to copy the way that Nettle had done it, all those weeks ago. If only Nettle were here now. She would know what to do.

She found another silver chain in a jewelry box on her dresser, but it was shorter than the last, leaving the dragon to rest below the hollow of her collarbone. It rattled every time she moved.

She set off before dawn the next day, dressed in a fresh tunic and trousers, her hair pulled back in a sloppy bun. Her dagger was shoved in her belt. The flat of it bumped against her thigh with every step.

The dock was deserted except for a couple of fishermen, preparing their boats for the day. The boat waited where they had left it, secured to the dock by some loyal soul after Aurora had run to the palace. She walked across to it. Nobody gave her a second glance.

"Girl!"

Lucas strode across the dock behind her.

"What are you doing, girl? You're not going out alone, are you?"

She gripped the rope tying the boat to the dock. "I have to," she said. "There's something I need to do."

"Out there? You'll get yourself killed. What help to Finnegan will that be?"

She stared at him. His shoulders were tense, almost aggressive. Her hand flew instinctively to the dragon pendant.

"I want to go back to the mountain," she said. "To see what's there, like we planned before. It's the only thing I can think of that might help."

"I understand the impulse, girl, but it won't make a difference."

"Perhaps not," Aurora said. "I have to try." She continued to stare at him. "What are you doing here? Were you trying to go to the waste?"

"I was," he said, as though challenging her to argue. "I thought if I had a little more information, I might be able to figure out a cure. But I'm an expert, girl. I know what I'm dealing with. You can't go."

He was lying. He knew about her power, knew what she was capable of. If anything, she was safer in the waste than he was. Lucas was hiding something from her.

"You won't stop me," she said. "You should stay with Finnegan. He needs your expertise."

Lucas shook his head. "I can't help him right now," he said. "And if I can't stop you, I suppose we'd better go together. Two sets of eyes'll be better than one, and Finnegan'll never forgive me if anything happens to you." He untied the knot with a few steady movements.

She should refuse him. She did not need more complications. But she needed to move quickly, and Lucas knew his way around the waste better than anyone. She would be no use to Finnegan if she got lost. And she was curious. What, exactly, did he intend to do? He had seen her fire magic. He knew he could not hurt her. So what was lurking out there that he needed to see?

"All right," she said. "Let's go."

They walked across the waste in silence, following the path they had taken on their struggling walk back with Finnegan. The world had been quiet then, as though the kingdom had been holding its breath. Or perhaps Aurora had been too focused on Finnegan's pain and her panic to notice anything that was happening around her. Now the air seemed full of dragons. Their journey was interrupted by screams and shadows. Every time they left the melted ruins behind, limping onto open ground, they broke into something like a run, ducking as though that few-inch difference in height would prevent the dragons spotting them from above.

For the first time, Aurora saw the dragons and felt truly afraid. She had not been able to control the one in the mountains. What if she had been wrong, what if she *couldn't* control them? She could be walking into a trap.

But no. Celestine wanted a dragon heart, and she needed Aurora to get it. That meant she had been right, that she was connected to the dragons, that they shared blood. She had lost control in the mountains, but she would not do so again.

She and Lucas did not speak. Hour after hour, Aurora tried to think of how to deal with Celestine, how to deal with Lucas. The scholar complicated things. Celestine might be unwilling to speak with Aurora while he was there, and Aurora did not know how she could sneak off for a private conversation in this derelict place.

Perhaps she could use him to her advantage. His presence

could create a distraction for Celestine. But Celestine would kill him if he threatened her or her scheme.

She ran over her plan in her mind. She would let Celestine touch the heart, place it in her hands, and then burn it into nothing. If she had an affinity with the dragons, if they shared blood, she might be able to tap into the heart's magic, make it burn from the inside. Celestine would be left with nothing, but the bargain would have been fulfilled.

It was not a good plan, but it was the only one she had.

And she would get three questions. Three honest answers from the witch. The number was nowhere near enough. She could ask her about the curse, about her mother, about her magic and the dragons and Celestine's past. She could find out what Celestine wanted, or what she intended to do now. But she could only pack so much nuance into three questions.

She needed to learn more about Celestine's plans, before anything else. But there were other things that she *longed* to learn. Should she sacrifice her one chance for answers, to help people who hated her?

She didn't know.

They reached a village that was half-intact as the sun began to set. A few buildings still had their roofs, at least, and a small pool of water waited in the middle of the central square. Aurora sank onto the ground and scooped the water in her hands. It tasted of ash, like everything else here, yet it was still cool to the touch. The stars glistened, and fire wove across the sky.

"We should stop," Lucas said. He sounded out of breath. "It will be too dangerous to go on tonight, and this will be the safest place to rest until morning."

"We need to go as quickly as we can," Aurora said. Her whole body ached, but they had to keep going. "Finnegan can't wait."

"It'll be better for us to wait one more night than for us to not return at all."

"We can rest for an hour," Aurora said. "But then I'm moving on, with or without you."

Lucas sank to the ground beside her, letting out a sigh. "It's risky," he said.

"So is staying here."

She let her fingers trail in the water as they sat, staring at the sky. Dragons were all around them, flashing in and out of view.

"Were they what you expected?" she said. "The dragons? You studied them for years before they came back. Were they what you thought they'd be?"

"No," he said. "No, they weren't."

"What did you expect?"

"I didn't expect them to be killers," Lucas said. "I didn't expect them to destroy the kingdom. I knew that the dragons killed and burned, it's not hard to figure out, but there's a difference between knowing it and really *accepting* it. Taking it in. I didn't really *know* it until I saw my first smoldering village. The creatures can't be the same after you've seen that."

"No," Aurora said. "No, I suppose not." An itch ran through her legs, and suddenly she needed to walk, to leave this haunted town and finish what she'd set out to do. She scrambled to her feet. "You can wait here if you like," she said. "But I'm going on now."

Lucas stood without a word, and, together, they continued across the waste.

The sun rose, and the mountain grew before them, until it was all that Aurora could see, blocking out the sky, filling the world above and ahead. A few dragons circled the jagged mountain top. Aurora climbed, her legs aching, gripping outcroppings and boulders to drag herself farther up the mountainside.

Then the ground sloped away, and the cave engulfed them, all sound muffled. This time, Aurora did not dare to create a light. They would stumble blindly downward, and the dragons would light the way.

Perhaps it was the shaking of the earth that warned her, the sound of someone walking too close to her back. Perhaps it was the sound of Lucas's frightened, heavy breathing close to her ear, or the whisper of *I'm sorry* as he leaned in. Perhaps it was the anticipation of the cold glint of steel as it moved toward her throat. Pain sliced under her chin, and magic slammed out of her.

Lucas yelled. The knife fell out of his hand, burning red. It clattered onto the ground, and Aurora kicked it, one arm outstretched to shove him away, the other reaching for her own dagger. Light flickered between them, illuminating Lucas's panicked face.

"What are you doing?" she hissed.

"I had to," he said. "If you understood—"

"Had to what? Try to kill me?"

"I'm sorry," he said. "I can't let you go down there."

"Why?" she spat. "Because it's too *dangerous*?"

Her fist tightened around the dagger. She stepped forward, forcing Lucas back against the wall. "Why did you attack me?" she said.

"You don't understand." He glanced down the tunnel. His whole body shook now. "You're fools, you and Finnegan both. The dragons already destroyed most of the kingdom. Who knows what they'll do if you interfere with them? What if you make them cross the water? I can't let you do that.'"

Farther down the tunnel, a dragon screamed.

"So you came all the way here to kill me?" Her hand shook around the dagger. "Why not stab me on the docks and be done with it?"

"I hoped you'd turn back," Lucas said. "I didn't want it to come to this."

"But you tore off my necklace," she said. "You thought it would stop us; you knew it would upset the dragon. This is your fault. You got Finnegan hurt."

"No," he said. He did not flinch. "You did."

But she would not back down now. She *had* to do this. "Go," she said. She gestured down into the tunnel with her dagger. "You can lead the way."

TWENTY-FIVE

THE PATH FLATTENED OUT, BECOMING SO NARROW that no more than three people could have walked side by side. Now she understood why they had only encountered one dragon while climbing down here. Most of the creatures would not fit. There must have been many similar tunnels, a hundred paths into the heart of the mountain, vast entryways where dragons flew.

They turned a corner, and Lucas stopped so suddenly that Aurora almost slammed into him. She had to drop her hand at the last moment, her dagger narrowly missing his back.

The tunnel ended in a huge cavern, a dome of heat and stone.

The walls gleamed with jewels, and the ceiling was so high that Aurora could barely see it, except for the points where dragons skimmed it with their burning wings. Their shrieks echoed from wall to wall, magnified a hundred times.

For a moment, all she could do was stare, taking in every inch of it. There were so many dragons. So much fire.

She began to walk to the center of the cavern, weaving around stalagmites that glistened as though magic had been caught in the stone. She ran her hand along one, almost expecting it to scorch her palm. It was cool and rough to the touch, tugging on her skin.

She craned her neck, watching the shadows swoop around the stalactites.

Come, she thought.

The air swelled with heat, and Aurora's magic pounded in response, making her dizzy. *Come here,* she thought again, and this time she sent out magic, too, a ball of flame that darted around her.

Behind her, a dragon roared. Aurora turned as it thudded to the ground, its neck writhing, eyes gleaming.

Aurora took one shaky step forward. It would not hurt her, she knew. They were alike, fire and blood and Celestine's magic pounding through their veins. The dragons would not hurt her.

She stretched out her hand, palm turned upward. Heat sank into her skin.

She glanced at the dragon's chest, searching for a weakness, for some hint of how to take its heart. But she could not harm a creature that was so fearsome, so awe-striking as this. She could not pull out its heart and place it under her thrall.

The dragon continued to watch her.

But neither of them was watching Lucas. He snatched Aurora's wrist, twisting it until the dagger fell from her hand. She yelped, magic sparking within her, but Lucas had already grabbed the weapon. He slashed at her side as she jerked away. The tip of the knife sliced her skin. Blood stained her tunic red.

Lucas lurched forward with the dagger again, and she scrambled away. The dragon rose onto its hind legs. Its scream shook every stone in the cavern. It twisted its head, nostrils flaring, eyes staring at the wound at Aurora's side. Its head snapped to Lucas. He stumbled backward, dagger shaking in his hand. And Aurora knew that it was going to kill him. The blood had set something off in the creature, and it was going to burn them away.

She moved on instinct, all of her fear for Finnegan, all of her fascination, all of her need for answers swelling inside her and driving her forward. Her free hand snatched at the dragon's chest, and she reached for the connection, for the way their blood sang together, her dragon pendant burning at her throat, hot enough for its wings to imprint on her skin.

And her hand slipped, brushing against the dragon's smooth scales and then sinking deeper, slipping into pure heat that pulsed and writhed and caressed her skin. She bit back a scream.

Her hand snatched at the fire. She wrenched it backward, and the scream escaped her throat.

She held a heart, no larger than her own. A fierce red thing that glowed in the darkness.

The dragon looked at her. She looked back. And she felt the sadness in its eyes as though it were her own. It tore at her, the pain searing through her own veins, so intense that she almost shoved the heart back, almost abandoned Finnegan, almost left all the answers she wanted in this cave, to give the murderous creature its life again. To give it the freedom she had wanted for herself.

But then the instant was over, and the dragon began to smolder. Not the air-bending heat she had seen before, the steam rising from its nostrils, but a crackling and burning, smoke rushing from its scales, singeing the air. The dragon opened its mouth, but nothing came out except a strangled shriek. Then its scales, its powerful wings, its cavernous eyes were all glowing red, crinkling into black like burning paper, the fire spreading from the inside out, until it was consumed by its own heat. It crumbled, skin and scales and fire all blackening and falling to the ground as the heat pushed out and out and out.

Aurora ran. She clutched the heart, and she ran, scrambling around the stalagmites, tripping over stones, the heart beating in time with her own. The other dragons were screaming now, not the death scream of the first, but screams of anger, of hatred. Aurora ran faster. She risked a glance over her shoulder and saw

Lucas following. Behind him, the once great dragon was nothing more than a huge ball of flame and smoke, still growing, lighting the entire cavern so that Aurora could see the cracks in the ceiling. The ground rumbled, and she ran, twisting into the narrow corridor, forcing herself up and up and up the slope, terrified that the fire would catch them at any second, that one of the dragons would swoop down and roast them as they fled.

Behind her, Lucas screamed.

She plunged out of the mouth of the cave and tumbled to the ground, the rocks scraping her knees raw. She threw down her free hand to stop her fall, and little stones embedded themselves in her skin. She came to a stop a few feet from the cave, hidden in the shadow of a boulder.

She looked at the heart in her hand. It was so small, almost delicate, like one squeeze would make it burst. Such a fragile thing, to keep that terrible creature intact. But she could still feel it beating. Her hand was scorched black.

She pulled up her tunic to inspect the wound in her side. It was shallower than she had expected, and the blood had already clotted. Painful, but not life-threatening. She had dealt with worse before.

Aurora staggered to her feet, ignoring the sting in her knees and her side. If Lucas emerged from the cave, he would have to make his way back alone. Perhaps he was waiting for her to leave. Perhaps it would be safer if they walked back to the capital separately anyway. Perhaps.

She scrambled down the slope. The mountain rumbled beneath her feet, and she could still hear the dragons' screams. The earth rushed toward her, faster and faster as she slid over the stones, desperate to reach level ground, to reach the ghosts of the villages, to run and run until those horrible cries were miles behind her.

Celestine was waiting for her in the village at the base of the mountain. The witch stood beside a melted wall, framed by black soot and white stone. She glanced at the heart in Aurora's hand, and she smiled, a mad, grasping smile that matched the starved look in her eyes.

"You did it," Celestine said. "I knew that you would." She stepped forward, snatching for the heart, but Aurora stepped back, clutching it against her chest. She could feel it beat. She thought, wildly, of Finnegan, how his heart had beat against her chest as they'd kissed out here in the waste. Yet this was fiercer, a persistent, terrifying beat.

"I can take it from you," Celestine said. "I can take it from you and leave your precious prince to die. We had a deal."

"You said you would answer my questions if I brought you the heart," Aurora said. "And I've brought it to you. Questions for bringing the heart. Finnegan for putting it in your hand. A deal is a deal."

"Yes," she said. "A deal is a deal. Ask me your questions."

The heat of the heart beat into her, making her bolder. *Three questions*, Celestine had promised her. Only three, and there was so much she needed to learn. She needed to be careful how she spoke. "You brought the dragons back."

"That is not a question."

"You made a potion, using my blood."

Celestine only smiled.

"My blood has magic in it, because I was made with magic, wa—" She almost said *wasn't I?*, but she caught the question at the last moment, biting her lip. Celestine's grin grew.

"It took you so long to figure out why your magic is different. I must admit, I thought you smarter than that. I told you all you needed to know. But you stumbled around with your prince, wondering *why*, *why* did you have such spectacular magic, *how* could you have such a gift? You should have known it was because of me, Princess. It has always been because of me."

"You're weak," Aurora said. "You could not get the heart without me. You have no magic here without me."

"I wouldn't say *weak*," Celestine said. "You are relying on me to save your dear prince. But I never had magic in Vanhelm before. There was no magic in the air here, nothing to draw from . . . and now I have your blood in me, your magic, for now at least. And I am grateful for that. But you will not get more answers from me by goading me with statements. Three questions. Ask them."

Aurora's fingers tightened around the heart. She could think of a hundred questions to ask, but she had to be careful, to gain as much knowledge as she could from every word.

"Why do you want this dragon heart?"

"I want what should be mine, Aurora. I want my magic back. I am just a shadow of what I was before, and the dragons . . . they will give me magic like yours. Magic that no one can take away."

Aurora bit her lip. She could not return Celestine to full strength. She couldn't. But Celestine only laughed. "Do not look so afraid. I am not going to hurt you. I want back what I used to have. I want to give the people in these kingdoms the magic that they crave."

"And use it to hurt them."

"Magic always hurts the weak. People unable to see the paths their wishes might take. People who think they can gain their dreams for free. Your mother was one of those people."

"And me," Aurora said. "Now."

"No," Celestine said. "Not you. You are like me, Aurora. I want you by my side."

If Celestine still wanted Aurora by her side, she must have plans for her beyond fetching the dragon heart, beyond the return of her magic. But what use would Aurora be to her, once Celestine had all the power she wanted of her own?

She had to know what Celestine intended, what she thought Aurora would be. "What do you want to happen," she asked, "after I join you?"

Celestine tilted her head, and her smile faded slightly. "I want you as an ally," she said. "That's all. It's what I've been hoping for, from the very beginning. There has never been anyone like me, Aurora. And now there is you. That is why I accepted your mother's bargain, you see. I knew who you would be. I knew we would be magnificent together." She slid closer, running her fingers through Aurora's hair. "It needed time, of course. You need to see what the world is really like. Everyone wants something from you, and they all turn against you in the end. But once you've seen the truth, you will think as I think, feel what I have felt. I want you to be my ally, so you're free to be who you're meant to be. So that no one will ever control you again."

"*You* will control me."

"No," Celestine said. "Why would I? You'll see things as I see them. If not yet, then soon. Soon you'll see." And she stepped forward, her fingers reaching for the heart. Everything about her seemed frantic, unbalanced, from the quirk of her lips to the tilt of her head, but she looked so *convinced*. She truly thought that Aurora would join her. Because of the curse. Because of the life that Celestine had woven for her.

Aurora fought the urge to step backward, to flinch away. The dragons screamed above them. *Let them come,* she thought. Let them burn her into ash. She would not back down.

"What did my mother offer you?" Aurora said. "In return for me?"

"Oh, dear child," Celestine said. "She offered *you*."

Aurora's heart beat in time with the dragon's. "What?"

"I promise you, it is true. She asked for a child, and in return, she promised that the child would belong to *me*. She sold you away, even as she ensured your existence. Your mother thought she could outwit me, because she did not say *when* she must hand you over. She thought to delay, to protect you. She told me that her baby might *belong* to me, but that I had said nothing about taking you from the castle. She believed herself so clever, to point out that no person can belong to another, and that our bargain had no real price."

"So she didn't betray you. She was smarter than you."

"No," Celestine said. "She simply brought the curse upon you. I would have kept you in my tower, helped you to grow into a fearsome witch, if she had let me. But she did not. I could not physically move you from the castle, so I cursed you, to get what I wanted and to reward your mother for thinking herself smarter than me. I thank her for it now. Your mother gave me *such* a sweet opportunity, to craft another woman like me. All that power, all that betrayal, all that *hatred* . . . far stronger than a girl who grew up with all the freedom she required, do you not agree?"

"But you said you cursed me to wake to the kiss of true love. That hardly seems like a good way to crush me."

"Oh, Aurora, you are still so naïve. Have you learned nothing since you awoke? True love is meaningless. You could have loved Rodric. You *would* have loved him, if it had not been thrust upon you, if you had not been told that you had no choice, that the security of your entire kingdom rested on your happiness.

But when your supposed love is a cage, preventing you from living the life you wish to live . . . no. You could not love him then. You had the *potential* to love him, but the world beat it out of you." Celestine's smile grew. "Without the curse, you could never meet him, but with the curse, you cannot love him. Strange, is it not, how magic works?"

"It only works that way because you made it that way."

"Perhaps. I suppose there have been many people you could have loved, over the years. Many people who suited you. Some of them may even have kissed you. But I did not curse you to make you *happy,* Princess. I cursed you to suffering, to a love that was doomed before it began. That is what true love is, Aurora, not flirtations with foreign princes and fire. And your mother gave me the chance to teach you that, as she gave me the chance to teach you many things."

It could not be true. Her mother could not have sold her to Celestine, given away her life in the same breath that created it. But Celestine had promised to tell the truth, and Celestine always seemed a woman of her word.

"My mother wouldn't bargain for my life by offering my life," Aurora said. "It wouldn't make sense."

"Desperate people will do desperate things," Celestine said. "And if a queen cannot have a child, if people are already against her, if whispers spread that she needs to be replaced, for the good of the kingdom . . . well, she may convince herself that the bargain is worth the risk."

"But—"

"Ah ah ha." Celestine held a figure before Aurora's lips. "Three questions, Aurora. I have kept my side of the bargain. Now give me the heart. Unless you want Prince Finnegan to die."

She could not give Celestine her power back. She could not restore the witch to her former strength.

But Finnegan still lay dying in his palace, his skin burned away by dragon fire, and if Aurora did not help Celestine, if she did not become complicit in her plan, one of the few things she cared about, one of the few people who cared about her, for her, would suffer and wither away.

And what was she trying to protect? A kingdom that was already in flames? A king who had tried to murder her, who had killed his own daughter in the attempt? Was placing power here any worse than struggling on alone, allowing the existing chaos to continue?

Yes, a voice said. *Yes, it was worse.* But when she thought of Finnegan, when she thought of the insults scrawled on that poster, she found that she didn't much care. Her own mother had sold her away. Everyone had betrayed her, hated her, used her. Why should she not make a decision for herself?

And Celestine had said she would cure Finnegan if Aurora put the heart in her hand. All she had to do was *place it in her hands.* Then she could destroy it. Then she could stop her.

She did not believe she could. But it was possible. It was *possible.*

"I could take it from you," Celestine said. "Do not doubt that for a second."

Slowly, Aurora loosened her hold on the heart. She held it out with shaking hands, and Celestine snatched it, the hungry look back in her eyes. As Aurora released the heart, some of the heat went out of her, some of the fury, and regret rushed in its place. Celestine pressed the heart to her lips, kissing it, almost caressing it. Then she bit into it, tearing at the muscle, red blood staining her lips. Aurora gasped, grasping for her magic, for the ability to *burn*. The power flickered out of her reach, and Celestine took another bite, blood smeared across her face, eyes gleaming. Aurora's instinct told her to take the heart from the witch, *now*, before it was too late, but Celestine was already devouring it, and her skin glowed red, like the heart had done, like the skin of a dragon.

Aurora snatched at the heart. Her fingers caught a scrap of gristle, and she yanked it away, blood spilling over her own burned fingers.

One moment the scrap of heart was in her hand, inches away from Celestine's bloody lips, and then Aurora had placed it in her own mouth, desperate to keep it from the witch, desperate to regain control.

It did not taste as she had expected. Her mouth burned from the inside out, and heat filled her, power flowing down her throat and into her lungs. The blood covered her own lips too now, and Aurora shuddered. The witch grinned at her then, and all her teeth were red, red with blood and magic.

"You will regret that," Celestine said. "But it is no matter to me."

"Finnegan," Aurora said, her voice hoarse. "You promised to help him. You promised."

"I did," Celestine said. "And unlike your mother, I *always* keep my promises." She moved closer, pausing inches from Aurora, her mouth still sticky with blood. "I have the perfect thing for you." She stretched out her hand and pressed a single, bloodstained fingertip to Aurora's lips. She dug in slightly, so that Aurora could taste more of the dragons' blood, the metal and flame, and then slipped her finger away. Aurora's lips tingled where the witch's skin had been. "A kiss, I think," Celestine said. "Go to him, and kiss him, and think of how *desperately* you want him restored. If you do this, he will live. For now, at least."

Aurora pressed her own fingers to her lips. "The kiss of true love?" she asked.

Celestine laughed. "It's just a kiss, my dear."

TWENTY-SIX

AURORA'S LEGS SHOOK WITH EXHAUSTION BY THE time she reached the city. The sun had set, and the sun had risen, and Aurora had dragged herself on, putting one foot in front of the other, all the way to the palace doors, and then through the maze of rooms, into the library, up the winding stairs, around and around, as Finnegan must have traveled to her tower door years ago, as Rodric had done while she slept.

Beyond Finnegan's rooms, she could hear people talking in low voices. Orla, she thought, and someone else. A doctor perhaps. She could not make out the words.

His bedroom door swung open without a sound. The

room beyond was dark, the curtains blocking out the sunlight. Aurora summoned a small ball of light, making sure to keep the magic gentle and controlled. The flame flickered and danced as though caught in a breeze, but it did not grow larger, and it did not blow out.

She held the light aloft. Finnegan's bed was piled high with blankets, but his head was visible, his black hair mussed with sleep. Aurora hurried across the room, her footsteps muffled by the plush carpet. She left dusty footprints as she went, dirt and ash falling from her clothes like rain.

The entire right side of Finnegan's face was covered in thick white cream and sprinkled with herbs, but Aurora could still smell the deadened flesh beneath. Flakes of black lingered on his skin.

One kiss. Then he would be all right. He had to be all right.

She rested a hand on his shoulder. "Finnegan," she whispered. "Finnegan, wake up."

He groaned, but he did not move.

"Finnegan, I need you to wake up," she said. "Come on. We have a deal, remember? You can't abandon me now."

He groaned again, and this time, he opened his eyes. "Rora," he said. "Can't you see I'm trying to sleep?"

"It's after noon," she said. "Time to wake up." She sat on the edge of the bed. The mattress sank under her weight, and she tumbled closer to the prince.

He gave her a small smile, and then winced in pain. "Here to seduce me, dragon girl?"

"Not likely." She reached forward, her hand gripping the edge of the blankets. "I wouldn't need to."

"You're smart," he said. "That's why I like you."

"I'm going to kiss you, though," she said. "Is that okay?"

"It's been a few days since you did. Started to feel like forever."

She forced herself to smile. Then she leaned closer, brushing her lips against his. One soft kiss. His lips tasted hot, like a burst of dragon fire, but then the kiss deepened, and the heat faded away, melting into something soothing, like cool rain on a sweltering summer day. And she forced her thoughts away from fire, away from frantic kisses in the wilderness, away from witches grinning with blood staining their teeth. Instead, she thought of Finnegan with his arm around her, his face close, as the thrill of magic ran through her. She thought of him lying beside her in the park, and the intensity in his eyes as he told her that she would conquer them all.

She pulled back, his breath on her cheek.

"What was that?" Finnegan said.

She ran her fingers along the line of his jaw. Already, the skin was cooler, softer to touch. "A kiss," Aurora said. "What did you think it was?"

"Magic," he said. "You used magic."

"Yes," she said. "To help you to get better."

"Don't trust me to get better by myself?"

She kissed him again, and it was like it had been out in the waste, like nothing in the world mattered but them. He pressed his hands to the back of her head, running his fingers through her hair, and she grabbed his shoulders, barely able to stand a shred of space between them. Finnegan was there. He was *there*, and he was hers, for that moment at least. For that second, and the next.

When she finally returned to her room to sleep, her dreams were full of fire.

Aurora awoke to the taste of ashes. She blinked at the sunlight streaming across the wall. Her legs ached. Then she remembered. The blood on her tongue. The gristle between her teeth. The red on Celestine's lips, as the witch laughed and laughed and called her *my dear*.

She had killed a dragon. She had given Celestine a dragon heart.

Aurora scrambled out of bed and grabbed a basin. She threw up, her muscles screaming, eyes stinging. Then she sat back on her heels. Acid burned her throat.

Her right hand was charred black.

She flexed her fingers. They did not hurt, but they were the color of the ruined cities in the waste. The nightgown she wore suggested that she had at least changed before collapsing, but everything after her kiss with Finnegan was a blur, irrelevant to her too-tired brain. Finnegan's burns had healed under her fingers, and that had been enough.

Celestine had kept her promise, at least. Finnegan would live.

She dressed quickly, pulling on a blue cotton dress, and then attempted to untangle the knots in her hair. The sun was high in the sky—at least a day must have passed since she collapsed. An entire day. She should have been planning, should have been figuring out what to *do*. Instead, she had slept.

Someone knocked on the door. The handle turned before she had time to answer, and Finnegan stepped into the room.

"Aurora," he said. "I thought I heard someone moving. You slept for a long time." His black hair was still mussed with sleep, but the burns had completely faded, the skin as smooth as it had ever been, except for a single red scar that ran along his jawline.

"You have a scar," she said.

"Don't you think it makes me look dashing?"

She crossed the space between them and pressed her fingertips to his skin. Warmth pulsed from it, like fire pulsing from a dragon. It was not a burn scar. It was like a cut.

She had marked him. The scar followed the line of his jaw, where she had touched him after their kiss.

"Upset about the loss of my perfect face?"

"No," she said. "No, of course not." But she could not take her eyes from the scar.

"No comment about how my face was never perfect?" he said. "No attempt to reassure me that the scar isn't *that* bad? I'm almost disappointed."

She did not reply.

"So," he said. "What did you do?"

She looked away. "Magic," she whispered. "I found a spell."

"Seems strange," he said, "that you were unable to help me for the entire walk back to the city, and then could heal me with one kiss within the walls of the palace."

"I panicked," Aurora said. "The dragon, your injuries . . . I couldn't focus. Once I got back, I found a book to help. I'm sorry it took so long, but it was all I could do."

"A book?" Finnegan said. He rested a hand on her wrist. "Which one?"

"I don't remember." She pulled away. "A book in the library."

"You're going to have to learn to lie, or learn to stop lying. Either would do." He watched her steadily, and the scar seemed to glare in accusation.

"I had to help you," she said. She tugged at her hair. "I didn't know what to do."

"I'm flattered you value my life so much," Finnegan said. "What did you do?"

"I can't tell you. I can't."

"I've heard that Lucas is missing. You both disappeared, they said, but only you came back. Does that have anything to do with it?"

She could not lie to him. But the truth felt illicit, like she was confessing to murder. "Yes," she said. "And no. He won't be coming back."

"Aurora," Finnegan said. "What did you *do*?" He rested his hands on her shoulders, and looked all over her face, as though the answer might be written there. "Did you go back to the mountains? Did you find something?" He glanced down, and then paused. "Aurora, your hand," he said. "What happened to your hand?"

"A dragon," she said. She pulled it away. "Why does it matter?"

"Because it *matters*. How could a dragon—did it burn you? I won't care, Aurora. I won't blame you, even if you burned all of Petrichor to do it. You know how I think."

She did. That was why she could not tell him. She needed to work through her feelings for herself, without Finnegan there to tell her how to feel. To dismiss it like it was nothing.

Burn them all, little dragon.

"I saved you," she said. "That's all there is to say."

"I'll find out eventually," he said. "You know I will."

"Then *eventually*, we'll talk about it."

He laughed. "All right, Aurora," he said. "I'm grateful, whatever you did. Thank you."

On impulse, she darted forward and kissed him. "I'm glad you're okay," she said. Celestine had not broken her word, at least. One kiss, and he was exactly as he had been before. Or almost exactly.

"I'm glad to be okay."

She leaned in to kiss him again.

A scream rattled through the air. Aurora spun to face the window.

Fire raced across the sky.

Dragons.

TWENTY-SEVEN

AURORA AND FINNEGAN RAN OUT OF THE PALACE, through the courtyard and onto the street. Flames seared the paving stones. The dragon had gone, but Aurora could feel its heat, drumming a few streets away.

Another shadow fell over them, and Aurora and Finnegan leapt back. A crowd surged down the street, some people ducking into buildings for protection, others struggling to escape into the open. And among the screams, among the panic, voices boomed: "Repent. Repent!"

There were four of of them. She could sense it, although

she did not know how she knew. Four dragons had crossed the water.

A cannonball rushed past. It slammed into the building behind them, scattering fragments across the street. Giant cross-bows and catapults were firing from the roofs. But no weapon could kill a dragon. Perhaps cannons would deter them, but they could not end this.

Lucas had told her not to interfere with the dragons. He had died trying to stop her. And now they were attacking the city.

"I have to stop them." She stepped forward. Finnegan grabbed her arm, tugging her back.

"They'll kill you."

"No," she said. "They won't. I'm the only one who stands a chance against them."

Finnegan looked around, his face pale. He nodded. "What do you need to do?"

The sky burned red above them. "Take me to the tallest building in the city."

They hurtled down the street, weaving past scorched stones and huddles of people. Even the cobblestones glowed hot beneath their feet.

"Prince Finnegan!" one person yelled. "What should we do?"

"Find water," Finnegan said. "Get to the docks."

"But they crossed the water. They crossed—"

"They flew over it," Finnegan said, barely slowing down.

"They didn't fly *in* it. And water is still the best weapon against fire I ever heard of."

Another shadow flew across their path, another wave of scorching heat. The dragon spat fire, setting a nearby building alight. It landed on the roof, amid the flames. One huge green eye settled on Aurora, and she stumbled to a halt.

"Aurora—"

A cannonball crashed into the building, a few feet below the dragon's claws. The dragon screeched and took off, neck snapping from side to side, looking for the source of the onslaught.

"The tallest building," Aurora said. "Now."

They swerved onto another road, narrower than the first. A few people were huddled against the wall, as though the shadows would protect them. One woman was clutching her knee and sobbing. Her whole lower leg was black.

"Can you—" Finnegan began, but Aurora shook her head. Whatever magic Celestine had given her, she was sure it was gone. It could only save one.

One building towered ahead. It was half-built, the outside held up with metal supports and a staircase that wove around and around, up and up. A sign hung over the entrance, declaring it dangerous. Aurora skidded to the stairs and tore the sign aside.

The stairs shook as she climbed. She gripped the barrier to hold herself steady, the clank of her feet mixing with the screams of the dragons, the screams of the people, the smoke that filled the air. Finnegan ran one step behind her.

A dragon whipped past, its tail smashing into the side of the building. The tower swayed, and Aurora crashed to her knees, the metal digging into her skin. Finnegan slammed forward as well, his hands landing on her back. Then he grabbed her by the upper arm, half using her to regain his feet, half pulling her up as well.

The dragon screeched. Water crashed into its side, making its scales hiss. Several rooftops away, a line of soldiers reloaded their catapults with barrels. The dragon lunged for the soldiers, teeth bared, but a barrel struck it in the chest with a sickening crunch, and the explosion of water sent the dragon reeling backward, its jaw slamming into its tail. Aurora flinched.

The dragon struggled to regain its balance, but another barrel sent it sprawling into a nearby building. It bounced off the roof and gave its wings a determined furl, but it was smaller than other dragons Aurora had seen, and it couldn't right itself. Its struggling sent it more off-balance, and it flew sideways, past more roofs, its skin fizzing, before it was struck again, and it plummeted like a stone.

The moment it hit the river, a chill ran through Aurora, like she had been plunged in ice. She gasped, clutching the railing to keep herself upright. Water flew up and surged down the streets. Even high in the air, it splashed Aurora's skin.

"One down," Finnegan said.

"That one was small," Aurora said. "It won't be enough." And if throwing water at dragons was enough to kill them,

Vanhelm would have done it long ago.

The top of the building was an uneven expanse of metal, wood, and stone, some parts solid, others covered by planks that wobbled underfoot. Aurora grabbed the railing and looked out, the wind blowing her hair over her eyes. Far below, to the west, the river sizzled, waves crashing outward, as the dragon continued to struggle and cry. A second beast was perched on top of a building farther inland, its head hanging below its feet, snarling and burning the street. The third and fourth were circling, swerving in the sky as though anticipating an attack.

As Aurora stared at them, the world stilled. The screams faded away, until all she knew was the heat, the creatures that burned before her. She could *feel* them, deep in her chest where the magic burned, as though their anger was part of her, and she was part of them.

She could feel all of it. The rage, the hunger, the *desire* that drove the creatures forward, a desire for something indistinct, unnamed, unattainable. A desire that just *was*. A pounding *beside* her heart, tiny and irregular and strong, and she could almost taste the sliver of muscle on her lips again. Power and fury and fire.

The dragons paused. Their heads snapped in her direction.

"Stop," she said, her voice quiet and steady. "Stop. Go home."

The dragons did not move. Did not attack, did not retreat. And Aurora felt curiosity grow inside her, tugging at her ribs. Curiosity at this girl who was a dragon and yet was not, a girl with the same fire, the same blood, with the heart they had lost, or something like it. They listened to her, but Aurora knew her control was tentative, incomplete. They listened because they *wanted* to listen.

One of them snapped its jaws, and its eyes were black like scorched flesh. Its tongue flicked around its teeth. "No!" Aurora screamed. Fire crackled around her feet. "No. Go home."

She did not move, did not flinch. She stared at them, Finnegan close to her shoulder, the air burning around her.

"Go," she shouted. "Or I'll tear out your heart too."

The creatures still watched her. Then the one on the building took off, ripping part of the roof with it. It circled once, twice, dodging the barrels and stones with ease.

Something caught Aurora's eye. A flash of blond hair, familiar and terrible. She whipped her head around, knowing in her gut that she would see Celestine, that the witch would smile, and curtsy, and mock her. But when she turned, there was no one there, nothing except a small scorch mark on the stone, forming the now-familiar shape of a dragon.

A dragon swooped and paused above them, rising and falling several feet with each beat of its wings. Aurora stared at it. It stared back. Then, with a final snap of its jaws, it spun and took off east over the water. The others followed, screams tearing through the air.

Aurora watched them leave, until they were nothing more than specks against the morning sky.

"You did it," Finnegan said.

She collapsed to her knees, all the strength rushing away. Her hands shook. "No," she said. "It wasn't just me. There was something . . ."

Celestine, she thought. She had been here. She had interfered, unleashed the dragons and then reined them in once her point had been made. The fire, this attack . . . it had meant nothing. A laughing attempt to show them what she was capable of, now that Aurora had helped her. Now the dragon blood pumped through Celestine's veins as well.

She had lied about her intentions. She had lied about everything.

"Aurora," Finnegan said. "What did you do? How did you help me?"

"I made a deal," she said. She forced herself to keep looking at him, to face what she had done. "I had to."

"What sort of deal?"

"With Celestine. She told me that she'd give me the magic to save you, if I returned to the waste and fetched her a dragon's heart."

"And you did it." It wasn't a question.

"I got her the heart. And it killed the dragon, the dragon died, like . . . like it couldn't contain its own fire any more, like it burned from the inside out. And when Celestine took the heart, she—she ate it. Like she was absorbing its magic." *And she told me things,* Aurora thought. *She told me what I was meant to be.* "And then she gave me the magic to save you. With a kiss, because she's cruel, and—and mad. She's insane, Finnegan, absolutely insane, and I don't know what she plans to do, but I helped her anyway, and now—"

He cut her off with a kiss. Lips burning into hers, frantic, pulling her so close that she could barely breathe. She clung to him, her fingers digging into his shoulders, and for a moment it was like they were out in the waste again, locked away from the rest of the world, the rest of her worries. Pressure grew in her chest, and the dragon pendant burned against her throat, the need so strong that she thought it would consume her.

"If she comes to you again," he said, his face a breath away from hers, "you should burn her into nothing."

"She's stronger than me," Aurora said. "She'll always be stronger than me."

"Not always," Finnegan said. "Not forever."

"She has the dragons."

"Weren't you paying attention?" he asked. "So do you."

TWENTY-EIGHT

A SMALL CROWD GATHERED ON THE BANK WHERE THE dragon had crashed. Soldiers had pulled it out of the river with chains, and it now lay sprawled across the ground, its wings beating with all the energy of a dying fly.

"Stay back," one of the soldiers said, as they approached. "It's still dangerous."

Aurora ignored him. She moved closer, her hand reaching out to touch the tip of the dragon's wing. It was cold and clammy.

"It's in pain," she said.

"Good," the soldier said. "But it'll recover if it dries off."

Finnegan moved closer, carefully avoiding the dragon's

head. "What do you plan to do with it?" he asked.

"We haven't yet reached a decision on that, Your Highness," the soldier said. "We thought to chain it underwater, but we'll need your mother's approval, and it could take time to—"

"No." Aurora released the dragon's wing and turned to face him. "You can't do that." She could feel the dragon's pain, like the memory of a wound that had never quite healed. They couldn't chain it under the river, to suffer and smolder until the dragons faded from the world again. A dragon without fire, without anything. There had to be another way.

"Who are you to tell me what to do?" the soldier said.

"I am the one who stopped them," she said, in a low, clear voice. It barely felt like a lie. "So you will listen to me."

"You stopped them, did you?" Orla strode toward them. Her face was lined with exhaustion, but her expression was sharp, alert. "We must speak alone." Orla turned to the soldier. "Keep the crowds away from it," she said, "and keep water on hand. I'll return to tell you my decision."

"No disrespect, Your Majesty," another soldier said, "but we should kill it now. Before it has a chance to recover."

She shook her head as she turned away, already dismissing the conversation. "You cannot kill a dragon."

"You can try."

"No," she said. "You cannot. Do your job, and listen to me." She flicked her hand in Aurora and Finnegan's direction, silently commanding them to follow her. Then she strode away.

Aurora ran her hand along the edge of the dragon's wing, feeling the delicate webbing, the power beneath it. Already, the scales were beginning to warm.

Stay still, she thought, brushing the words into the dragon's skin. *I'll come back.*

"You took a dragon's heart."

Orla leaned on her desk. Her long black braid had fallen over her shoulder, and her face was covered with soot. The weight of the attack, and of Aurora's explanation, seemed to press her farther toward the ground, hunching her entire body. She spoke as though she could not believe what Aurora had told her.

"Yes."

"With magic?"

"Yes."

"And now fifty people are dead," Orla said. "Fifty, *so far.* I'm sure there'll be many more, once we finish searching damaged buildings, once more people succumb to their injuries." She glanced at Finnegan, standing a few paces behind Aurora. Erin sat straight-backed in the corner, her red hair flowing to her elbows. "I hope my son uses his life well. It was bought at quite a cost."

Aurora closed her eyes. Fifty people, dead because of her. Dead, because she could not bear for Finnegan to die. This was the cost of her selfishness.

"You must stop this from happening again." Orla looked at

Aurora's charred hand. "You claim that taking the heart killed the dragon, and that *eating* it gives a person the power to control them. That, then, is our best hope. You will take another heart, and we will use the dragons to defend our city against further attacks."

"No," Aurora said. She couldn't put more of that power into the world. Celestine already had one dragon heart. What would happen if she got more? What would happen if other people took that magic too? "I won't do it again."

Orla's eyebrows flew upward. She looked at Aurora for a long moment, seemingly genuinely lost for words. "You won't? You would save countless lives."

"Or destroy them. We can't predict what would happen if I took more hearts. It could increase Celestine's power."

"That witch has already half destroyed my city. What does it matter if she gains *more* power, if she already has far more than we do, and this could give us the chance to fight her?"

"If you took the hearts of all the dragons," Erin said slowly, "the witch wouldn't have anything to control."

"You want me to wipe them out?"

"No," Orla said firmly. "But with a heart or five, with you here, we could have them under control. They could be an asset."

"And you want me to give that power to you?"

She certainly owed it to them. She had been the one to let the dragons across the water, the one who inspired a direct attack on the city. Orla had helped Aurora, protected her, and this destruction was her reward.

But dragons were not a defensive force. What would Orla do, with all this fire at her command? Every other kingdom would be terrified of her. They would bow to any of her demands. And although Orla seemed fair and just, the needs of her kingdom would come before anything else. They would certainly come before the needs of Alyssinia.

And Aurora remembered their conversation, when Orla had spoken of Vanhelm's right to Alyssinia. She did not want revenge, she had said. But she said had nothing about her plans for the throne.

Aurora wanted to help her. Wanted to trust her. But as a princess, as a witch, as someone with responsibilities that she had avoided for too long . . . no. She could not take that risk.

"I'm sorry," she said. "I can't."

"You can't?" Orla stared at her in disbelief. "You can't stop more dragons attacking my city? They're gone for now, but they will come back. We need to be ready for them."

"You will be," Aurora said. "I'll help you. But I can't give you the dragons."

Orla's lips were pressed into a thin line. "You and Finnegan created this mess," she said. "You acted like fools, both of you. It's your responsibility to fix it."

"And it's my responsibility to Alyssinia to protect them."

Finnegan stepped forward. "She did the best she could, mother," he said.

"Do not speak back to me," Orla snapped. "You'd better hope that she agrees to this. If you were true king material, you would not have created this mess. Vanhelm cannot have a prince who endangers the city for his own ridiculous whims."

"I was working to protect the city," Finnegan said. "The dragons have been coming closer for years. We needed to find a way to defend ourselves from them."

"And instead, we got *attacked*."

"And we fought them off."

"That is not good enough," Orla said. "And if you do not fix this, I don't see how I could allow you to be king."

"Are you threatening to disinherit me?"

"I am saying that you had better do what is *right*," Orla said. "As your sister would do."

"That's unfair," Erin said. Her voice was soft and clear. "I don't know what I would do."

"You would not have created this mess in the first place."

Aurora had heard enough. "I will not do it," she said. "And it has nothing to do with Finnegan, and it has nothing to do with Erin. It's just *me*. And you will not convince me to change my mind."

Orla stared at her, disgust all over her face. "Then go."

Aurora nodded, conceding to Orla's anger, and walked out of her room.

She had remained in Vanhelm too long. She had as strong a control over her magic as she ever would, had learned as much as she could from this kingdom. And she had definitely outstayed her welcome.

If she left, Celestine would surely follow her, as she had followed her here. It would be safest for everyone if she left.

Aurora hurried to her rooms. Her hair smelled of smoke, her feet throbbed, and the world had become hazy after days without enough sleep, but she pulled her bag toward her and started piling her possessions into it.

Footsteps echoed in the corridor outside. She did not need to look to know it was Finnegan.

"Have you come here to convince me to change my mind?"

The footsteps paused.

"No," Finnegan said. "I know you won't."

"How do you know?"

"You're a terrible liar, remember? I can read your face like a book." Silence. Then: "I have news." His voice was too light, too casual. Bad news, then.

"About the dragons?"

"About Alyssinia."

She turned to look at him. He stood in the doorway, a roll of parchment clutched in his hand. "What is it?"

He stepped inside and closed the door. "A letter came for me while I was injured," he said. "A guard just gave it to me. It was from Nettle."

"What does it say?"

"You're not going to like it."

"Then tell me faster."

Finnegan unrolled the letter, but he spoke without really looking at it. "John's arrested Rodric," he said. "Everyone in the kingdom will know by now, but Nettle says she heard it early, from a reliable source. She says he's being charged with treason."

Treason. Aurora had been afraid this would happen, but that had been before. Before Finnegan's burn, before Celestine, before the dragons. In all the more immediate danger, she had almost forgotten Rodric. But he had been caught.

And John burned people for treason. He burned people for less.

The thought was too huge, too terrifying after everything else, so she grasped for another detail, something else to focus on. "A reliable source?" she said. "What does that mean?"

"Someone in the castle, I assume. Did you hear what I said? Rodric is being charged with treason."

She had heard. But what was there to say? "I suppose the rumors were true."

"Perhaps," Finnegan said. "He was connected to you, and the king's not exactly reasonable. John must have decided his son was too much of a threat."

Aurora reached for the parchment, as though she could make any sense of Nettle's code, as though she could drag some other meaning from the page. Finnegan did not give it to her. "That's not all," he said.

"What else could there possibly be?"

"He claims that he has arrested you as well. You will be tried together, but the verdict seems set."

Aurora closed her eyes, but it did little to calm the buzzing in her head. "He has someone he's pretending is me?"

"Nettle certainly thinks so."

It was possible the king was bluffing. But why would he risk that, when he could use any blond girl off the street? She was a story, after all. Any girl could play her part. "When?" she said. "When's the trial?"

"Seven days from now."

A long wait, from capturing them to putting them on show. Was he doing it on purpose, trying to tempt her back to save Rodric and the innocent girl he had taken in her place? Or was he dragging it out, to get a confession from Rodric, to get the greatest advantage from the promised burning of the princess?

"I have to go back," she said. "Now."

"You're going to fight him?"

"Yes," she said. "I have to."

"For Rodric?"

"Of course for Rodric. He's a good person. He's my friend." She couldn't make a deal with Celestine to save Finnegan, and not even *try* to help Rodric, not after his kindness to her, not when she ran and left him to help the people in Alyssinia alone. "He needs to live through this, so he can be king, so things can be *better*." She had the answers she'd wanted; she had control over her magic; she had a piece of dragon heart beating beside her own. She was as ready as she would ever be.

"What's your plan?" Finnegan said. "My mother won't help you, not after that."

"I have something that she wants," Aurora said. "She'll listen to me." Aurora had never been good at negotiation, but she could not back down now. And their kingdoms had a long history of unbalanced bargains and broken promises.

She might not be fit to be queen, but she had the power to help. She had to use it, whatever that would mean.

"As for the king . . . I can fight him," she said, the certainty building inside her. Finally, she had conviction. Finally, she knew what to do. "I have you. I have magic. And I have a dragon."

TWENTY-NINE

"THESE ARE MY TERMS." AURORA STARED AT ORLA, determined to look the part of a queen, negotiating with an equal. "I will take the captured dragon to Alyssinia and overthrow the king, to what I believe will be our mutual benefit."

Orla raised her eyebrows. "Finally seizing the throne for yourself?"

"I'm not seizing anything," Aurora said. "John is killing my people, including his own son for his association with me. Maybe Rodric will be king, maybe someone else, maybe I will rule. Regardless, the path seems simple to me."

"And you expect me to let you take a dragon there? How

will I know you won't turn around and attack my kingdom?"

"You can send soldiers with me as well," she said. "As many as you like. Help me to defeat John. And once that is done, I will help you deal with the dragons. Whatever you need."

Orla domed her fingers under her chin. Her expression was impossible to read. "And how can I trust you?"

"You'll have to," Aurora said. "I'm the only one who can help you."

"If you go," Erin said, "how will we stop the dragons if they attack again? We'll be defenseless."

"I don't think you will be," Aurora said. "The dragons are after me. Celestine was sending a message to *me*. She won't attack when I'm not here."

"You can't know that."

"No," she said. "I can't know it. But I believe it."

Orla walked around her desk, never taking her eyes from Aurora. "I gave you refuge," she said. "Resources. I believe you already owe me."

"I appreciate all you've done for me," Aurora said. "I do. And I'm sorry for the problems I've caused. But I *must* think about Alyssinia first. If you want an alliance, you must give me this."

"And what inspired this sudden change of heart?" Orla said. "An hour ago, you said you would never help me."

"I spent the last several days hiking through the waste and fighting dragons. I needed time to think it through."

"Time to scheme, you mean." But Orla looked contemplative.

"All right," she said. "You can take the dragon, and I will lend you a few soldiers as well. But I want a dragon's heart in return. Do we have a deal?"

"Yes," Aurora said. "After I've dealt with John, after you help me, I'll give you that dragon's heart." The lie almost stuck in her throat, but she shoved it forward, refusing to flinch. Finnegan always said she was a terrible liar, but she had to be believable now. She had to make Orla think she would cooperate. There was no backing down from this.

She could sense Finnegan watching her, and she knew, she *knew*, that he had seen the truth of her. She would not kill another dragon. She would not give that power away.

Orla stuck out a hand, and Aurora shook it, her grip firm. "A deal," Orla said.

"A deal."

"You lied to my mother," Finnegan said in an undertone, as they walked back to the docks. "Impressive."

"Do you think she knew?"

"If she'd known, she wouldn't have made the deal." He looked out across the river. "So, how are we going to get this dragon across the ocean?"

She stopped. "You're really going to come with me?"

"My mother was wrong. The best way to protect Vanhelm is to get you out of here. And you're not losing me now, Rora. I'm going to see how this ends."

"And the dragon?" she said. "That doesn't influence your decision at all?"

"The last attempt to use them to help Vanhelm didn't go that well. I'm not about to try and seize one for myself." He grabbed her hand, pulling her close. "I'm not going to betray you, Aurora. Not now."

She tilted her head to look at him. "I believe you," she said. And she did. She trusted him, whatever happened next.

The dragon still lay by the docks. The soldiers had chained it to the ground, but the fire in it was awakening again. Every few minutes, it thrashed its tail or beat its wings, sending the men around it grasping for water. Aurora ran up as it whipped its tail again, smashing against the stone.

"Unchain him," she said, in her most commanding voice. "Queen Orla has ordered that he come with me."

The soldiers looked to Finnegan, who held out a paper with the royal seal. "It's all here," he said. "We'll take a small boat. Soldiers will follow in the other. And . . . what do you think, Aurora? We'll chain the dragon to ours so it can fly behind?"

"No," Aurora said. She rested a hand on the ridge above the dragon's nose. Its eyes followed her movements with a lazy flicker. She could still feel the connection there, the extra beat in her chest, the desire and anger muted now to something more like longing. *You will stay with me,* she thought, as she ran her fingers along the dragon's nose. *We are meant to be together, you and I.*

And the second heartbeat whispered *yes.*

"No chains," she said. "He'll follow."

"Miss, I don't think—"

"I am not a miss," Aurora said. "I am Princess Aurora, heir to the throne of Alyssinia, and your queen has commanded you to help me. Do you want to be the one who defies her? I hear she does not suffer fools gladly."

The man stared at her for a long moment, and then he bowed. "As you wish, my lady."

"Impressive," Finnegan whispered in her ear. The hum of the word made her shiver.

"What can I say?" she murmured. "I was born to be a queen."

Aurora stood by the side of the boat until Vanhelm faded from sight. The dragon circled overhead. Every now and again, it screamed or thrashed its wings, but Aurora simply glanced upward, and it quieted again. The heat of it, the smolder, was less over the water, like it had left part of itself on the shore. But the heat inside Aurora, the burning in her heart . . . that was fiercer than ever, a heartbeat that grew stronger every mile they sailed from the shore, as though she were driving the dragon onward, as though her own heart were keeping it alive.

Night fell, and still the dragon circled, lighting up the sky. Not a single breath of fire slipped past its teeth. It just flew, around and around and around, as though tethered to her somehow, as though waiting for the moment when it could land again.

Finnegan waited in her cabin below. "I don't know if I can do it," she said, as she paused in the doorway. It seemed safer, admitting the truth in the dark.

Finnegan was leaning back on the bed. "You can do anything you want to, dragon girl. I knew that from the start."

"I don't know if I want to," she said. "If I *kill* him . . . I'll be as bad as he is. Won't I?"

"Sometimes you have to do terrible things," Finnegan said. "Sometimes it's the only thing to do."

"That shouldn't be true."

"It shouldn't, but it is."

"Celestine . . ." She trailed off, searching for the words. "She said that I was only good for destruction. Maybe she's right. Maybe this is exactly what she wants."

"Maybe," Finnegan said. "Is that going to stop you?"

She thought of Rodric, of flames, of the hunger in Celestine's eyes when she looked at her. Of the whisper of dragons, and the power that was hers and hers alone. "No," she said. "It won't."

The journey to Petrichor seemed endless. They marched through the day and the night, weaving through forests and around villages in order to reach the capital before Rodric's trial. Crowds gathered wherever they went, people come to stare at the soldiers and the dragon, mouths open in astonishment, eyes wide with fear. No one attempted to speak to them or question their presence. Did they know who she was, Aurora wondered, or did they see the dragon and assume she was from Vanhelm, a long-feared enemy invading them at last? She had felt so trapped before, hating their desperation for her to save them, but now was almost worse. Now she was a creature from their nightmares, come to tear them apart.

Aurora kept the dragon's fire tight within her chest, but her control hardly mattered. As they walked, they passed burned-out fields, whole villages that had been torn to pieces or reduced to ash. Endless groups of travelers limped along the road, heading to and from the capital. Nowhere, it seemed, had been safe while Aurora was gone.

Aurora swallowed her guilt. A few more fires, one more fight, and things would start anew.

And perhaps it would not come to that. Fear of dragons was a powerful thing. Who would face one, when surrender was an option?

They did not meet any Alyssinian soldiers on the road. Either King John had chosen not to fight, or he had pulled his men back to guard the capital.

One day's journey outside Petrichor, their group paused at the edge of the forest for food and rest. The trees loomed over them, whispering with the wind, and Aurora shifted closer to the fire, trying to focus on Finnegan's conversation, trying not to think about what the following evening might bring. The men had caught deer for dinner, and it tasted rich after days of increasingly stale food, but her stomach would not settle, and she could hardly eat a bite.

The dragon flew above them, swooping in and out of sight. It had grown stronger with every step away from the water, so that Aurora could feel the heat of its skin again, the anger and desire rushing through it. At first, it had taken every molecule of willpower inside her to keep it in check, but now it seemed easier, like their thoughts were falling in sync.

A guard cleared his throat. "You have a visitor, Your Highnesses," he said.

Finnegan stood. His hand went to the hilt of his sword. "The kind we want to see?"

"She claims so." The guard shouted over his shoulder. "Bring her here!" Two more men strode forward, a woman between them. Nettle. Her arms were hooked around theirs, but she stood with all the dignity of a queen, a braid falling over her right shoulder.

"Please tell them to release me, Finnegan."

Finnegan waved his hand, and the guards stepped back. Aurora hurried toward Nettle, but uncertainty seized her at the last moment, and she paused a few inches away. Nettle smiled and ran her fingers through Aurora's hair. "You are okay?" Nettle said.

"As okay as I can be. It is good to see you."

"You too." She slipped onto the ground by the fire. Aurora settled beside her. "I have missed you."

"For Nettle, that's practically a declaration of undying love," Finnegan said. He did not sit. "Why are you here? Not that it isn't good to see your beautiful face, but we arranged to meet outside Petrichor."

"I have information," she said. "And you were not difficult to find." She glanced at the sky as she spoke.

Aurora grabbed her arm. "Is it about Rodric? Is he all right?"

"Yes and no," Nettle said. "He and the girl are locked in the dungeons of the castle, awaiting their trial. If it can be called a trial. They will be found guilty of treason either way."

"You're sure?" Aurora said.

"Yes, Princess. The pyre is already being built. The king wants to show how *dedicated* he is to protecting the throne. He will make a show about how all traitors must be treated equally. He's saying that your death will end all the kingdom's problems, that it will end the curse on Alyssinia, whether magic comes back or not."

"And everyone believes it?"

"Not everyone. But enough people do. And enough others *want* to. Desperate people will believe many unbelievable things."

"So they'll accept that this other girl is me as well?"

Nettle nodded.

Aurora hugged her knees to her chest and thought of the imposter princess. A girl, imprisoned, alone, for no crime at all. "Who is she?"

"Her name is Eliza," Nettle said. "She looks similar to you. Small and blond and beautiful. A little like the slightest breeze would destroy her, but haughtier than you too. I believe she is the daughter of some out-of-favor noble, one who never came to court. People will not recognize her as herself, and her parents have been killed for some treason or another."

"Before or after he decided she could pretend to be me?"

"After you ran," Nettle said. "But before she was arrested. No one will protect her, and no one wants to believe that she is not who the king claims."

"What's your source on this?" Finnegan asked. "Rumors?"

"I do not rely on rumors," Nettle said. "I was told this by the queen."

"The *queen*?" Aurora's grip on Nettle's arm tightened. "You've been speaking to Iris?"

"I have," Nettle said. "She is unhappy that her husband has arrested her son. Unhappy enough to speak to me and to help your cause, as long as it also helps Rodric."

"How will she help us?" Finnegan asked.

"Not directly. Information is all she will offer. But that is useful, at least."

"What has she told you?"

Nettle picked up a stick from the ground and began to draw in the dust. A large circle for the city walls, a smaller one for the castle, with roads and squares in between. "The city walls are manned and the gates locked," she said, "so you will not get past them without alerting the king. Nor will you be able to reach Rodric and Eliza before the trial. They are under heavy guard here." She poked part of her castle with the stick. "You might be able to get to them as they're escorted out of the castle, but unless you want to slaughter an army of guards, the best chance will be during the trial itself. Everyone in the city will be forced to attend, in the courtyard outside the castle. The dragon will help as a distraction there, I would think."

"Good," Aurora said. "I want it to be memorable." She looked over the map in the dust. "But what if we get there before the trial? Or what if he comes to fight us here?"

"Neither will be a problem. The king wants a spectacle as much as you do. The imposter princess, tearing through the kingdom, coming to save his traitor son. He will want everyone to see you fail."

"He'd abandon strategy for that?"

"That *is* his strategy. He's a showman, Aurora. You know this. He cares about getting the message right. He wants people to see your defeat. And he is arrogant enough not to doubt that it *will* be a defeat."

"And what about the people?" Aurora said. "Will they support me, do you think?"

"There has been unrest since Rodric's condemnation, but everyone is afraid to speak, and the rebels are mostly gone. But you should be able to rally some support. And I have seen Tristan in the city. He will help you all he can."

"*Tristan?*" Tristan could not help her. "He's in Vanhelm. I saw him."

"He decided to return. It seems he thinks there is hope after all."

She was glad to hear it. She had not always approved of his methods, but Tristan had not seemed like *Tristan* without that fierce belief inside him. "But why would he help me?" she said.

"You both want to be rid of the king, Princess. And since you have an army and a dragon, you may stand a better chance than he does."

The firelight danced across the side of Nettle's face, elongating her features. Aurora shivered. Had she finally become brutal enough for Tristan to approve of her? Or were they simply both desperate for any kind of plan now?

Nettle stood. "I should return to Petrichor," she said. "I'll watch things until you arrive tomorrow."

Aurora nodded and bid her good night, but although she settled under her blankets, she could not sleep. Anticipation buzzed through her, visions of tomorrow crowding her thoughts. She saw Rodric's death, Finnegan cut through with a sword, the city burning.

The dragon soaring behind her, their magic as one.

She would not fail now. Tomorrow, she would show them. They would see everything that she could be.

THIRTY

NETTLE WAS WAITING FOR THEM ON THE ROAD TO Petrichor as the sun set the next day.

"The king has moved the trial," she said, in lieu of a greeting. "To tonight. His guards were rounding up the people of the city when I slipped away."

So this was it. She would fight the king, and things would fall as they would. "How much time do we have?" she asked.

"I am not sure," Nettle said. "An hour or two at most. The king may choose to delay until you arrive at the gates. Or he may speed up to spite you, once he sees you approach. He is difficult to predict."

"Then let's hurry," Aurora said. "Before he gets the chance."

Trees stretched above their heads, and the air was heavy. They walked in silence, surrounded by Finnegan's men.

The walls of the city emerged gradually ahead of them. The road was completely straight, cutting through the forest with brutal precision, so they could see the entrance to the city for almost a mile before they reached it. Every few steps brought more into focus. The metal portcullis blocking the way. Soldiers lining the wall. Crossbows aimed at the road.

When they were within shouting distance, a guard raised an arm. "Halt!" he said.

Aurora stopped. She stared at the soldiers. "Let us pass," she shouted. "We are here to stop the king. We have no quarrel with you."

Her dragon screamed in accord. It circled above her, snapping its jaws in the direction of the men on the wall. It took all of Aurora's willpower to keep it under control, to cool the fire in its throat and keep it close. "Surrender," one of the guards shouted. He had a crossbow aimed directly at her heart.

"Let us pass," she said again, "or I'll be forced to attack."

An arrow shot through the air. Aurora engulfed it in flames. She looked at the soldier who had attacked her, taking in the details of his face.

She could not make threats she did not intend to keep.

"Burn the way through," she whispered. It was enough. With a screech, the dragon dove and let out a jet of flame. The gate caught fire. The metal melted almost instantly, and even the stone warped under the heat. The guards scrambled aside, and Aurora focused her magic on their weapons, turning them to flames in their hands.

The guards screamed, throwing their crossbows away. And Aurora felt a rush of triumph. The fire was hers to command.

But the closest entrance to the city was now blocked by the dragon flames. "We can't wait for this," she said. "I can't wait for the stone to cool enough to pass. I'm going in another way."

"I'll go with you," Finnegan said. "And Nettle."

"All right," Aurora said. "But the soldiers should stay here." They would make a good distraction, at least. She looked at the dragon. It continued to circle, snapping its wings. Leaving it would be a risk. How far away could she get before the dragon broke free, before it burned the whole forest into dust? But it was a powerful distraction, and if it flew above her, she would lose any element of surprise.

Her performance here would be key. She was not a usurper. She was not a spy, an assassin crawling through the dust. She was the princess, and they would know when she returned.

"I've changed my mind," she said. "You and Nettle stay here, with the soldiers. I can't have you with me."

"Aurora—"

"You don't have magic, and you can't fight all those guards. All your presence will do is make me look like an agent of Vanhelm. I'm going to face the king alone. With my magic, and with the dragon. No one else."

"Aurora—"

"Stay safe, Finnegan," she said. "I'll see you when it's over." And before he could react, before he could argue or say good-bye, she turned and ran into the trees. She followed the curve of the city walls, until she reached brambles and trees that seemed familiar. The point where she had escaped, all those weeks ago.

She did not hesitate. She crawled into the city.

Not a single living thing stirred. There was no panic, no fear, nothing but empty streets, lost in the shadow of the wall.

She looked east toward the gates. Smoke curled upward, casually, almost lovingly. The flames sent orange light skitter-ing across the darkening sky. The dragon gripped the roof of the gate tower, its tail wrapped around the spikes and stone. She would call it to her soon.

Still, there were no screams in the city below.

Aurora ran.

Ahead, she could see her tower, see the castle, stern and forbidden and untouched by the chaos. The dragon's screams echoed in her ears, but she could hear more shouting now too, the booming voice of the king, like the voices of the preachers shouting for Vanhelm to repent.

"Do not be afraid of the cowards' fire!"

Aurora used a stack of crates to climb onto a low-hanging roof, and crawled closer. A pyre had been built at the top of the steps, the wood piled higher than the great doors of the castle.

King John stood before it, wearing a golden crown. He stabbed the air with a long, jeweled sword as he spoke. The steel glinted.

The castle square was crammed with people. Guards stood all around them, forming a solid wall of flesh and steel. Few people were paying attention to the king. They looked in the direction of the fire, the dragon's screams, and some tried to scramble away, but nobody moved from the square. Nobody would let them.

"Do not fear them!" the king shouted again. "These traitors, these *monsters* have infiltrated the castle, have brought my *own son* under their thrall. Now they are here to save him from our justice, but they will not succeed. We do not abide traitors, and we do not abide threats. Alyssinia is strong."

Iris stood a few paces away from her husband. Her black hair was pinned back, her dress and face plain. Rodric was on the other side of the pyre, held by more soldiers. His hair had grown longer since she had last seen him and was matted around his eyes. He had a bruise on his jaw, and his clothes were dirty and torn, but he stood straight-backed, no trace of fear on his face. A blond girl stood beside him, her hair silver-white and as fine as gossamer. She too looked filthy and worn, but she stood unmoving, glaring at the crowd. Every inch of her screamed defiance.

"Two weeks ago, my son was caught dealing with rebels and traitors in our city. Plotting our downfall on the false princess's behalf." Aurora tightened her grip on the edge of the roof. "My son instigated the riots that left parts of the city in ruins. He spread the rebellion that left so many of our loved ones dead. I had hoped, with a father's blindness, that I was mistaken, but now he has brought our enemies across the water to burn us, to save himself. It is the ultimate betrayal. They want to make us burn, but we will burn them first! Starting with the so-called princess!"

The guards dragged the blond girl forward. She struggled every step of the way, her heels dug into the stone, her arms locked against them. She looked similar to Aurora, but not similar enough. Few people could genuinely believe they were the same person. Not if they had paid her the slightest attention before.

But the crowd was still distracted by the dragon's screams.

"This witch has infiltrated our city," the king said. "She has mocked us, and mocked our hopes. We will show her what we do to people who betray us! She will burn, and a new era in Alyssinia will begin!"

A few people in the crowd screamed in approval, but it was not the stirring response that the king must have hoped for. Too many people were still staring in the direction of the dragon, too scared to get into the fever of the moment.

The guards yanked the false princess toward the pyre.

Aurora stood. She could feel the heat of the dragon in the air, the flames caressing the walls. She reached out, tugging on the thread inside her, the second heartbeat. *Come,* she thought. And the dragon obeyed.

"Stop!" she shouted.

Heads in the crowd turned. Crossbows clicked and pointed at her chest. King John held out a hand, and the soldiers dragging the girl paused. John smiled. "Oh, we have another pretender," he said. "How many false princesses is Vanhelm going to send us?"

"None," she said. "How stupid do you think people are, to hope they'll have forgotten my face?" She stepped forward. The crossbows jerked, but none of them fired. "You wanted a princess? Well now you have one. The throne is mine. It was mine for generations before you were even born. So I suggest you stop. Now."

John laughed. "And if I don't?"

Aurora clenched her fists, and the roof exploded behind her, tiles and debris flying into the air. The crowd screamed.

The dragon roared as it plunged from the sky, its wings casting her into shadow. The crowd surged again, people falling over their own feet, over children, to escape. They crashed into the wall of guards, but some of the guards were running too, breaking line to flee down the side streets. Others shoved back, swords out. Panic rippled through the square, bodies heaving back and forth. And scattered through the group, onlookers stood still, staring up at the dragon with wide eyes, as though unable to look away.

Aurora kept her eyes fixed on the king.

"You think you can defeat us with this?" he said. "You think you can take the throne by force?"

"Why not? You did."

Someone scrambled up the roof to Aurora's left. She turned, fire building inside her, ready to fight, expecting to see a weapon pointed at her heart.

It was Tristan. His eyes met hers for a moment, and then he turned to face the crowd. "The king has been lying to us," Tristan shouted. "*This* is Princess Aurora. Anyone who looks at her for more than a second must know that. And if the king's lied about this, what else has he been hiding? If he's willing to kill an innocent girl and his *own son*, what will he be willing to do to us?"

People weren't listening. They were still struggling away from the dragon, pushing against the guards. A crossbow fired. The bolt flew into the crowd, and the screaming grew angry, otherworldly, as the crowd swarmed toward the guard. The man raised his sword, ready to cut his way through.

Tristan leapt from the roof and vanished into the crowd. In the moment of distraction, someone had stabbed the guard who had attacked. He gaped at the dagger in his chest as though uncertain what it was doing there, and then fell to his knees. The soldiers beside him also drew their swords, some bearing down on the crowds, some challenging one another, some pointing toward the king.

"Stop!" Aurora screamed. "We won't hurt you. We won't

hurt any of you, as long as the king stands down."

The dragon snapped its jaws, the scent of blood, of chaos, pounding through its veins. And Aurora could feel it too, the burning.

She had to end it.

She leapt from the roof as well, and the dragon dove with her. Her knees landed with an ungainly jolt, and she started to run. The crowd made a path for her, whether from fear, or support, or the burn of her magic, Aurora did not know. But she ran across the square, her feet moving so fast she felt as though she were flying, past the guards, up the stairs, onto the platform where it had all begun, where a marriage arch had become a pyre.

"You little witch," the king said. He raised his sword and swung at her. Aurora dodged away, the air crackling around her. He swung again, shouting for his guards, but they were all caught in the growing riot. Aurora willed John's blade to burn. It glowed white, and John dropped it with a shout. When she snatched it up, it was cool under her fingers. She pointed it at the king's chest.

He laughed. "You won't kill me," he said. "You don't have the nerve."

"You don't know what I'm capable of."

He reached for the sword. She drove him back, blade swinging, magic burning. He tripped, and his back slammed against the stone, scant feet from the pyre.

Her sword point rested under his chin. And Aurora felt that whisper of a second heartbeat again, urging her on.

She looked at the rioting crowd. "Stop," she said again, and this time the dragon screamed with her, fire bursting through the sky. "Stop!" The air pulsed as she shouted the word, and the square froze, every person caught in place. They stared at her.

Magic again, she thought. Unexpected, uncontrolled magic. She did not just have fire. She could influence people, as Celestine did. She could *control* them.

How much magic did she have?

She wanted calm, she wanted *peace*, but she did not want to bend everyone to her will, a magic cage dropped upon them all. "Please stop this," she said. "I will bring justice to the king, and there will be magic. Things will be better. But this must stop."

"Kill him!" One voice from the crowd, but then another, and another, until all the panic and bloodlust was directed at the dais. Kill the king.

His shallow breaths jerked under the point of the sword. He had tried to capture her, to control her, to kill her. He had killed so many others. He had been about to kill Rodric, his own *son*. He deserved death. But her hand shook. The sword shook. Could she take a life, even one such as his? Taint her hands with his blood, become as brutal as the king himself?

"Don't."

She looked up. Rodric had escaped his guards. He looked thin and worn, but he hurried toward Aurora with a determined expression on his face.

"Rodric—"

"Don't kill him, Aurora."

"I have to," she said. "It has to end."

"It will." He shouted louder now, his voice echoing over the crowd. "Lock him up. Give him a trial. He'll pay for what he's done. But you're not a killer, Aurora. You're not a monster. Don't do this."

She was a monster. Dragon fire, dragon blood. That was who she was. But still she hesitated, sword brushing against the king's throat.

"Do this right, Princess. Don't be like him."

Neither of them had been watching the king. He grabbed the sword around the edges and shoved it backward. The hilt crashed into Aurora's stomach, and she dropped it, gasping for breath. John pulled a knife from his boot, and then he was gripping Rodric, the dagger pressed against his throat.

"I am the king," he said, barely louder than a whisper. "You can't stop me. You can't defeat me. I am—"

He gurgled. Blood spurted across his lips to match the red now staining his hands. His grip on Rodric loosened, and Rodric shoved him away. The king fell to his knees. Blood was spreading down his chest. He keeled forward, and his chin cracked against the stone.

Queen Iris stood behind him. She held a small dagger. Her dress was covered in blood.

She stared at her husband as though surprised at what she had done. Then she looked up, skin flushed. She nodded.

The crowd was quiet. They stared at the dais, held still by shock or magic.

"Rodric?" Aurora rested a hand on his arm. She was surprised at how solid it felt. He was alive. "Are you okay?"

The prince stared at her hand. "I think so," he said. "Yes. I didn't expect to see you." He wrapped an arm around her shoulders, pulling her toward him. Her hands crashed against his chest and then settled around his waist. Safe. "Are you okay?"

"Yes," she said. "Yes." She pulled back. "I heard you've been supporting the rebellion."

"Rebellion is my father's word," Rodric said. He ducked his head. "I thought of it more as helping people. Things have been worse since you left. The food shortage, the deaths . . . someone had to do something. And my father . . . well. You saw my father." He looked up at the sky. "Care to explain the dragon?"

"It will take a while," she said. "But it isn't Vanhelm's. They're here, but it's mine. It follows me."

"What exactly—"

Magic crackled in the air, and Aurora felt a rush of heat,

a rush of fury and yearning that almost choked her. And she knew what she would see before she turned, knew before the fire ripped across the square.

A horde of dragons, swooping out of the sky.

THIRTY-ONE

THE CREATURES CIRCLED THE CASTLE, THEIR SHRIEKS tearing through the air. One let out a burst of flame, and the west tower buckled under the heat.

"Vanhelm," Rodric said. "They're attacking."

"No," Aurora said. "No, they're not."

"Aurora?"

She ran to the edge of the dais, reaching for the connection between her and the dragons. If she could find it, if she could calm them, lure them down from the sky . . . but the dragons burned too hot, driven on by vengeance and rage.

Her dragon was still there, a separate beat from the others, shrieking but not burning, not attacking . . . not yet.

Rodric ran up beside her. "If it's not Vanhelm, then who? Aurora?"

"It's Celestine," Aurora said. Another dragon dove over the square. Fire raced across the cobblestones. "It's my fault."

"Celestine?" Rodric flinched from another rush of dragon fire. "The witch? She's dead."

"No," Aurora said. "No, she's not."

She ran down the steps, but she could see nothing but fire. She did not know where Celestine would hide. She did not know where to look. The screams rattled around her head.

If she were Celestine, if she wanted Aurora to find her, wanted to make a point, where would she wait?

And then she knew.

She looked up at the castle, searching for her own tower. A green light danced around the window. The screams of the dragons distorted, replaced by far-off laughter, and a singing that sent prickles down Aurora's arms.

Aurora ran. The light floated in front of her eyes now, brushing around her hair, luring her onward. She ducked around the blazing pyre, around the remaining guards and through the castle doors.

"Aurora!"

Rodric's footsteps pounded behind her. "Stay here!" she shouted. "Get people to the river. I'm going to stop this."

"How?" he said. "Where are you going?"

She ignored him. She ran faster than she had known was possible, tearing through the corridors, her arms catching on tables and flower vases, until she reached her tower door. It was still unlocked. She kept running, around and around, past the tapestries, through the dust, until she crashed into her bedroom. That room was empty too, but the fireplace was open, lights gleaming above the ashes.

Celestine waited in the room above. She sat on a stool, turning the spinning wheel with flicks of her fingers. The air glowed.

"It is a pity," Celestine said, "that a beautiful thing like you spent her whole life locked in this tower. This spindle was the thing that brought you your freedom, in the end. Do you not think?" She turned her head to look at Aurora, and her smile was wide and hungry, like the smile of a dragon.

"Stop them," Aurora said. Her voice was hoarse. "Stop the dragons."

"Stop them?" Celestine tilted her head. "But you were the one who brought them here."

"I didn't—"

"You did not what? You did not take a dragon's heart?"

"I didn't summon them here."

Celestine laughed, and the spinning wheel clicked. "Are you really so dim, Aurora? *You* brought them here. *You.* I told you that you would regret eating that piece of dragon heart. They are drawn to you. They were drawn to you in Vanhelm, they are drawn to you now. They are following *you.*"

Aurora stepped closer. "No," she said. "I saw you in Vanhelm, when the dragons attacked—"

"I *helped* you in Vanhelm," Celestine said. "You were trying so hard to send the dragons away, but they were not listening, were they? Poor thing, fighting to control your magic, your new link to the dragons, and still knowing so little. You are too weak to handle them all, so I was offering my assistance. We both have that link now, thanks to you, and since I actually understand how to control it, I thought I might help."

"And is that what you're doing now? *Helping?*"

"Observing," Celestine said. "To see what you will do. To see if you will accept who you are after all."

But Celestine had to be lying. It did not make sense. "But you brought the dragons back," Aurora said. "You used my blood, you wanted my magic—"

Celestine's laugh was decidedly mocking now, mingling with the dragons' screams. "You are so ready to put all evils at my feet. I suppose I must find it flattering. Did it flatter you, I wonder, to think your blood awoke dragons, to think you were part of them? I did not awaken them. How could I have? I had no magic in Vanhelm, and dragons know their own minds. They awoke, Aurora, because they awoke, because this was their time. I merely took advantage of the circumstances."

"But—the things you wrote in the ruins—"

"I was weak. There was so little magic left, none I could access in Vanhelm. I saw the potential of the dragons, remembered legends, but without magic to begin with, I could not take the heart myself. I needed you. And since you awoke, I've *wanted* you to do it. I've wanted to show you how brutal you really are. So think on that, Aurora, before you judge me."

"But my connection with them. My fire magic—"

"You do not have *fire magic*. You have magic. But you were too narrow-minded to use it for anything but fire. The dragons were intrigued by you because you are a creature of magic. And you deluded yourself into thinking you controlled them, that you could use them like tools, because that is what you wanted to be true."

Celestine stood up and slid toward her. "You could have healed your prince yourself, you know. I did not give you power. I simply told you how to do it. If only you had listened to me, my dear. If only you had joined me when I asked. Think how different things would have been."

Aurora's heart crashed against her ribs. The air stank of blood and scorched flesh, and the dragon's blood pounded with fury, with a need that no amount of destruction could quench. "What do you want?" she said. "I can make another deal—"

Celestine laughed. "Oh, you sweet thing. Did you not hate your mother, not so many weeks ago, for bargaining with me? And now you would like to deal with me again?"

"If you know how to stop the dragons, then stop them."

"I do not think so," Celestine said. "Not yet. These people wanted magic, did they not? And they deserve to be punished, for the way they have treated you. Let them remember how fearsome magic can be."

Aurora stepped back, reaching for that connection with the dragons again. If she could just calm this fury, if she could soothe the dragons, guide them away . . .

Celestine's nails dug into her arm. "Do you not understand, Aurora? You are not the one to stop this. You should not want to stop this. This is what you are meant to do, what you are meant to be. You tried so hard to be good, to play the little hero, and look where you have ended up. Look what you have done. You are not the good, sweet hero in this story. There is no good, sweet hero here. You are *twisted*, my dear. Just. Like. Me."

"You don't know me," Aurora said. "I'm nothing like you." But she remembered her words to Finnegan, less than two weeks ago. *If I let out everything I felt, I'd burn the whole city to the ground.*

"But you *are*." Celestine pressed her hands around Aurora's face, crushing her hair. Her voice was gentle. "Do you think I did not want to be good, once? That I did not want to be loved? But I learned, as you learned, that that cannot be done. They will despise you for your power, even as they beg you for more. You were happy to pretend to be the villain, weren't you, Aurora? To be the witch they feared, if it would help? Too naïve to accept that things are not so black and white. Too stubborn to think I might ever have reached the same conclusion." She smoothed Aurora's hair. "I wanted them to *love* me, as you did. And they betrayed me, as they betrayed you. They dismissed me, feared me, loathed me, when all I did, I did for them."

Her nails dug into Aurora's scalp. "The throne was meant to be mine," she said. "And I ruled, in my own way. I was the only one who could give them their wishes, for all that they feared me."

"What are you talking about?" Aurora said. "What—"

"You know," Celestine said. "You must know. I am Alysse, Aurora. It has always been me."

No. Alysse had died, hundreds of years ago. Everyone knew that. Everyone *knew*. She was not Celestine. She was not twisted.

Celestine brushed a stray hair away from Aurora's forehead. "You do not want to believe it," she said. "I know, I know. But it is true. I saved them all. They wove myths about me, but they did not want me. They did not want my power." Her voice sped up, rising in pitch, the mad smile spreading across her face again. "They made me an outcast. Yet I was still their queen, when it counted. They came running to me, under all my different names, *begging* for my magic. Begging to make deals with me. They loved me, in their own way, or feared me. Oh, I was queen. And now I will be again. Now I will have you. Our stories are the same, you see. We belong together. We can give Alyssinia the magic it wants, together. Give them what they need. Make them bow to us. Even if they hate us for it."

"I don't want that," Aurora whispered.

"Not after they cast you out? Tried to kill you, called you a witch, called you a whore? They tried to kill you, and those you love. They begged you for magic and feared you because you had it. And do I not deserve your sympathy too, Aurora? For what *I* have suffered? For what they did to me?"

"You cursed me," Aurora said. "You took away my *life*."

"I *gave* you your life. A prick of your finger, and you were free to come here. To see dragons and kiss princes and feel what true power is like. Was that not a gift, Aurora? Was I not good to you?" Her voice was soft. "This was what your mother wished. This is the bargain she made. And surely you see now how tricky magic can be. How bad consequences do not make the witch herself evil. We give people what they wish for, and things fall as they fall." She cupped Aurora's cheek, her long fingernails digging around her jawbone. "Trust me, Aurora. I care for you. I can teach you so much. We will save the kingdom from these dragons, together. I meant what I said. I want to return to my rightful place. The people cannot be trusted, Aurora. They *need* us. And you would be glorious as queen."

The words wove through Aurora's thoughts. So simple. So *appealing*.

"I will stop this, as soon as you agree. I will teach *you* to stop this. To control your power, to control your magic, to be everything you could be. Do not reject me, Aurora, for some ancient grudge. Is that not what people have always been doing to you?"

Celestine would make Aurora magnificent, as she had promised. Celestine had said it herself: she could use magic, but Aurora *was* magic. With practice, she could be more powerful than Celestine could even dream.

And if Celestine was Alysse, if her life had led to this . . .
Aurora knew what it was like to be lied about, to have the facts
of your life twisted into something new.

Celestine's heartbeat thudded against her arm. Not Alysse.
Celestine.

"No!" She shoved Celestine back, so that the witch stumbled against the stone wall. Fire engulfed Celestine, and she
laughed. She watched Aurora through the flames, her mouth
gaping, laughing and laughing, until the spell petered out, and
Aurora stepped back, exhausted, uncertain. Celestine continued
to laugh, unscathed.

"Was that supposed to prove me wrong? I am not threatening you. I am doing nothing to you. And yet you want to
burn me away, because you are so convinced that you are good.
Accept it, Aurora. You know you are meant to be with me."

She would not accept it. Celestine was lying, she had to be
lying. She had brought the dragons here, she was manipulating
Aurora, like she had manipulated her mother, like she manipulated everybody. Aurora had to stop her.

Celestine's power had come from the dragon's heart. She
had devoured the heart, and she had found that magic again. If
Celestine lost her own heart, would she lose her magic too?

Aurora lunged. Her fingers scraped against Celestine's chest,
but Celestine grabbed her wrist and twisted, until Aurora turned,
her back to the witch, arm contorted between them. Celestine's

nails dug into Aurora's skin. She gripped Aurora's hair, close to the scalp, and yanked her head backward.

"You think you can fight me?" Celestine hissed in her ear. "Do you think you can stop any of this without me?" She pulled Aurora's neck farther back, and Aurora fought not to cry out in pain. "Shall I show you?" she said. "The final lesson? Do you want to see what your defiance has done? Yes," she said. "Let us see."

Her hand still tight on Aurora's hair, Celestine dragged her down the stairs, out of the tower, out onto the dais again. Flames swirled around them, the heat so intense that Aurora flinched back. The square itself was scattered with scorched corpses, and a few living people too, injured and unable to run, huddled by the castle as though it would protect them, frozen by fear. The pyre burned, and fire leapt from roof to roof, chasing back toward the city wall.

"Look," Celestine said. "Look at what you have done. You need me, Aurora. You need to join me."

"Never," Aurora said. She struggled against Celestine's grip, but she could not break free. "I will *never* join you. Not even if you burn the whole world away."

Out of the corner of her eye, she could see Iris, struggling to hold Rodric back, as he watched them, sword in hand.

"And still you refuse to listen," Celestine said. "*You* are burning the whole world away."

Finnegan and Nettle plunged into the square, the soldiers

limping behind them. They were ash-covered, scratched, but did not seem seriously hurt. Finnegan mouthed Aurora's name, but she couldn't hear him. She couldn't hear anything except the rush of her own blood and the hiss of Celestine's voice. Yet she saw his eyes, focused on something descending behind Celestine's head, and she felt the heat in the air, that yearning and starving in her chest. "You are *nothing* without me. So look at this world. Look at the world you have created, and tell me you're *better* than me. Tell me."

Aurora struck with her free hand. Her nails scratched Celestine's face, across her eyelids, down her cheeks, scraping, gouging. Celestine screeched, and Aurora jerked her elbow backward, catching the witch in the stomach and twisting away.

Aurora summoned flame, and her dragon screamed, engulfing Celestine in fire. The witch laughed and screamed, the sounds melting together as her hair crackled and crumbled away.

The dragon landed behind Aurora, its tail curled around her feet, the heat from its scales filling the air. And Celestine grinned at them, her skin blackened, blood dripping down her face where Aurora had attacked her, hair falling away. "I can cure a little dragon burn," she said. Her voice scratched against her throat, like it too was turning to ash. "Can you?"

"Shall we try it again and see?"

Rodric stepped behind Aurora, sword held out in front of him. Then Finnegan was on the other side of her, swordless but defiant, while the dragon snapped its teeth.

Celestine tossed what remained of her hair, even as her skin crumbled away. Her grin was wider now, her lips shriveled, so Aurora could see all of her teeth. "I only wanted to help you, Aurora," she said. "I only want a return to what is right. But I see you are not yet ready. You have not accepted who you are." She glanced from one prince to the other, taking in the dragon, the melted castle, the flames. "You will destroy yourself, you know. Or they will. You'll see. You'll see how right I am." She turned away, looking over the destruction of the square. "You want magic?" she shouted to the quivering crowd. "You want justice? You want what you *deserve*? Come and find me. Your new queen does not want the power that I offer, but she is a fool. If you want magic, come to me." She twisted back to Aurora. "I am not your enemy," she said. "I do not wish to hurt you. You shall see." She swept into a curtsy. "Enjoy your new kingdom, Your Majesty. I'll see you in the ashes."

And then she was gone, leaving nothing but the smell of burning flesh and an army of screaming dragons.

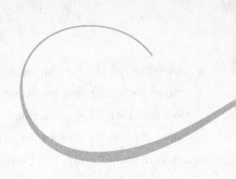

THIRTY-TWO

ONE OF THE DRAGONS CLUNG TO THE CASTLE'S EAST tower, its claws gorging the stone. Another gripped the city walls, and several more still swept through the sky, their wings blocking out the stars.

"Aurora," Rodric said. "What do we do?"

She didn't know. She stared as another dragon dove over the city, its breath setting several more rooftops alight.

She had been wrong. She had been wrong about everything. She had ignored Celestine's warnings, and now an army of dragons was burning her city away, and people were asking her for a plan. They were looking to her to save them.

She had no time for self-doubt now.

"Get as many people as you can into the river," she said. "It'll protect them, at least a little."

"It's on the other side of the city," Finnegan said. "They won't make it."

"Then get people into the castle," she said. "Down in the dungeons." The basement room at the Alysse museum had been mostly untouched by dragon fire. Perhaps the ground would protect people here, too. She turned to the few guards that remained. "What are you waiting for? Find people, get them here. Rodric, make sure that they're safe. Guide them, keep them calm. . . . You'll know what to do."

A king for another time, she had thought. He was certainly the right king for this. Rodric grabbed her hand and squeezed. His face was ashen with fear, but his expression did not waver. "I'll do everything I can," he said.

"I know you will."

He hurried away, racing toward the nearest group of cowering people. He rested a hand on the back of one girl, pointing to the castle with the other. The girl nodded and began to run.

"Finnegan, you have to stay out of sight. If anyone realizes who you are, they'll blame you. I don't want you hurt."

"And you?" Finnegan said. "What are you going to do?"

"I'm going to stop them."

He grabbed her arm. "Then I'm coming with you."

"You can't. Celestine said they were drawn to me. If that's

true, then anyone near me is in danger."

"Then I'll be in danger," he said. "I'm not leaving you now."

"No." She pushed his hand away. "I have to do this alone." Last time Finnegan had supported her like this, he had been burned by the dragons; he had almost died. She couldn't risk it happening again. "You know more about dealing with dragons than anyone here. If you won't stay out of sight, help. Tell people what to do. But don't let anyone try to fight the dragons. And come back alive."

He pulled her up on her toes, pressing his lips against hers in a fierce kiss. "You too, dragon girl," he said. Then he turned and ran.

The air was thick with smoke now, the stench of fire. The dragons screamed, and the people screamed, and crowds shoved toward the castle, and Aurora could feel all of it, the panic, the rage, the desperation.

She needed to *think*. She could run out of the city, luring the dragons with her. But the city would be destroyed before she reached the gates. She needed to control them, needed to force them down. Make them sleep, as she had once intended.

That plan had been based on delusions. She had never had any connection with the dragons, beyond the shared existence of their magic. She had wanted answers so desperately that she had woven her own, and her blindness had hurt Finnegan, it had given Celestine more power, it had brought the dragons to burn Vanhelm and Alyssinia.

She had achieved everything she'd wanted. She'd saved Finnegan, learned more about her magic, got rid of the king. She had been so convinced of her connection with the dragons that she'd ended up forging one herself. But things were never supposed to end like this.

And the dragons had not intoxicated her, not in the way she had assumed. She had not been overwhelmed by her connection to them or their magic, had not been turned into someone other than herself when the creatures were near or when she used that magic. Her giddiness, her fascination, her recklessness . . . it had all been her. She had not been in danger of corruption. She had already been corrupt.

But now she had the connection she had wanted. Now she had to use it to help. She searched the burning square for a vantage point, but the only good place was the castle, and she could not lead the dragons there with people hiding inside. King John's pyre was already burning, as were the houses around the square. But the fountain she had destroyed at her wedding was still there, half rubble, left as a monument to her wickedness. She scrambled onto it and closed her eyes, searching for the sliver of dragon heart inside her, reaching for the magic she felt filling the sky.

There. Heartbeats pounding beside her own. She tugged them closer, and fury raced through her, stealing her breath. She felt the fire, and she wanted to burn with it too.

Stop it, she thought. *You have to stop.* But her desperation only seemed to drive them onward, spurring their rage, spurring her rage too. The city deserved to burn, didn't it, for what it had done? Why should she worry for them?

She shoved the thought away, and took a deep breath, trying to calm her pounding heart. What had Finnegan said in the practice room, all those weeks ago? You couldn't think about magic, just as you couldn't think about walking and expect your foot to move. Her connection with her own dragon had been instant, effortless, an instinct that she had never questioned. She could not command the dragons with her thoughts. She needed to feel it. *Calm.*

She thought of the moment in the park, when her magic had felt so easy, so *freeing,* and of the love and happiness she had poured into the kiss that healed Finnegan's burns. Another dragon screamed, and she squeezed her eyes closed to help block out the sound. If she wished to calm them, she had to be calm herself.

She took a deep breath, in and out. Her heartbeat slowed. And once she felt that calmness, she searched inside herself for the dragons again. Their rage still burned, but she held it back, refused to let it overwhelm her. They stood in equilibrium for a moment, feeling each other's presence, the power there. Then she reached out, pushing that quiet toward them as she had once sent out tendrils of flame.

The fire softened. The frantic pound of their hearts calmed to a steady beat.

She opened her eyes. The dragons had paused. The people below still screamed, but the sound was warped, far away. The dragons were all that mattered, the bond between them, this world of peace and fire.

But they could not stay here, she knew. Not when they were so powerful, not when the very idea of the dragons had corrupted her before. Not when Celestine could influence them too. She had to make them sleep again, for now, at least.

She breathed slower, deeper, letting her tenseness wash away. *Sleep,* she thought, and she felt it too, felt the heaviness in her bones, the weariness of an ancient beast.

But if she had to feel the magic, feel the connection, how could she make them sleep without sleeping too?

She felt a surge of panic, and the dragons screamed. She could not sleep again. She couldn't fall back into that oblivion, couldn't open her eyes to find another new world, lose everything she had gained and start again. She would not sacrifice herself, not like that, no matter what it meant. She wouldn't.

But there were other ways, she thought. She took a deep breath, focusing on the calm again, pushing for control. Dragons could not exist without magic. They needed the power in their hearts, the power she now seemed to share.

But could she do it? Could she use her magic to destroy so much beauty, so much life, no matter what destruction they had caused? She would become everything Celestine said she was meant to be. Powerful. Destructive. Arrogant in her attempts to bend the world to her will.

The dragons shifted, her own doubt rattling them. She took another deep breath, letting the thoughts float through her head, emotionless, detached. She had told Orla that she could *never* do that, but she had been so wrong, about everything. She had already become the person Celestine wanted her to be. She had brought the dragons here. It was her responsibility to stop them. And she had already proved that she wasn't as good as she believed.

So she reached past the calmness, reached for each flicker of fire, letting her own magic caress it.

Calm, she thought. *Calm.*

And once she felt it, once she believed it, she seized that flicker of power, all but the part that was her dragon, the part that was *hers*, and she ripped it away. Ripped it toward herself.

The dragons shrieked, not their usual screams of wrath and fire, but that ear-splitting cry she had heard in the cavern, like the thing they loved most in the world had been torn from them. They cracked and burned, screaming, still screaming, while flames exploded around Aurora, whirling, dancing against her skin. She fell to her knees, the fire scorching her throat. The world was burning and red.

Then the flames were gone, and the dragons, too, all but the one she had rescued and brought across the sea. For a breath, everything was still.

Ashes floated on the breeze across the empty square.

THIRTY-THREE

THE REMAINING GUARDS LAID OUT KING JOHN'S BODY in the throne room. Iris stood over it, eyes fixed on her husband's face. She seemed, at most, vaguely satisfied, like she had been proved right about some inconsequential matter.

Rodric paced the room, reaching the thrones and then turning on his heel again, all restless energy and confusion.

Aurora could still sense her dragon, circling the castle. The one remnant of their power, unless more had remained across the sea. A legend that Aurora had bent to her will and then torn apart.

Aurora could not think about it now. Not when the

kingdom lay broken at her feet.

"Rodric," she said. "Are you all right?"

"Am I all right?" He shook his head, as though astonished by the question. "My father tried to kill me today. Twice. My mother killed him. My home was attacked by dragons. And you reappeared out of nowhere and used magic to fight them. Am I all right?"

"I'm sorry," Aurora said. "I shouldn't have abandoned you."

"Abandoned me?" Rodric stopped pacing, only a few feet from her. "You didn't abandon me. You did what you had to do. And things worked out, didn't they?"

"The city is burning," she said. "People are dead, dragons attacked—"

"But it's a start," Rodric said. "The start of a new world. Like we said we wanted."

Aurora suddenly had the overwhelming urge to hug him. Her arms twitched. She could not find the energy to take the step, but Rodric seemed to understand what she meant. His arms slipped around her. For once, his embrace wasn't stiff or awkward. For a moment, she felt safe.

"Why did you come back?" Rodric said into her hair. "You had escaped. You didn't need to come back."

She looked up at his earnest face, filled with concern for her, the face she had run from, the prince she cared for but could never love, could never feel for in the way people expected. The prince who genuinely believed that she should not have helped him. "Of course I came back," she said softly. "Your father . . . he had to be stopped." She squeezed tighter, just for a breath, then stepped away.

"Do you think Celestine will still be a threat? Will she bring more dragons to attack us?"

"I don't think she'll attack again," Aurora said. "And I don't think she intends to be malicious to us, not yet. But who knows what trouble she'll cause, when people go to her with their wishes?"

"It does not matter. She is not your greatest concern." Iris was still standing by her husband, still staring at his body, but her voice rang out across the room. "She can be fought with magic. The people won't be dealt with so easily."

"Dealt with?" Aurora said.

"Do you think you can control them? Things have been on the brink of revolution for so long. Chaotic for decades. And now they have been attacked by dragons, now the king is dead and two witches claim to rule. My husband called you a traitor, and you might well be, as Vanhelm provided you support. You are a foreign invader now, claiming to be a princess. And trust me, they do not take kindly to foreigners."

"Then Rodric can rule," Aurora said. "Someone they can trust—"

"Oh no, Aurora," Iris said. "You cannot overthrow the king,

call him a usurper, and then put his son on the throne. If you are who you claim to be, it has to be you. Or else things will fall apart again."

"Things have already fallen apart."

"And you have made it your job to put them back together. No one else can repair this now."

A figure at the side of the room laughed. Aurora had forgotten that the false her, John's decoy, was there, seated on the floor, dressed in tatters. She had a fierce look in her eyes. She stood now, still laughing. "Would you like me to do it, Your Majesty?" She swept into a mocking curtsy. "Princess Aurora, at your service. But you can call me Eliza."

"Eliza," Aurora said. "I'm sorry for what happened to you."

"As you should be." She was almost skeletal under her rags, worn down by days or weeks in captivity, but Aurora could see why John had chosen her. She had something regal about her, a command and a dignity that Aurora herself had not possessed. Her expression matched that of the girl in the wanted posters, a little haughty, passionate, ready to fight.

"I'm sorry," Aurora said again, and she was. "I'm glad I got here in time to help."

"I wouldn't have let him kill me," Eliza said, but her voice shook. Aurora didn't ask how she had planned to stop them.

"I'm glad," Aurora said. "I wouldn't want anyone's fate to rest on me." But that was part of what being queen would mean. It was part of her curse. Part of her magic.

Aurora glanced at Iris. She had looked up from her husband's body, and was watching the exchange with sharp eyes. "Rodric," Aurora said. "Why don't you find Eliza somewhere to stay? I need to speak to Iris."

Eliza frowned. "Dismissing me already?"

"No," Aurora said. "We'll talk soon enough."

Eliza swept into another mocking curtsy, her head bowed, perfectly balanced despite her stick-thin legs and rag-like dress. "Until then, Your Majesty." Rodric gave Aurora and his mother a more authentic-looking bow, and then led the still-furious-looking Eliza out of the throne room.

"I would watch that one," Iris said. "She might be dangerous."

"No," Aurora said. "She's just angry. I would be too."

"It is not how a princess should behave."

"Then it's a good thing she's not really a princess." Aurora walked slowly toward the queen, the woman who had guided her and imprisoned her, so powerful yet powerless. "You stabbed your husband," she said. "Why?"

Iris stared straight back at her, no guilt on her face, no pain at all, not even resignation. It was the same slightly pinched yet dignified expression Aurora had seen her wear again and again. The expression of a queen. "He was going to kill my son," she said. "He may have already killed my daughter. It was too much."

"He was going to burn your son," Aurora said. "And Eliza.

But you didn't fight back then."

"And you know that for a certainty?" Iris's glanced at her husband's body. "I wrote to you. In Vanhelm. I told that insufferable Prince Finnegan what was happening. And I gave information to his spy. I hoped you would arrive in time. And if you did not, I was more than prepared to step in. I can conceal daggers too."

"Now you're no longer queen."

Iris pressed her lips together. "You think that matters to me?"

"Yes," Aurora said. "I think it matters to you very much."

"Rodric matters more," she said. "And what good is power if I cannot stop my own son from dying in front of me? Perhaps it was time to be free of it. Give you the trouble instead."

Aurora thought of Orla, so confident, so determined, so in control. Elegant, sophisticated Erin. Aurora was not like that. She would never be like that. "I don't know how to be queen," she said.

Iris clasped her hands in front of her and looked at her husband again. Her expression did not change, but when she spoke, her voice was almost gentle. "I could teach you."

Aurora hesitated. "I don't want to be queen like you."

"Neither did I." Iris sighed. "You cannot keep control, you know. Not unless you make them fear you, as they did my husband. And if they fear you, they may only fight you more fiercely. Because what is more fearsome and unnatural that a woman who does not do what she is told?"

"I have to try," Aurora said. "Not to be feared, but to do something. To make it work. I have to *try*."

Now Iris looked at her. "Do you want to be queen?"

"No," Aurora said. "I want to be free."

"None of us is free."

"And so I am queen."

Iris brushed her hands down her dress, as though sweeping away imaginary crumbs from the bloodstained cloth. "I can still advise you," she said. "I have learned a lot, about how to gain people's trust, how to play this game. About the kingdom and the people in it. I always listened, and I always knew. You will need as many people on your side as you can get, Aurora. Accept my help in this."

Aurora thought of all her past lessons with Iris, the berating, the locked doors, the instructions to curtsy and be meek. The slap across her face after Isabelle's death, and the tiny, subtle ways she'd tried to help, in her own, infuriating way. Aurora did not have to listen to her, not all the time. But she did need help. She needed someone who knew how to be queen. "All right," she said. "Yes. Thank you."

"I will begin preparations for the coronation," Iris said. "It should be as soon as possible."

There were words Aurora had heard before. Her stomach twisted. She could already feel the weight of the crown on her head, the responsibility, the restriction pushing her in.

She would not be afraid. She would do what needed to be done.

Aurora found Finnegan pacing the palace gardens. The flowers were in bloom now, an explosion of yellows and reds, and blossom had fallen from the trees, leaving a carpet of pink on the path.

"Your Majesty," Finnegan said, when he saw her approach. "I suppose that is the proper way to address you now."

"I'm not queen yet," she said. "Not officially."

"But you will be. Soon."

"Yes," she murmured. "Yes, I will be." She sank onto a bench. The garden was quiet, no one there but Finnegan and her, but she could still feel the presence of her dragon, swooping over the city, its heartbeat next to her own.

Finnegan sat beside her. Aurora seized her necklace, almost on instinct, and looked up at the castle walls. The last time she had sat here, it had been with Rodric, her storybook open between them. She had told him she didn't love him, the one thing she was never supposed to say. And now she was here again, in *her* castle, with a different prince, her emotions exposed and raw. With no idea what to do.

Finnegan shifted on the bench beside her, his shoulders tense. "So, are you going to marry Rodric now? Be with your true love?"

She laughed. It was inappropriate, she knew, but so

ridiculous, that the all-knowing Finnegan was out of touch with her thoughts. "He is not my true love," she said. "And no. *No.* I will be queen, I don't have a choice in that, but if you think I'm marrying a boy because a prophecy told me so, you are very much mistaken. I'm rather tired of fate. Aren't you?"

Finnegan grasped her hand. When he spoke, he almost sounded tentative. "There's another choice, you know," he said. "This isn't what you want, Aurora. You don't want to play princess. You don't want to be queen. Come with me. Run, and leave all of this behind you. You did it before."

"I can't," she said.

"You can. You can do anything you want."

"And I want to be here." She looked at him, only inches away, all uncertainty gone. If she had wishes, she would change all this, wash it all away so that she could kiss Finnegan and run and never look back. But she couldn't. She had to fix her mistakes, to save the people around her. And she couldn't do that from afar. "After," she said, and she trailed off, uncertain of the words. "After this is all dealt with, then maybe . . ."

"After," he said. "Right." He looked away, staring at the few blossoms clinging to the nearby tree. "Is this the part where you ask me to leave, tell me you can't be associated with me anymore?"

"What?" She tightened her hold on his hand. "No. Why would I say that?"

"Well, you have queenly duties to consider now. And as my mother has mentioned, I would make a *terrible* king."

An insecure Finnegan. She almost laughed again. "You're not going to be king of Alyssinia, Finnegan. That doesn't mean I want you to *leave*. Who would I have to irritate me if you weren't around?"

"I'm sure that Iris is up to the task."

"Finnegan." She pulled on his hand. "I thought you were smarter than that. I gave Celestine her powers back in order to save your life. Why would I send you away now?"

"Well," he said. "It would be insane for you to do so. But it has been said about you." He relaxed beside her. "It does make things more complicated, you realize, when you become queen. Especially considering your promise to my mother. I can't go back to Vanhelm."

She tightened her grip on his hand. "Why not?"

"My mother made it quite clear. I come back with that dragon heart, or I don't come back at all."

"But you're heir to the throne."

"I'm *an* heir. And my mother doesn't exactly think I'm capable of taking on the role. She blames me for what happened. I can't go back without the heart."

"But the dragons are gone," she said. "I destroyed them."

"Not all of them." He looked up to the sky to prove his point. Aurora's dragon still circled the castle, and there might be others, still in the waste across the sea.

She let go of his hand. "I can't give it to you. You know I can't."

"I know," he said. But did he, really? Aurora had seen the lengths he had gone to prove his worth before. He was insightful and inventive and utterly fearless in his execution. If he needed that dragon heart to be king . . . she did not know what he would do.

She had to balance her own desires with the needs of the kingdom. But she would not throw away everything, not for them, not for anyone. She could do this. She could be queen and still be Aurora, use her magic to help and still hold on to herself. Orla had managed it. It *had* to be possible.

"I want you here," she said. "I want you to stay."

"Well," he said. "I suppose I could. For a little while. If you insist."

"I suppose I do."

"Then I guess you're stuck with me."

She nestled her head against his shoulder. "However will I cope?"

"You're resourceful, Rora. I'm sure you'll find a way."

Aurora's tower was still coated with dust. The torches had burned out, so she pulled a ball of fire into her hand to light the way. The tapestries of her story hung there, almost accusingly. She would ask someone to take them down, to lock them out of sight.

When she reached her room, she let the flame float beside her and hurried over to the fireplace. It opened easily enough, and then she was climbing again, until she stood in the rafters, hidden in a rickety room that should never have existed.

The spinning wheel still clicked.

She sat on the stool and stared at the wall above the stairway, at the words scorched into the stone. *She is mine,* Celestine had written, so long ago. And below that: *Nothing can stop it now.* Aurora stared at the letters, listening to the wheel click-click-click beside her.

She was not Celestine's. She was not anybody's. She would take on her responsibilities and she would make her *own* choices, and no dragon fire, no threats from ancient witches and twisted stories from long ago would stop her.

She ran a hand around the spinning wheel, catching its spokes with her fingers. The needle still gleamed, as inviting as it had seemed a hundred years ago. Magic crackled across her skin, and she itched to let it loose, to burn this spinning wheel into char and ash. But burning the spinning wheels had not stopped the curse. Something told her to wait, to save this remnant of before, this one harmless object that had changed everything. She could not burn her past away.

Instead, she walked down the stairs to her old bedroom and crossed to the window. The view had changed again since she had last looked out, revealing a city of ruined buildings and lingering smoke. Another era had ended, another world was beginning.

And she would be queen of it. She would make sure that it was as good as it could be.

She held out her palm and called to the second heartbeat that whispered beside her own. The breeze brushed through her fingers, and then heat, as her dragon burst into view, its huge wings barely moving to keep it aloft. She ran her hand along the scales of its neck, feeling the smoothness, the fire.

So much power. And it was *hers*.

She looked over the kingdom—half beauty, half ash—and she smiled.

ACKNOWLEDGMENTS

Many, many amazing people were involved in the creation of this book, and it's impossible to fully express how grateful I am for them all.

First, a huge thank-you to my agent extraordinaire, Kristin Nelson, whose wisdom, dedication, and humor make everything possible.

Massive thanks to everyone at HarperTeen, especially my editor, Catherine Wallace, who takes my words and helps to shape them into novels. Big thanks are also due to Jennifer Klonsky; to my wonderful publicist, Stephanie Hoover; to Jenna

Stempel, who made the book look gorgeous; and to everyone else who played a part, big or small, in making the novel happen.

Alexandra Zaleski was the first to read this novel, and to make me think there might be something in it after all. My work would not be the same without her thoughts, and I would not be the same without her love and support.

Rachel Thompson provided invaluable feedback on this novel, along with her even more invaluable friendship. If the whole saving-the-world-from-disease-using-physics thing doesn't work out, she should really consider a second career as an editor. Thanks for all her patience and support, for her speed-reading when I really needed a second opinion, and for generally being awesome.

When I told Phoebe Cattle I was writing my acknowledgments, she said not to mention her, because she "hasn't read it yet." She clearly doesn't realize how much she means to me, and how much her friendship helps me to write. Thank you to Phoebe for all the jokes, all the Sunday pancakes, all the random shouts of "And I'm Javert!"—for being a best friend, in short, and keeping me sane(ish).

I'm lucky enough to be surrounded by fantastic friends on both sides of the Atlantic. Massive thank-yous to James Cattle, Matt Goodyear, and Oz Shepherdson; to Kelly Smith; to Shelina Kurwa; to my roommates, Meg Lee and Anna Liu; and to Will Nguyen, for being generally wonderful and for inspiring me to write.

I'm also eternally grateful to Tracy Cochran, whose kindness and wisdom keep me steady through all the ups and downs of publishing.

And of course, no thank-you is big enough for my parents, Brian and Gaynor Thomas, who gave me a love of stories and encouraged me to pursue all this in the first place.

A HUNDRED DOVES BURST OUT OF THE PIE.

I don't know why I was surprised. Of course there were a hundred doves in the pie. The king wouldn't open his birthday celebration by actually feeding his guests. Not when he could amaze us all with his extravagance instead.

I just wished someone had considered what would happen to the doves *after* they were released. The king had skewered a couple in his enthusiasm to cut open the pastry, and the survivors were determined to get as far away from that knife-wielding maniac as possible. Many of them settled in the rafters of the banquet hall, forty feet above us. More crashed against the huge arched windows. One settled in the bell of a trumpet and refused to move, no matter how violently the player waved his hands.

I sank into my chair and kept watch on the doves overhead. I wasn't afraid of them, not exactly, but I already felt on edge.

If only the king would serve the first course. Then I'd be one step closer to leaving. My father usually allowed me to skip the king's festivities—as the king's fourth cousin once removed, I was hardly considered *important*—but this time my father had insisted I attend. To represent the family. To show we were people who mattered.

He couldn't really have believed that would work. No one had spoken to me since I'd arrived. Even my father had abandoned me for "necessary business conversations" on the other side of the hall. So I sat at my table near the door, empty seats on either side of me, half wanting to join in the conversation of the people opposite, too scared to appear to be eavesdropping on them to try.

King Jorgen, for his part, looked completely relaxed, and completely unconcerned about his potentially starving guests. He lounged on his throne, legs thrown over one arm, his golden goblet full of wine, his golden plate free of food, while the golden paneling glittered on the wall behind him. He was talking to a girl about my age, whose smile was so wide that the corners might have been pinned to her cheeks.

The king raised his goblet to her lips. When she shook her

head, still smiling that strained smile, he tossed the goblet over his shoulder, wine and all. "This drink does not please my lady!" he shouted. "Bring us something better."

Queen Martha sat on his right. I'd always thought she looked like a praying mantis—tall, thin, and bug-eyed, with a ruthless personality to match. Her dress was the biggest in the room, with silk ribbon at the end of every layer like icing on a cake. Her hair reached up toward the ceiling, studded with berries. She held a peacock-feather fan in front of her mouth to hide her yawn, and pointedly avoided looking at her husband.

A dove landed next to my still-empty plate and fluffed its wings. It looked at the foodless platter, and then looked at me, as though blaming me for the lack of treats.

"I know." I ran my fingers along the feathers at its neck. They were softer than I'd expected, and pristine white. Only the best could be baked in the king's pies, I supposed. "I'm hungry, too."

"Freya, what are you doing?" Sophia, the woman sitting opposite me, waved a ring-covered hand in my direction. She was in her forties, her hair a rich henna red. A black-silk moon and two stars had been stuck to her forehead, either as an affectation or to conceal any scars. "Don't encourage it. It's filthy."

"Pigeons all over the tables," Sophia's neighbor, Claire, said. She was in her forties, too, and rather portly, with a silk heart placed to the right of her pink lips. "I suppose the pie was entertaining, but—"

"Doves," I said, without thinking.

Claire raised a single, perfectly arched eyebrow. "What was that?"

"Doves," I repeated, a little louder, forcing the word out. "They're not pigeons, they're doves."

Claire laughed. "Oh, Freya, you are strange." She waved carelessly at the bird. "Pigeon, dove, whatever it is. We really don't want it on the table."

I pulled my hand back and stared at my plate as she shooed the bird away.

People had been calling me "strange" since I learned how to talk, although usually they only said it when they thought I couldn't hear. When I was younger, I had chattered constantly, stumbling over the words in my eagerness to express them, asking question after question until I was at least five explanations deep. People commented on my strangeness to my mother, as though she had somehow missed it and would surely take action now it was revealed to her, but she would just laugh and say, "Isn't it wonderful?" like my strangeness was my greatest strength.

Even then I'd known what it meant. That something was wrong with me. That I didn't belong.

Then my mother had died, and my strangeness had become far more concerning. An insult to her memory. An accusation: "Why can't you be more like your mother, and less like *you*?"

It was fine, I told myself. Claire should have been the one embarrassed, for making such a stupid mistake about the birds. It was fine.

But whenever I tried to convince myself my worries were all imaginary, that no one judged me, I remembered every scrap of evidence I'd ever gathered to the contrary. Every time someone had sniggered after I spoke. Every sideways glance shared by friends when I approached. The moment I had walked away from Rosaline Hayes and her friends and heard them repeating my words in high-pitched, laughing voices.

I'd been reluctant to say anything to anyone after that.

At first, my father had comforted me—"Court is an odd place, but you'll get used to it, you'll make friends, you'll figure it out"—but I continued to stumble, and "You'll make friends" became "You'll survive" became "Freya, could you at least try, for my sake?"

Five years later, I still had no place here. Or, I did, but it was sitting by the wall, practically invisible, the butt of jokes if I was mentioned at all. Awkward Freya, strange Freya, silent stuttering Freya who said rude things by accident and was so very, very plain. Did you hear she does experiments in her cellar? Did you hear she nearly burned her house to the ground? What was she even doing in court, behaving like that?

Or that's what I assumed. No one gossiped about me in front of my face. No one said much to or about me at all.

I'd decided long ago that I didn't care. I was going to escape this court as soon as I could. My father insisted I had to *try* and find a good match, to get married and play a role in court life, but no one had ever shown any interest in me. I'd never found anyone who interested *me,* either. As soon as my father accepted that, I'd be gone. I'd travel to the continent, perhaps, where research was taken far more seriously, and conduct my experiments there. One day soon.

Because, it turned out, I did care. I cared what people thought of me. I cared what they were saying. And I needed to get out, before their judgment changed me.

"Hi, Freya."

I turned toward the voice, smiling. I'd only ever had one good friend, but Naomi was so wonderful that I couldn't imagine needing anyone else. She'd been drawn to me, somehow, when she first moved to the capital with her brother, Jacob, joining me in the corner of awkwardness and pulling me into quiet conversation. We had little in common as far as interests went—she loved novels, stories, romance, and adventure, while I was much happier with equations and research—but our souls clicked.

She looked pretty tonight. She always looked pretty—not the court's version of beauty, but something softer and sweeter. She had large brown eyes, a tiny pug nose, and ever-present dimples. Her black hair was piled in a dome on top of her head, every twist studded with a gem, and her dark skin shimmered with whichever crushed-jewel powder was currently in fashion.

"Hi," I said. She slipped onto the chair beside me, wobbling slightly as she maneuvered her massive skirts into place.

"The people at my table are horrid," she murmured.

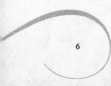

"And you're surprised?"

"I guess not. But then my brother abandoned me, so it was just me thrown to the wolves. How are you coping?"

"I'm alive. That's something, isn't it?"

"Here? Definitely."

"What are you girls whispering about?" Claire said. "It's awfully rude to have secrets, you know. We'll be thinking you're talking about us next."

"We'd never gossip about you," Naomi said. She glanced at the table again, then quickly back at Claire, correcting her gaze. "What would we even say?"

Lots of things, I thought. But Naomi probably meant it. She made fun of the court, but she was always eager to forgive the courtiers themselves for their cruelty and vanity. Every insult became a harmless misunderstanding or good people having a bad day if you allowed Naomi to sit with the story long enough.

"Well, I hope I'm not *that* boring," Claire said.

"Tell us," Sophia said, leaning forward slightly. "How is your brother, Jacob?"

"He's—well. Thank you."

"What a handsome young man. I suppose he'll be finding a girl soon? Or is he enjoying life too much to settle down?"

Naomi was saved from answering by a hush that descended on the room. The king had stood, arms swept out toward the crowd. "Before we enjoy our next course," he said, "I've arranged a little entertainment."

Other rulers probably had entertainments arranged *for* them on their birthday. But the king would never leave anything to chance. He had to show how extravagant and benevolent he was, and that meant planning every detail himself.

A troupe of performers ran into the hall through its rear doors. One woman backflipped her way along the hall, passing just behind my and Naomi's chairs. She shot us a sideways grin as she went. She was followed by more acrobats, people cartwheeling, a man walking on his hands, and jugglers, too, knives flying through the air. Their outfits sparkled, catching the light as they danced, so it almost hurt to look at them.

One of the performers clapped her hands, and the juggling knives burst into flame. The court gasped and applauded as the group continued to juggle, continued to dance and contort, the flames flying through the air so fast they became a blur. More performers ran in from the sides, holding torches aloft. They threw them into the paths of the burning knives, so they caught fire, too, and then the performers bent back, faces to the ceiling, mouths open wide, as they seemed to swallow the fire.

Then they started to *breathe* fire, shooting streams into the air. It caught on ribbon hung across the ceiling, too thin to be visible before, and raced along it, spelling out the king's name.

The crowd applauded again, and the king grinned. "Ah, now, our performers need a volunteer." He glanced up and down the high table in faux contemplation. "Fitzroy! Why don't you come up here?"

Fitzroy. Even I heard the danger in that word. William Fitz-roy was the king's bastard son, and although most people referred to him by his surname, the king's name for him changed with his mood. He was "my son" when Fitzroy was in favor, or "William" if a name was really needed. *Fitzroy* was a hint of dismissal, a reminder of his place in court. A surname they invented for the bastard son, the boy who wasn't supposed to exist.

But Fitzroy sauntered forward without hesitation. His blond hair fell across his eyes, giving him an air of casual confidence, and he was smiling, like he couldn't wait to suffer what his father had planned.

"Whatever my adoring fans demand," he said. People laughed, and danger flashed in the king's eyes. The performers positioned Fitzroy in the middle of their group, and then began their show again, tossing flaming rings to one another over Fitzroy's head, sending knives spinning inches from his arms, breathing fire so close that his hair must have been singed.

Fitzroy did not flinch. He mugged for the audience as the flames flew past, like nothing was more fun than nearly dying for everyone's entertainment.

Fitzroy, I decided, was an idiot.

The performance ended, Fitzroy bowed, and his father flicked a hand to send him back to his seat without a word.

The performers departed the way they'd come, tumbling and dancing. The backflipper passed behind us again, and as she did, her foot caught on my shoulder. She didn't pause to apologize—she probably hadn't even noticed, so focused on her performance—but I jerked, shoved forward by her momentum, and my heart sputtered into triple time.

The conversation in the hall started again, and Sophia and Claire leaped straight back into interrogating Naomi about her brother. I couldn't concentrate on the words. They were at once too loud and too far away to understand. My hands began to shake.

The kick had triggered something in me, the awareness that people were too close. There were too many of them, and I couldn't leave, couldn't escape, couldn't do *anything*.

No, I thought. Not here. I was safe. I was fine.

It was too late. There were too many bodies, too much breath and too many eyes. It was so loud, so crowded, and I couldn't leave.

No, I told myself again. I would be calm. I tugged at the pins in my hair, and looked around the room again, searching for something to ground me. The fountains of wine, the cascading flowers, the doves that still seemed confused about their inability to fly through the windows. Everything was safe. I'd be all right.

I tugged at another hairpin, my hand shaking, and it slipped free, sending a section of hair tumbling to my shoulder. I grabbed it and tried to shove it back in place.

"Freya?" Naomi said again. "Are you all right?"

I nodded, up and down and up. The world had turned fuzzy,

and all the sounds were too loud, and people were so *close,* even those far away seemed to loom and press toward me, and I couldn't breathe, and—

"Come on," Naomi said. "Let's get some air."

I couldn't leave the table, it wasn't allowed, but Naomi was already standing, not touching me, just standing and waiting, and I felt myself standing, too.

Naomi led the way to the doors at the back of the hall. They hadn't seemed far away before, twenty feet at most, but the distance stretched out now. Everyone was watching us leave, I knew, thinking about how *odd* we were behaving, and my father would be watching, too, glowering . . .

The doors stood slightly open, and we stepped out into the gardens beyond. An October chill was in the air, and I gulped it in, stumbling farther from the palace. Calm. I was calm.

The world slowly came back into focus. The vast lawn had been decorated with floating lanterns and glistening ice statues, and couples walked between them, hands entwined, faces close.

Naomi hovered about a foot away, watching me closely. "Are you all right?"

I nodded. "Yes. Yes, I'm fine." If I said it enough, it had to be true.

"You don't have to be fine, you know. If you're not."

Naomi said that every time this happened, and I always nodded, like I actually believed her. It was one thing to be uncomfortable in court, to hate all the pretenses and be desperate to leave. It was quite another to panic, to become so frightened of the people around me that I forgot how to breathe.

But she understood. She said her father reacted the same way to court, or to anything too crowded. That was why her parents lived out in the country, while she and her brother represented the family in the capital. Whenever I panicked, she would appear beside me, ready to talk me back to reality.

She swept her thirty-six layers of skirts forward and sank onto the grass. It must have been cold, but she simply looked up at me with a smile until I settled beside her.

At least I could breathe again. The chatter and music floated through the hall's open door, but it felt safer now, farther away.

"Want me to take your hair down?" Naomi asked.

I nodded. Naomi moved behind me and began pulling the pins loose with quick fingers. With every tug, my lungs relaxed, just a little.

"How's the experiment going?" she said. "Any luck?"

I shook my head. I'd been working on a way to create portable heat for weeks, something that could keep your hands warm and perhaps even banish the cold from my laboratory without fire. So far, all I had for my efforts were a whole lot of notes, and a whole lot of burns.

I plucked one of the loose hairpins from the grass and began to twist it between my fingers. The diamonds gleamed. "I've been experimenting with different metals," I said. "But nothing yet. I'll figure it out." Naomi tugged the last of my hair free, and

I leaned back, falling onto the grass beside her.

"When you figure it out, you'll be famous."

"Of course."

"Cold hands are the worst, Freya. People'll pay you a lot of money if you figure it out. You could do anything you wanted after that."

I shook my head. But secretly, I agreed. Not that I'd be famous, perhaps, but that this would work, that *this* was my solution. If I could solve this, and sell it, I'd have my own money. I could travel wherever I pleased. Travel to the continent, convince a scientist to teach me there. Stop living on the edge of other people's lives and start living my own.

I couldn't admit it, though. Not even to Naomi. The thought was too thrilling and terrifying to share. If I said it out loud, even nodded at Naomi's suggestion, I felt, madly, irrationally, that it would be snatched away from me, just to punish me for believing.

Naomi tucked her legs underneath her. "Well, you can be boring and unromantic if you like. *I* believe it'll happen. I'll miss you, though. When you're gone."

"I won't leave you." It was the one downside to the plan, the one detail that made me hesitate. I wouldn't know what to do without Naomi beside me. "You'll come with me."

I knew she wouldn't, she *couldn't*, not with her parents' approval, at least. But I wanted to pretend.

"I suppose I would like to see the continent. But what would

Jacob do without me? He gets into too much trouble as it is."

"He'll have to come and help you on your adventures," I said. "Rescue you when that dashing rogue you meet turns out to like girl-bone soup."

"Because of course that'll happen to me."

"It happens to all the best heroines. And if your brother doesn't have to rush to your aid, how will he employ that handsome stranger to assist him who falls madly in love at the sight of you?"

She laughed. "Well, when you put it like that." She glanced toward the palace. "Should we go back inside soon? They'll be missing us."

"They won't miss us." Everyone had already seen us go, and my father was going to be furious about that, whatever I did. At this point, I might as well leave entirely.

I tapped my fingernail on the hairpin. Brand-new, special for the banquet. Made from aluminum, which was the stupidest thing I'd ever heard. Someone on the continent had discovered a new metal, and what did everyone here do? Rush to make it into jewelry, without a thought to what better uses it might have.

I'd be there soon. On the continent, with real intellectuals, with people who actually cared, rather than the vapid, fashion-hungry mob here. I just had to solve this one problem.

Another tap of the hairpin. Metal hadn't worked. Not even close.

But I hadn't tried aluminum.

I sat up.

"What is it?" Naomi said.

"Aluminum. I haven't tried it yet. For my experiment." My thoughts were racing. "What if—what if I combined it with something? Maybe iodine?" Yes. *Yes.* That would produce heat. Wouldn't it?

There were carriages around the front of the palace, waiting until they were needed. Surely one of them could take me home. My father must have noticed me leaving the hall, but he hadn't come looking for me. I could slip out for an hour or two, then come back, and say I'd been in the gardens all along. He'd be angry, but he wouldn't be able to disprove it. The gardens were huge. He couldn't search them while I was gone, not without leaving the ball for longer than he'd deem acceptable himself.

I could go back to the laboratory, try out my thoughts, and be back before the end of the feast.

And if this worked—if it worked, I'd never have to go to a banquet like this again.

Naomi grinned back at me. "All right," she said. "Let's go make your fortune."

DON'T MISS THESE BOOKS BY
RHIANNON THOMAS

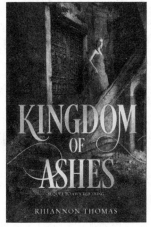

JOIN THE

Epic Reads

COMMUNITY

THE ULTIMATE YA DESTINATION

◀ DISCOVER ▶
your next favorite read

◀ MEET ▶
new authors to love

◀ WIN ▶
free books

◀ SHARE ▶
infographics, playlists, quizzes, and more

◀ WATCH ▶
the latest videos

www.epicreads.com